Kay Stoc ... **for people in Del's profession**

"The last consultant I had dealings with decided I was not the right material to be a politician's wife," she told Del. "And my fiancé apparently agreed."

"Obviously a mistake on his part," Del said quietly, his admiring glance telling her he would never have made the same error. "No wonder you have such an aversion to consultants, Kay. Why didn't you tell me?"

"What was I going to say? That I'd already gone a few rounds with someone in your profession and come away bruised, if not the definite loser?"

Del shook his head. He reached out and put a hand on her arm. The close, intimate contact sent shock waves zinging through her.

"I don't want to change you, Kay," he said softly. "I like you just the way you are."

ABOUT THE AUTHOR

Risa Kirk found her curiosity about robots
piqued when she saw one picture of a
complicated robotic hand holding a rose, and
a second one of a robotic arm lifting heavy
construction equipment. "The contrast
fascinated me enough to explore the subject,"
says this successful Californian author, who
has written several mainstream novels as well
as category romances.

Risa's expert light touch is evident in *Made to
Order*, her eighth Superromance novel, as is
her obvious pleasure in writing about a
heroine who is bright and talented enough to
challenge the power structure of a
predominantly masculine field.

Books by Risa Kirk

HARLEQUIN SUPERROMANCE
238–TEMPTING FATE
273–DREAMS TO MEND
300–WITHOUT A DOUBT
361–PLAYING WITH FIRE
408–UNDERCOVER AFFAIR
441–SEND NO REGRETS

Don't miss any of our special offers. Write to us at the
following address for information on our newest releases.

Harlequin Reader Service
P.O. Box 1397, Buffalo, NY 14240
Canadian address: P.O. Box 603,
Fort Erie, Ont. L2A 5X3

Made to Order

RISA KIRK

Harlequin Books

TORONTO • NEW YORK • LONDON
AMSTERDAM • PARIS • SYDNEY • HAMBURG
STOCKHOLM • ATHENS • TOKYO • MILAN

Published November 1991

ISBN 0-373-70476-3

MADE TO ORDER

Copyright © 1991 by Janis Flores. All rights reserved.
Except for use in any review, the reproduction or utilization
of this work in whole or in part in any form by any electronic,
mechanical or other means, now known or hereafter invented,
including xerography, photocopying and recording,
or in any information storage or retrieval system, is forbidden without
the permission of the publisher, Harlequin Enterprises Limited,
225 Duncan Mill Road, Don Mills, Ontario, Canada M3B 3K9.

All the characters in this book have no existence outside the
imagination of the author and have no relation whatsoever to
anyone bearing the same name or names. They are not even
distantly inspired by any individual known or unknown to the
author, and all incidents are pure invention.

® are Trademarks registered in the United States Patent and
Trademark Office and in other countries.

Printed in U.S.A.

CHAPTER ONE

CRASH! The rock came flying through the window, smashing the glass and sending fragments in all directions. With a thud, it landed on Kay Stockwell's desk and rolled off onto the floor.

"What in the world...?" Kay exclaimed.

Moments before she had been standing at that very window, staring down at the demonstration taking place beyond the front gates of Stockwell Engineering, her company based here in Springfield, Illinois. The protestors were carrying crude, hand-drawn placards, some with pictures of robots piloting Stealth bombers, others with such slogans as Men Need Work, Not Machines, and Women And Business Don't Mix.

As the rock came to rest by her foot, Kay moved again toward the window. "All right, that's it!" she said furiously.

Brice Moreland, her vice president, reached across the desk and jerked her back out of the way. "Are you out of your mind, Kay? What if someone throws another?"

She hadn't thought of that. Her face paled as she stood back while Brice moved cautiously to the side of the window and looked down. After a moment, he breathed a sigh of relief.

"Security just arrived," he said over his shoulder. "And it looks as though the demonstrators are just as shocked as we are at what happened. I don't think anybody expected it." He turned and saw how white Kay looked as she stood by the desk, gripping the edge tightly. "Kay... are you all right?" he asked anxiously. "You weren't hit, were you?"

She hadn't been injured, but she was shaken to the core. She wanted to sit down, but she couldn't take her desk chair; it was covered with glass, and more was scattered all over the floor behind it.

"No," she said faintly, "I'm okay." Shakily, she took a deep breath. "I never expected... violence."

Looking a little shaken himself, Brice put his arm around her shoulders and led her to the couch along one wall of the office. Once she was seated, he brought her a glass of water and forced her to take a sip.

"I don't think it will happen again," he said. "It's my guess that things just... got out of hand."

Kay's first shock was passing; soon she was in control again. But her green eyes were wary as she set the water glass aside, and after a moment, when she was sure her legs would hold her, she got up and went back to the window. The demonstrators were leaving, looking subdued as they went to their cars. She had to admit that they looked as scared as she'd felt when the rock crashed through the window, but she also knew that as contrite as they might be right now, they'd be back. Not with potential weapons, perhaps; she felt instinctively that they'd learned their lesson about that. But with more signs and demonstrations and protests, to be sure. And already some of her people who had elected to continue working during this latest crisis were becoming reluctant to cross that picket line; she had been hearing reports about absenteeism and stress, and if they heard about this...

Brice was right, she thought as she gazed somberly down into the now-empty street in front of the gates: something had to be done. But what?

Then she began to feel angry again. How could this have happened? She'd known when she took over the company after her father died that things might not go so smoothly, but she had never anticipated the situation would come to this. Had George Mott been right? She didn't want to believe it, but before she had fired him, George had claimed that she should step down and let someone else run Stockwell Engineering, and heaven only knew, the decisions she'd made since becoming president hadn't made her the most popular person around. Now, with demonstrations against her policies going on outside the gates, things were even worse.

But I know I'm right, she thought fiercely. *Despite what some of these old mossbacks say, robotics is the wave of the future.*

And she intended for Stockwell Engineering to ride that wave. Her father wouldn't have entrusted her with his company if he hadn't thought that she could carry on ably in his place, and she knew she could do it. All she asked was to be given a chance. From the beginning, she had encountered resistance. It had begun the day of that first board meeting after her father died, when she had announced that she had not only inherited the company but intended to take Jim Stockwell's place. Immediately, a hue and cry had been raised.

She had been prepared for argument and some jealousy; what she hadn't anticipated at all was the outright hostility from George Mott and a few others. She had barely concluded her speech about making a smooth transition and being open and available for suggestions and advice, when Mott had startled everyone by banging his fist on the conference table.

"This is outrageous!" he cried, his face turning red with anger. "We all know that Jim was a dreamer, not the most practical of men at times, but to...to hand over this company, lock, stock and barrel, to an untried, inexperienced young...*girl,* is beyond belief! I, for one, won't stand for it!"

All eyes moved to the head of the table, where she was standing. She caught Brice looking worriedly at her, and she knew that if she indicated, he'd do something to try and defuse the tense situation. But this was the first challenge to her position and authority, and she couldn't back down. Instinctively, she realized that her conduct in the next few minutes would determine just which of these men would give her their loyalty and support and which would probably walk out.

"I'm sorry you feel that way, George," she said, deliberately using his first name. "And I agree with you that acting as my father's chief assistant these past six months means I have little *direct* experience running this company." She glanced around the table. "But that doesn't mean I don't learn quickly. And, as I've said, my door will always be open."

Then she met Mott's furious glance again. "But I take exception to a few of your other remarks, George," she said calmly. "For one thing, I am not the untried youngster you seem to believe I am. As many of you are already aware, I hold a master's degree in electronics engineering and ten years' experience in the field. I won't bore you with a recital of the positions I've held—my résumé is available to you all...including details of the months I was assigned as a consultant to NASA." She paused just a second or two to make sure that informa-

tion sank in, then she softened her stand slightly with a
small smile. "And, as much as I might like to at times,
I'm afraid I can no longer lay claim to being a *girl*. Unfortunately, at thirty-five, those carefree days are far behind me." She looked down the table again at Mott. "But
thank you, George," she finished serenely, "for the
compliment."

During the spontaneous applause from everyone but
Mott and the four men who were his closest cronies, Brice
gave her a surreptitious thumbs-up gesture from which
she took heart. But she knew that while she had safely
negotiated one section of a very tricky course, the most
difficult part was still to come. It did, a few moments
later, when she handed out her prospectus for the new
robotics division. Instantly, applause turned to conster-
nation.

"Robotics! Stockwell has never been involved in robotics!" someone exclaimed.

"That doesn't mean we can't be," she replied, more
calmly than she felt. She knew there would be outrage
and argument, and she had armed herself with facts and
statistics and more data than anyone could possibly want.

"But why?" someone else moaned. "We can't possibly compete! It's too expensive to develop prototypes!"

"We'll get venture capital," she said, much more confidently than she felt.

"Which field of robotics?" a third man demanded.
"There are service robots, medical robots, automotive
robots...defense robots." He stopped, looking scandalized. "Surely you don't intend to get us involved with
the Department of Defense!"

"I intend to go after government contracts, yes," she
said, and caused another uproar, which she quieted by
using the authority of her new position.

"Gentlemen, please!" she commanded, holding up her hand. Again, she looked around the table. "This isn't a new decision. My father and I not only talked about a robotics division many times, but right before he died, he gave me permission to go ahead. And I know he discussed it at great length with all of you."

"But we never *dreamed* it would be put into action!" someone protested.

And that was the problem, Kay had thought at the time. They hadn't *dreamed*.

Well, she'd decided to do their dreaming for them. And now, despite the fact that there had been one crisis after another in the six months since she had taken over, she and Stockwell Engineering were surviving...if barely. She'd eventually had to fire George Mott and two of his cronies; they'd been so antagonistic that she hadn't had any choice. She had managed to weather that setback. The rest of Mott's colleagues stayed, but it was a tenuous truce and she suspected many were just waiting to see what would happen. She knew it was Brice who had bought her some time. Brice, who believed in her and what she was doing, even if sometimes—especially late at night or when she was tired or depressed—she questioned it herself. Without his wholehearted support and his quiet working behind the scenes on her behalf, the defection would have been much worse, and she was more grateful to him than she could ever say.

But George had had his revenge after all, she thought, remembering the demonstrators. However, she had also had her triumphs. Stockwell Engineering had a robotics division, and—her expression turned even more grim— if she had anything to say about it, and she did, it was here to stay. Inch by inch, she had consolidated her position, and no matter how many rallies they put on to convince her she'd made a bad mistake turning to robots to pull Stockwell Engineering out of a financial slump, she would persevere. She intended to make the robotics division even bigger than it was. She was right about this; she knew it.

On that thought, she turned back to Brice, who was regarding the mess on the floor and the desk with a mixture of distaste and anger. "I'd better call someone to have this cleaned up," he muttered.

"Wait," she said, and when he gave her a questioning look, she shook her head resignedly. "I'm beginning to realize you were right and I was wrong. It's obvious the situation is more serious than I thought." Then she turned stubborn again. "But I still don't like your idea. I don't believe we need an image consultant."

Just the way she said the last words—her voice dripping with contempt—made Brice wince. But since this was the very reason he had requested their meeting, he had no choice but to pursue the topic. "Now, Kay. We've talked about it—you know we have. And it's not as bad as all that."

She glanced away. "It's bad enough," she muttered.

"Out there, it is," he agreed, deliberately mistaking her meaning. "That's why I think it's time to bring in help."

Even though she had conceded the point, she still felt cornered, and she began to pace, tall and slender in the business suit she always wore to work, even if most of the time she threw off her jacket and put on a white coat to go to the lab and observe some problem her engineers were working on. But she hadn't had time to do that lately; she'd had too many other things to deal with. George Mott had promised to make trouble, and judging from the increased negative publicity—and those damned demonstrators who had been outside every morning now for the past three weeks—he was keeping that vow.

Just thinking about it made her despair. She still missed her father so much. She had been so devastated by his death that sometimes she thought that the heart attack that had killed him had wounded her heart in some way, too. She had lost her mother so young, but her father—and her grandfather Emmett, who still lived on the farm outside Springfield—had almost made up for that maternal absence during her childhood. Both men had always been there for her, never more than last year when her relationship with Adam Cordell, her fiancé, had ended. When she had come back to Springfield with her pride in tatters, neither of them had questioned her; they had just welcomed her home with open arms, never once asking what had happened to her marriage plans, content to wait until she was ready to talk.

Her face tightened. She wasn't sure she'd ever be ready to talk about Adam. What could she say? That she had made a fool of herself over a man who had dumped her because she wasn't part of the *image* he was cultivating to get elected to Congress? When she thought about how Adam had treated her—and what she had done to try and keep him—she felt so humiliated and angry that she wanted to scream. To think that she had actually tried to make herself over to help his campaign…. She must have been out of her mind!

She still could hardly understand it even now. Before Adam had decided to run for office, he had been one of the most thoughtful, considerate and generous men she'd ever known. Even as an assistant district attorney, constantly exposed to the seamier side of life, he had never lost the magnetism that had initially attracted her. His charm and charisma were the reasons she had stayed with him long after she knew she should go.

But then he had decided he wanted to run for Congress, and everything had changed. *He* had changed, and it was all because of that damned political consultant he had hired to help him win. The consultant—she would never forget that name!—had been Martin Winslow. *Marty,* she thought with derision, who had taken over every aspect of Adam's life. From the time Adam got up in the morning to the time he went to bed, Marty was there—suggesting, advising, counseling, criticizing. According to Marty, Adam didn't even know how to dress himself properly. Single-breasted suits were no good; double-breasted jackets intimated more power. Paisley ties were out; a certain red had to be worn. The list went on and on until she thought she would scream. She couldn't understand how Adam—her Adam—could stand meekly by and let that man rule every aspect of his life.

But the worst was yet to come: Marty started on her. At first, she was willing to try a few of the consultant's suggestions. After all, she loved Adam, and she wanted what he wanted. Or she thought she did. She didn't really like blue, but according to Marty, it was more... retiring. And if she stood just slightly behind Adam's shoulder whenever reporters stopped them, she wouldn't be... in the way. Marty said it made for a better picture, but she knew, deep down, that what it did was make Adam look more in control while she seemed merely submissive.

Oh, when she thought of all she had done for Adam, she wanted to smash something. And for what? she asked herself bitterly. So that one night, when she was wearing a dress that didn't suit her, that putrid shade of blue she hated but wore because Marty thought it made her look *demure,* Adam could tell her that despite all she had done, he'd found someone more suitable?

"I'm sorry, Kay," Adam had told her that last time. "But you'll just never be a good political wife. You're too outspoken, too independent."

And just like that, as though he were discussing the weather or whether the Chicago Bears would win their next game, he added, "I really hate to tell you, but I've found someone else."

He hadn't even been apologetic, Kay thought—that's how much he had changed.

Then she felt furious all over again. It had all been Martin Winslow's fault, she thought wrathfully. Adam might have said the words, but he was just mouthing what Marty had told him to say. She had known it, and she knew by the furtive look in his eyes that Adam knew it, too. That's when she realized it wasn't only hopeless, but futile, as well. Adam had fallen so far under Winslow's spell that he would say or do anything to get elected—even break an engagement because his fiancée had become an impediment to his career.

After a long while, the thought finally occurred to her that not even an opportunist like Marty Winslow could have come between her and Adam if the seeds of discord hadn't already been there, but still...that didn't mean she had to like him—or the profession he represented. As far as she was concerned, all image consultants and spin doctors—the people hired to put the correct slant on things—could go to blazes.

Lost in reverie, she had forgotten Brice, but now he interrupted her roiling thoughts. "You really don't look well, Kay," he said in concern. "Maybe we should discuss this later."

For a moment, she couldn't remember what they had been talking about. Then she saw the rock, the shattered glass, and the situation flooded back all too clearly. "No, we'll discuss it now," she said, and then, despite herself, added almost pleadingly, "But Brice, there must be another way. Surely, we can think of another approach!"

She and Brice had known each other for fifteen years; he had worked for her father and had asked to stay on when she took over. Their long association was one reason he still spoke bluntly at times. "What? I'm open to suggestions. Do you have any?"

She was beginning to feel hemmed in again. "I don't know. If I knew, would we be discussing it?"

"I can guess why you're opposed to the idea, Kay, but—"

He knew about Adam and some of what had happened. But they had only discussed it once, and she had no intention of dwelling on it now. "Politicians hire image consultants," she said flatly. "Engineering companies don't."

"They do if they're in as much trouble as we are," he said calmly. He was in his early fifties and had worked at Stockwell Engineering all his adult life. Neither Kay's father nor Kay herself would have known what to do without him. In his role as advocate, adviser and peacemaker, he was invaluable.

Which was why she should listen to him now, Kay was telling herself as he added, "And we *are* in trouble, Kay. You can't deny it."

She couldn't deny it. But she couldn't forget Martin Winslow, either. Stubbornly, she said, "That doesn't mean we have an image problem."

"Doesn't it?"

"No! Image has nothing to do with it!" she insisted. "Regardless of what George Mott says, it's no one's business but ours what we do here. If I want to build an *army* of robots, I can. Or has everyone forgotten the concept of free enterprise?"

"It's more than that, Kay, and you know it," Brice countered. "Regardless of the rightness or wrongness of what George Mott has done, what he has succeeded in doing is building fear. People are afraid that any robots Stockwell builds here are going to take over jobs—"

"Well, they will," she said. "But not the kinds of jobs anyone wants these days—talk to the big fast-food chains, they'll tell you! Or hospitals or toxic waste sites or..." She waved her hand impatiently. "Oh, it's so *obvious!* I don't know why people can't understand!"

Patiently, Brice said, "It's because they don't know any better, Kay."

"Then maybe they should learn!"

"And how are they going to do that? What better way than to institute a campaign—"

"Oh, no you don't!" she warned. "I see where you're going with this!"

"If you would just talk to a consultant, Kay—"

"I've talked to all the consultants I'm going to in this life, Brice. I mean it! Never again!"

He hesitated. Then, because he was obviously feeling a little exasperated himself, he said, "Just because you had a bad experience with one doesn't mean the rest are all bad."

Wishing now that she hadn't told Brice anything about her experience with Adam and Martin Winslow, she glowered at him. "As far as I'm concerned they are. They're all cut from the same cloth."

"People could say that about engineers."

She was outraged. "Are you saying that George Mott and I are alike in any way?"

"No, no, of course not. Just like I wouldn't say that about that Washington consultant and Rafferty Associates. Rafferty does come highly recommended, Kay."

"Oh, really?" she said acidly. "Well, if that's so, what are they doing in Springfield? Why haven't they set up shop in a big city, like New York or Los Angeles or—" her lip curled "—Washington, D.C.?"

"Until last year, they were based in Houston."

"Oh, and what happened then? Did Texas run them out on a rail?"

"There's no need for sarcasm, Kay."

"Why not? It's what *they* do best!"

With obvious effort, he swallowed his retort. Instead, he said, "I can't believe you won't even consider it. It's just not like you."

"It is now."

"You won't even think about it?"

"I have thought about it. I know we can find another solution."

"Well, fine," he said, beginning to sound impatient despite himself. "And in the meantime, shall I have bars put over your window so if something else comes sailing in you won't get hurt?"

She fell silent. She knew he was right; she didn't need to look at the glass littering the desk and the floor to be reminded. But even more stinging was his accusation that she wasn't being fair. She prided herself on her objectivity, and after a moment she said ungraciously, "Oh, all right. I guess I can see your point."

"Great! Now we're getting somewhere. I'll call and—"

"I'm only going to talk to them," she said quickly, as he got up and started toward the door, intending to get out before she could change her mind. "Don't expect anything else!"

"One step at a time," he agreed, reaching for the knob. "What if I can get someone to come out tomorrow?"

"Tomorrow!"

"The sooner the better, don't you think?"

She was already retreating. "No, actually, I don't."

"Well, I do," he said. "The quicker we get started on this, the better. Oh, and I'll have someone come right away to clean up this mess and fix that window. We want to look our best, don't we?"

"Why? If we hire someone—and I said if, Brice, remember that," she warned him, "he's only going to try and change everything about us, anyway."

He opened the door. "I'll tell you what . . ."

"What?"

Smiling, he said, "We'll draw the line at changing the company's name. How about that?"

Her eyes narrowed. "I've got a better idea."

"What's that?"

"We'll draw the line after he eliminates the position of executive vice president. How about *that?*"

Grinning, Brice went to make his calls, leaving her alone to ponder the mistake she was sure she'd just made. How could she have agreed to such an absurd plan? she wondered. Hadn't one image consultant already brought her enough grief? She must be out of her mind to even consider talking to another one.

"He'd better not try to make me wear blue," she muttered, and sat down to wait for the cleanup crew.

CHAPTER TWO

FEELING INCREASINGLY out of sorts, Del Rafferty searched through the chaos on his desk for the file he needed. With everything such a mess, he couldn't find what he wanted and, as he flung papers here and there, he decided it was all Jennifer's fault. Ever since his fifteen-year-old daughter had come to live with him, it was like living in the middle of a hurricane. His office at Rafferty Associates proved it. Disorder was everywhere, and as he grabbed for a tall stack of folders perched precariously on the edge of the desk before it could slide off and join the mess on the floor, he shouted for his secretary. The intercom was somewhere beneath the rubble, but he was through trying to find things.

"Stella! Would you come in here a minute?"

His secretary, honey-haired and blue-eyed and looking younger than her twenty-four years, appeared in the doorway. Fortunately, she had decided to transfer with the company, for she always seemed to know where things were. Today, she took one look at the clutter and said, "If you're searching for the Spangler file, it's in your top drawer."

Giving her a wild look, he jerked open that drawer. Sure enough, the file marked Hollis Spangler was staring up at him. "Well, what's it doing there?" he muttered, and pulled it out as he sat down.

Stella hid her smile. "I thought it would be safer than on top of your desk," she said, straight-faced, and then added innocently, "Do you want me to clean up that mess for you?"

He glowered. "No. I like it this way."

Pursing her lips in that way she had, she said agreeably, "Okay, whatever you say." They both knew she would come in and rearrange everything after he left at the end of the day. She started out but paused again to remind him with a grin, "Don't forget you have an appointment with Chuck Turner tomorrow morning at eight." She knew how much he disliked Chuck, who was making a run for state senator this year. But before Del could complain about the early hour, she added, "And don't blame me. That's the only free time you had for weeks in your schedule. Oh, and if you want *that* file, it's under your right hand."

Waggling her fingers in his direction, she went back to her desk. Del looked down when she had gone. Naturally, the folder marked with Turner's name was right where Stella had said it would be. *How does she do that?* he wondered. He couldn't have found that file if it had jumped up and bit him on the...

Thinking how glad he was to have Stella, even if she was too smart at times, he sat back and glanced at the clock, relieved to see that it was almost five. The day was nearly over; he had no reason to feel so tired beyond the fact that he was obviously getting too old for this business. At forty, he felt a wreck. Maybe it was time for a vacation.

He nearly laughed at the thought. A vacation? He couldn't remember when he'd last had any time off; he'd been going nonstop, it seemed, these past dozen years or so since he'd started the agency. He couldn't deny that his hard work had paid off; Rafferty Associates was now one of the top image consulting firms in the country. His position was so secure that he'd been able to leave Houston, as he had always planned, and move to a smaller city. He had chosen Springfield for several reasons: it was the capital of his home state; it was more or less centrally located so that he could serve clients easily on both east and west coasts, and it still retained enough of a small town atmosphere so that when his daughter visited, he wouldn't worry as much as if he were still in the big city.

He'd wanted to make the move long ago, but there hadn't seemed any rush—not when Maxine barely let him see his little girl. Jennifer had just turned seven when he and Maxine had divorced, too young to understand why her parents couldn't get along. He hadn't understood it himself. He and Maxine had loved each other once, or he thought they had. Maybe, like so much of his work here, that had been an illusion, too.

Shifting uncomfortably at the thought, he decided that he had made the right choice about moving at this time, especially now that Jennifer was living with him this year. He had always wanted her with him. But Maxine had fought him bitterly about custody and visitations and everything else, until this summer when she had married again.

With Lyon or Lear or whatever the hell his name was, suddenly things changed. When Del found out that the guy was a tennis pro who traveled around a lot, he put his foot down. Jennifer was fifteen. Travel was broadening, but not when she would be changing schools every time a new tournament sprang up. He didn't want his daughter living out of a suitcase, and he insisted that she come to live with him in Springfield at least for this year. At the

end of the year, they could all reevaluate and decide what
to do. To his stunned surprise, Maxine had instantly
agreed to the plan. It wasn't until his shock wore off later
that he realized she'd been looking for an excuse all
along. Obviously, she had been wondering how to balance the needs of a much-younger husband with those of
a teenage girl.

Well, he had solved Maxine's problem, he thought,
putting his head in his hands; now all he had to do was
figure out the solution to his. Ever since Jennifer had
come to Springfield, she'd been impossible.

He had tried to be patient and understanding. He knew
that leaving her friends and her school behind in New
York and coming here had been a wrench, but still, it
wasn't as though he were a *complete* stranger. He was her
father, and he loved her. He would do anything in the
world for her—if only he could figure out what it was she
wanted. However, since she was still barely speaking to
him at this point, that was a little difficult to do.

It was his fault, he thought; he just didn't understand
females. Trying to fathom women was bad enough, but
girls... He turned grim, remembering what had happened the very first night he'd brought Jennifer home
from New York. He'd gone to collect her, and by the time
they got back, lugging all those boxes, suitcases, trunks
and other assorted treasures—with more to come by delivery—they were both tired and worn-out. He'd made
the arrangements so hurriedly that he hadn't had time to
fix up the extra bedroom, which was, he admitted, not
exactly a decorator's dream. He'd used that room as a
catchall during the months he'd lived in the house by
himself. Until Jennifer asked where she was going to be
staying, he had vaguely supposed that the den would do;
they could paint and paper and do whatever it was that

young girls like to do to the extra bedroom upstairs at some later date. More fool he, he'd believed that the most important thing was to let her know she was wanted and loved and very welcome.

Jennifer hadn't listened to his awkward, fatherly little speech; she'd taken one look at the sofa bed and the mustard-colored drapes that the previous owners had left and promptly burst into tears. She hated Illinois, she hated Springfield, and she hated this horrible house. She wanted to go home. She wanted her mother.

Del didn't know how to cope with tears. Caught off guard by the sudden flood of emotion, he was reaching to comfort her when she dropped the suitcase she was holding and started toward the stairs. The heavy bag landed on his foot, and as he hopped around in pain, she ran to the upstairs bathroom, locking herself in. She emerged with swollen eyes and tear-blotched cheeks shortly before midnight, and by then the celebration he'd planned had definitely fallen flat. Exhausted, they'd both gone to bed; he in the despised den; she in his bed.

Two months later things still weren't much better than they had been that first night. About the only improvement Del could point to was that Jennifer seemed content with the way they'd redone the extra bedroom. Once it was decorated in the frilly green and white she'd chosen herself, he'd been able to move back into his own bed.

But then, he thought bleakly, there hadn't been that much progression, after all. Now, instead of crying in the bathroom, she spent hours behind her own locked door. He could have handled that, he supposed, but what was even more disturbing was that she seemed to be gaining so much weight. Jennifer had always been a little chubby, but he'd just thought it was baby fat and that she would grow out of it. Now he wasn't so sure. Every time he saw her, it seemed she was eating some kind of junk food. He was no puritan, but he knew that too much of that stuff wasn't good for her, and a while ago, he'd made the mistake of trying to talk to her about it.

What a tactical error *that* had been, he thought. Jennifer had become hysterical, accusing him not only of ruining her life by making her come to live with him, but of thinking that she was fat and ugly, as well. He sighed. It seemed he couldn't win. Not even hiring a very sympathetic housekeeper named Mrs. Nivens to take care of the meals and the house and whatnot had helped. And then the other day, he'd gotten a call from Jennifer's school counselor, who was concerned that Jennifer was not making any friends.

Del hadn't been aware of it until that moment. Jennifer had always been popular and an excellent student, regularly bringing home all A's without any effort. If her studies plummeted he wouldn't know how to handle it. What did she *do* all that time she spent behind locked doors in her bedroom? He'd thought she was studying, but it seemed that what she was doing was lying on her bed listening to rock music through the headphones he'd bought her, imagining herself the tragic heroine in some domestic drama in which her father kept her captive.

Maxine hadn't been any help. He'd been so desperate the first month Jennifer had stayed with him that he'd finally tracked Maxine down in Europe to ask her what to do. That's when he had learned that his ex-wife had told their daughter that the move had been *his* idea.

"No wonder she thinks I'm the villain!" he had exclaimed. It had become clear to him then. Maxine didn't want Jennifer blaming her, so she'd told the girl Del was the one who'd insisted on ruining all the fun. She hadn't bothered to explain Del's reasons.

"Thanks a lot, Maxine," he'd said heavily. He was so close to losing his temper and telling her exactly what he thought that he didn't dare say much else.

Maxine knew that tone. "Jennifer'll be fine. She just has to get used to things," she assured him quickly, her voice sounding tinny and distant coming from wherever she and Lyon—was that his name?—were staying in Sweden. Last week it had been Italy, and before that, France. They were seeing a lot of country, but Lyon wasn't winning many tournaments, and Del wondered how they managed.

Not that it mattered, he realized angrily. The important thing was Jennifer. "She's had weeks to get used to things, Maxine," he said. "And it isn't getting any better."

"She'll be *fine*. You worry too much. And anyway," Maxine said defensively, "what do you think I can do about it from *here?*"

"You can talk to her," he said. "Tell her—"

He was about to say, tell her the truth, but Maxine forestalled him by exclaiming, "But I have talked to her, darling! We've been on the phone nearly every night!"

That was the first he'd heard of it. He didn't really believe her until he looked at the phone bill. The amount for all those overseas calls made him blanch. He wouldn't have minded so much if they had helped.

"Why didn't you tell me you've been calling your mother?" he asked Jennifer.

His daughter, the little girl he'd once thought so sweet, beautiful and charming, looked at him as though she hated him. With her thick black hair and deep blue eyes, she had his coloring, but that seemed to be the only thing they had in common these days. "I didn't know I had to ask permission!" she declared.

"You don't," he said. "I just thought—"

"If you want me to pay for it, I will!" she shouted.

"Don't be silly. That's not what I—"

"How did you know I called her? Are you spying on me or something?"

"Of course not. I just—"

"Oh, this is just great!" she cried. "First you make me come and live here, and then I have to go to a school I *hate,* and now I can't even call my own mother! It isn't fair!"

He didn't want to make things worse by telling her that her mother wasn't as blameless as she liked to think, so he started to say, "Jennifer, that's not—"

But he didn't get a chance to finish defending himself. Jennifer grabbed the peanut butter sandwich she'd just made and ran into her bedroom, slamming the door behind her. As the windows rattled and the floor shook, Del stood blankly in the hallway. What had he said?

He still wasn't sure, but it was obviously having a lasting effect. Jennifer wasn't talking to him at *all* now, and lately, she'd taken to leaving a dollar by the phone, presumably every time she called her mother. The first five times, he'd tried to return the money to her dresser, but when he'd found it a while later right back by the phone, he'd given up.

"Knock, knock...."

His thoughts interrupted, Del looked up and saw Stella in the doorway again. "Are you asleep in here or what?" she asked. "You've got a call on line two."

Blankly, he looked down at the phone. Sure enough, the second line was blinking. "Did you call me?"

"Only about ten times," Stella said. "I finally decided to see if you'd fainted or something."

"Very funny," he said. "Who is it?"

"Brice Moreland, out at Stockwell Engineering."

"Brice!" He had met Brice Moreland at some fund-raiser or other when he had first moved to Springfield. They had shared a pleasant few drinks and had seen each other off and on at various functions since. When Del remembered the troubles Stockwell had been having lately, he thought he knew why Brice was calling. Oh, not now, he thought with a groan. With all the work he had on his desk, plus the problems at home, he didn't have time to take on anything else, not even a campaign for a mouse.

Steeling himself to say no, he reached for the phone. "Brice!" he said heartily, hoping he could think of a graceful excuse before the man could ask. "How are you?"

"Not good," came the gloomy response.

"Oh. Sorry to hear that," Del said, and told himself, *Don't ask if there's anything you can do.* "Is there anything I can do?" he heard himself ask, and sat back with a sigh, closing his eyes. Now he'd done it. With an opening like that, Brice would be a fool not to pass right through.

"I was hoping you'd say that," Brice said quickly, just as Del had anticipated. "I know how busy you are, but we're really in a mess here at Stockwell."

"Yes, I know. I've seen the papers."

"Then you've probably guessed that we desperately need your help. Could you possibly take Stockwell on as a client?"

Just for a second, he was tempted. He liked Brice. And after their first meeting, Brice had steered some business his way. But he couldn't take on any more work right now; he was up to his ears, and it wouldn't be fair to

Stockwell. Feeling like a heel, he said, "I'd like to help, Brice, but—"

"Please, Del. You know I wouldn't ask if we didn't really need you."

Del tried one more time to extricate himself from the bonds of friendship. "Brice, your situation doesn't seem to warrant bringing in a consultant. I've seen things like this before. The publicity will all die down, and—"

"They're throwing rocks now," Brice said quietly. "One crashed through Kay's—I mean Kay Stockwell, the president of the company—it crashed through her office window. She was almost hit by flying glass."

Del was silent. Obviously the situation out at Stockwell had escalated without his being aware of it.

"Will you at least come out and talk to her?" Brice asked.

Del felt even more hesitant at that. Remembering the single interview Ms. Kay Stockwell had given to the press, wherein she had blasted not only every member of the media, past, future and present, but also George Mott, one of the executives she had fired, as well as all the fringe groups and demonstrators who were trying to storm her gates, Del felt less inclined to get involved.

Don't do it, he told himself. "Are you sure she wants me to?" he hedged.

Despite the seriousness of the situation, Brice still held on to his sense of humor. "Let's say she's accepted the inevitable."

"Well, that certainly sounds like an auspicious beginning to a successful business relationship," Del said dryly.

"Will you come?"

He didn't see how he could refuse. Brice had never asked him for anything, and as he'd already admitted, he owed him this much, at least. With a sigh, he said, "When do you want me there?"

"Yesterday," Brice said. "The day before. Whenever you can get here. *Now*. Take your pick."

Smiling despite himself, Del glanced at his calendar. The only time he had open in the next two weeks was tomorrow morning. He really didn't have that, but he'd never liked Chuck Turner, anyway. Tossing the potential state senator's file aside, he said, "How about tomorrow morning at eight?"

"So soon?" Sounding surprised and relieved at the same time, Brice recovered quickly. "That'd be great. And Del—I owe you."

Briefly, Del wondered if he'd have cause to regret his decision. He hoped not. After all, he was an expert in the field, and from what he'd read, Stockwell's problems were minor compared to other accounts he had. He'd just go out, interview Kay Stockwell and assign someone here at the office to the account. Piece of cake, he thought, and said comfortably, "Not at all, Brice. After all, what are friends for? I'll see you tomorrow morning."

"We'll be waiting," Brice said gratefully, and broke the connection.

As Del replaced his own receiver, he glanced up. Stella was in the doorway once more. "I *knew* you'd find a way out of the Turner meeting," she accused him. But she was smiling.

Del left the office soon after that, hoping that sometime between now and eight in the morning, he could think of an excuse to get out of this awkward position Brice had put him in. Pulling off his tie as he started the car, he tossed it onto the seat beside him, wondering what he had been thinking. He had no business accepting another client at this time in his life, especially one who clearly had been coerced into meeting with him. Despite Brice's obvious eagerness, he could imagine how the meeting would go tomorrow. He didn't know Kay Stockwell except by reputation, but she had already proved that she intended to do things her way.

But that was tomorrow; right now he had another difficult female to face, he thought, and realized with a sinking feeling that he was almost home. One of the reasons he'd moved here was the small town atmosphere, but sometimes it had its drawbacks—like right now. Tonight, when he could have used some extra time just driving around, he was turning onto his street before he knew it. Glancing up as he pulled into his driveway, he saw the living room lights on and tried to brace himself. Lights meant that Jennifer was home, and he reluctantly reached for his briefcase and got out of the car. His daughter had been in so many moods lately—all of them bad, ugly and nasty—that he never knew what he'd be dealing with when he went in, just that he probably wouldn't like it.

He saw to his surprise when he entered that Jennifer wasn't in her room, where she always seemed to be these days when she came home from school. Instead, she was sitting on the couch, holding a piece of cake in one hand and turning the pages of a magazine with the other. When he saw the cake, he repressed the automatic remark about it being so close to dinner and said neutrally, "Hi, Jen. How was school?"

For a moment, when she looked up at him, with those masses of thick black hair that fell past her shoulders and her eyes so much the color of his, she looked just like the little girl he remembered. Then she stuffed the rest of the cake into her mouth and wiped her fingers on jeans that were straining at the seams, and the illusion vanished.

Mumbling through the crumbs, she answered, "Horrible, just like it always is."

With another sigh—he seemed to be sighing a lot these days—he put his briefcase on the hall table. He could tell it was going to be a long night, and he briefly considered lifting the ban about reading at the dinner table. He had always forbidden it, but sometimes he thought that even the turning of pages was better than just sitting in strained silence. They both felt so awkward that they ended up gobbling down the tasty dinner Mrs. Nivens left for them every night, finishing quickly so they could escape again, he to the living room to finish up paperwork, Jennifer to her room to do...whatever it was she did in there. Heaven knew, from the state of her grades, it wasn't studying.

Determined not to let the thought get him down, he came in and sat in his favorite chair, a sagging old recliner. Because he didn't know how else to get her interest, he said, "I got a call from a new client this afternoon. It sounds like it could be interesting."

Jennifer had gone back to her reading. Since she was hunched over, with her head bowed over the pages so that her hair hid her face, he couldn't see her expression. Determinedly taking the indifferent shrug of her shoulders as a positive sign, he continued, "It's Stockwell Engineering. You might have heard about it. The company is involved in a big controversy about robotics, and—"

Jennifer's head had snapped up at the mention of the company. Any sign of attention from her about anything was so unexpected that he rattled on for a moment before he realized she was looking at him with interest.

"Did you meet Kay Stockwell?" she interrupted.

He looked at her in surprise. "Well, no, not yet. We have an appointment at eight in the morning."

She tossed the magazine aside. "Wow, I can't believe it," she said. "This is great."

"Why?" he asked warily.

She didn't answer directly. "Dad, you've got to tell me everything about her after you meet!" she said. "And you have to get her to take you on a tour of the plant. No one, and I mean *no one,* knows what's going on there because she won't let anybody in. And you have to find out how she really feels about the demonstrations and what she's going to be working on next and—"

"Wait, hold on!" he said, astonished. Was this the girl whose attention had been taken up with teen magazines these past two months? "How do you know about Kay Stockwell?"

"Don't you ever listen?" Jennifer said with a roll of her eyes. "I *told* you that my journalism project for this semester is analyzing all the articles about Stockwell Engineering. I know I told you that!"

She hadn't, but he wasn't going to argue about it, not when he saw that gleam of interest in her eyes. For the first time in months, she was talking to him as though he were her father and not some lower form of life. He decided not to correct her. "I must have forgotten. I'm sorry."

"That's *so* typical," she said heavily, but then brushed it aside. "But that's okay. Tell me—tell me everything!" She looked at him alertly from the edge of the couch.

The problem was that he didn't have anything to tell— not yet, anyway. Curious to know what impression she already had, he took refuge in his image consultant persona. "Tell me what you know about her, first."

To his amazement, she obeyed. "Well, I know she inherited Stockwell Engineering when her father died. And I know that when she decided to run the company herself, some of her executives didn't like it." She frowned, thinking. "A man named George Mott is trying to cause a lot of trouble—he's the one who's been giving all the stories to the press about the robots taking over and her being responsible for causing unemployment." Surprising him again, Jennifer suddenly grinned. She had beautiful white teeth, but since he hadn't seen them displayed for a long time in anything remotely resembling a smile, he was fascinated by the change in her expression. She no longer looked like a sullen teenager but a very pretty young girl. Before he could adjust to that, she was going on. "But she's been giving as good as she gets, Dad, I'll tell you that. Man! She can really stand up for herself!"

"You sound as though you admire her."

"Admire her?" She thought about it. "Well, you have to admit she's different, all right. How many women do *you* know who run engineering companies and have master's degrees and have worked at NASA, and—"

Delighted at this enthusiasm, he smiled. "I get the picture," he said. "She sounds like a paragon, all right."

"You don't agree?"

"I don't know. I'll tell you tomorrow."

"Maybe I should write down some questions for you to ask her."

He gave her a fond look. "Maybe you should, Button," he said, unconsciously using the name she had long ago disdainfully discarded as being too childish.

Suddenly preoccupied with something other than herself, she didn't appear to notice his slip of the tongue. Leaping up, she ran out of the room to get a pencil and paper, and as he waited for her to return, he shook his head. He wouldn't have believed such a transformation possible. He decided right then that if working for Stockwell Engineering could bridge the gap he'd felt with

Jennifer all this time, maybe he was being too hasty in thinking of assigning the account to someone else at the office, or worse yet, turning it down. In fact, he thought as Jennifer raced back in, maybe he should just handle it himself for the time being.

"Here's the list," Jennifer said a moment later, thrusting the hastily scribbled questions into his hand.

He looked down at the questions she had written. "How much prejudice have you encountered as a woman engineer in a so-called man's field?" was one. Another was "What do you think the future of women in robotics will be?" A third lower down was "What advice do you have for girls who want to follow in your footsteps?"

"Will you really ask her, Dad?" she asked anxiously.

Carefully he folded the paper and put it in his briefcase. "I'll do my best," he promised.

"All *right!*" she said. "Hey, this is great!"

Del couldn't have agreed more completely. Strange how things worked out, he thought, and was smiling to himself when he went in to see what Mrs. Nivens had fixed for dinner.

CHAPTER THREE

By THE TIME Del Rafferty arrived at eight the next morning, Kay knew all about him—or thought she did. Brice hadn't given her much notice, but her secretary, Rachel, could be quite efficient, and when Kay came in early she found the file already on her desk. She immediately sat down and read it completely. The impressive résumé confirmed what Brice had told her—Rafferty Associates was one of the top consulting firms in the country. She should have been reassured, but she wasn't. Martin Winslow had been with Taylor, Winslow, Ferris and Court, and they were big, too. Look what had happened with him, she thought, wishing she had never agreed to this meeting.

She felt even more tense when the hour arrived. Knowing that she had to do something about her problems at Stockwell didn't mean she had to like it. But she was a realist, too, and she knew there was no postponing the inevitable. She had really been shaken by that rock-throwing incident, and she knew now she couldn't count on the protesters just getting tired and going away. Even so, she had hedged her bets a little, informing Brice again when he checked in with her that the interview was only a trial balloon. She hadn't agreed to become anyone's client, much less sign on with an image consultant. Especially, she thought later, one who seemed as cocksure of himself as Del Rafferty did when he walked into her office carrying a briefcase.

His aura of unassailable confidence immediately set her teeth on edge. Her wariness increased as Brice introduced them and they shook hands.

She knew from her reading that Del was forty years old. She'd been surprised that so young a man owned such a prestigious agency. But when she saw how suavely he handled himself, she realized that he would have little trouble gaining clients. Many women would find such self-assurance appealing in a man, she thought, especially one as good-looking as Del was.

The idea made her even more cautious, and she felt increasingly off balance. For one thing, she couldn't understand why she was finding this man so attractive. Del Rafferty had thick black hair—a far cry from the blond men she usually preferred. His deep blue eyes interested her, too, until she realized he was staring. In fact, his gaze hadn't left her face since he'd come in. She decided he was probably planning to change her into someone he thought made a more suitable company president. The fact that his preconceived image most likely had nothing to do with what she was all about, probably didn't bother him at all, she thought angrily.

His handshake, like hers, had been firm and brisk, and she gave him a point for that, but her face still felt tight as they settled down for the meeting, she behind her desk, the two men in chairs in front of it. She knew—and knew Brice knew—that she was pulling a power play, but she couldn't help it. She was on her guard, and she didn't intend to drop her professional barriers by suggesting a cozy seating arrangement over by the couch.

Then she caught Rafferty's amused glance and felt even more annoyed. She saw that he was aware of what she was doing, too, and, feeling slightly foolish, she became more abrupt than she usually was with someone new.

Without preamble, she said, "You might as well know right from the outset, Mr. Rafferty, that this meeting was not my idea. I'm not convinced we need your agency's services, but Brice insisted I listen to what you have to say before I make up my mind."

With a glance toward her vice president that could have meant anything, Del Rafferty said. "It sounds to me as though you already have."

She flushed again but held her ground. "No, I promised him that I would hear you out, and I will," she answered. Realizing how rude she sounded, she tried to be a little less curt. "We do have a situation here, and if you have any suggestions—" she made herself say it "—I'd be happy to hear them."

"First it might be helpful if you would tell me exactly what you perceive the problem to be."

She couldn't hide her surprise. "You haven't been reading the papers?" she asked. From the furor, she would have thought everybody in the entire state had been avidly following the drama.

"Not the entire story, no," Rafferty said without apology. "But in any event, I prefer to get my information firsthand, if possible. It avoids misunderstandings and misrepresentations." He paused delicately. "If you see what I mean."

Was he mocking her in some subtle way? It was difficult to tell, and she frowned. "I wish more people felt like that," she ventured uncertainly. "If so, Stockwell wouldn't be in this mess."

"The demonstrations, you mean?"

Disturbed at the thought, she nodded curtly. "That, and everything else. George Mott, for one. The *Springfield Gazette,* for another." Despite herself, her voice rose. "Everyone seems to feel that my primary goal is to eliminate jobs and destroy the state's economy at the same time. I'm sure they all believe that the next step will be to take over the world! Why don't they realize—"

Abruptly, she stopped, embarrassed at how strident she sounded.

Rafferty looked as if he wanted to smile. "I take it, then, that the fall of the nation is not your intention."

She wasn't amused. "When I inherited this company, Stockwell Engineering was having financial problems. But no one ever mentions that we never laid off one single employee—not one, even though we've been through some rough times." She didn't add that she hadn't taken a salary in months or that she was rapidly depleting all her reserves and the company's, too, to keep everyone on the payroll.

"But you fired some of your top executives," Del pointed out.

"Only because they gave me no choice!" she said sharply. "Each of those men made no secret how they felt about my policies."

Brice decided it was time to enter the conversation. "Not to mention how they felt about Jim's daughter taking over the president's chair," he put in with an apologetic glance in Kay's direction.

Del looked his way. "Was that the reason for all the resentment?"

"That, and the fact that Kay is young—and a woman."

"No, that wasn't the problem," Kay interjected. She wasn't going to allow them to attribute everything to male chauvinism. "I've dealt with prejudice before, and while I won't deny it's infuriating at times, it's something I, and every other woman who enters a so-called man's field, have had to endure occasionally. Women are making inroads into the engineering profession, but we're still a resented minority. Until that changes, and it will in time, there are going to be problems. I was willing to deal with that—to overlook it." She took a deep breath. "But I couldn't overlook my top people fighting me about the direction in which I wanted to take the company. Regardless of how George Mott and those other men felt, I'm the one who's ultimately responsible for Stockwell Engineering, and I couldn't have anyone undermining my position. Those who didn't agree with me wouldn't have been happy here, anyway."

"So your decision to institute a robotics division was Mott's main objection?"

Kay started to reply angrily, but then, as though all the air had been let out of her, her shoulders slumped and her mouth turned down. "Yes," she said. "That's been the real problem with everything all along."

"Because of the jobs people think it might eliminate."

"Well, there's more to it than that," she said unwillingly.

"Oh?" Del glanced at the notebook he had taken out of his briefcase. "According to some figures I have here, estimates are that anywhere from one hundred to two hundred thousand jobs in this country are going to be directly eliminated within the next few years because of robots—thirty thousand jobs in the auto industry alone." He looked up, his eyes meeting hers. "That's a lot of people out of work."

"And a lot of people freed from dangerous jobs, as well," Kay shot back. "For instance, service robots have been at work in nuclear plants for several years, in positions where their human counterparts ran the risk of exposure to radiation. And robots have been utilized underwater in place of human divers who required cumbersome and costly life-support systems, which, despite the best technology, sometimes failed."

"It sounds like you're saying that it won't be long before human beings won't be needed in society at all," Del commented. "Robots will be able to do everything. Androids will take our place."

Kay laughed shortly. "You've been seeing too many movies, Mr. Rafferty. We're light-years away from actually producing any of the half man, half machines that you see on film—the so-called androids. Right now, even with the highest state of the art, the most intelligent robot is actually quite dense."

He looked surprised. "But I thought—"

This was her field; she leaned forward, intent on explaining it to him. "Let me give you an example of what we're talking about, then you'll see just how ridiculous the charges are that robots are somehow going to rise up and take over, or, even worse, that we're going to be enslaving machines against their will."

"Go ahead, I'm interested."

She saw that he really was. Taken aback for a few seconds because she hadn't expected him to be interested in anything other than changing her into something she wasn't, she said, "All right. Er . . . the key to making robots smarter lies in computer power that can enhance their intelligence—which as I've said, is still pretty poor."

"Why is that?" he asked curiously.

"One reason is because progress toward giving robots humanlike sight and hands has been so slow. We have yet to produce a fully workable robot hand, and trying to reproduce sight is even more difficult."

"I hadn't realized it was so complicated."

"Complicated isn't the word for it," she told him. "We're just now coming to appreciate how complex our human information processing systems really are. To translate all that into machine language is a formidable task we are just beginning to address. So you can see that these notions about robots and androids rising up to take over the world are *very* farfetched. However, robots taking over dangerous or repetitive tasks are already proving beneficial."

He looked impressed. "You certainly seem to know what you're talking about."

She saw the admiration in his eyes and, to her dismay, felt her guard going down. Why did he have to be so good-looking? she wondered. And worse, why did he have to seem so genuinely interested in her work?

And *why,* she wondered, really annoyed with herself, was she being so distracted? She *had* to keep her mind on who he was and what he represented. She couldn't afford to forget that, as charming as he appeared to be, Del Rafferty was still a professional brother to Martin Winslow. She didn't doubt that, despite Rafferty's undeniable charisma, he was entirely capable of doing what Marty had done.

On that thought, she brought herself back to the matter at hand. "Thank you," she said briskly, "but I've only scratched the surface, I'm afraid. Robotics is a vast subject, and I'm hardly an expert."

"You certainly sound like one to me."

"Thank you, but I wish more people would take the time to learn about the science. If they did, we wouldn't be getting all this bad press from a bunch of hysterical fanatics."

"I think what Kay is trying to say," Brice interjected quickly, "is that the entire industry is plagued with misunderstandings that have arisen because of ignorance or fear of what robots can—or might—do. I think lack of knowledge is the problem."

"It's not the only problem," Kay said flatly. "You can't tell me that the people carrying those signs and making all that noise at the gate really want to know anything about robotics. The only thing they want is to see themselves on TV."

With a sigh, Brice turned back to Del. "As you can see, we don't see eye-to-eye. I think information is the key, and Kay...doesn't."

"That's not true!" she exclaimed, annoyed. "I do believe in education. But the people who want to learn, will. Those who don't, just...picket!"

"So what do you think is the solution?" Del asked politely.

Kay was tempted to reply that if she knew, they wouldn't be having this meeting. Instead, she answered impatiently, "At the moment, I don't know. But I can tell you this. No matter what happens with the situation here at Stockwell Engineering, it's not going to make a difference. People can think what they like, but demographics are on the side of the robot industry. There will come a time when society has to accept the inevitable whether it wants to or not."

Demographics were Del's field, and he asked with interest, "What findings are you talking about?"

Kay shrugged. "It's a fact that the declining birth rate has already produced a shortage of teenagers available for minimum wage jobs," she said, and added when she saw their faces, "Now, I know how that sounds, but it's something society has to consider. And just as important, at the other end of the scale is the fact that people are living longer. It's no secret that older people require more services. Robot technology is one of the few fields that holds out the promise of helping this section of the population in ways they never could have been helped before—particularly in medicine."

"So it's not all about defense, then," Del said.

"It never was," Brice said, giving Kay a quick look before he turned back to Del. "That's why all this has been so unfair to Kay. She's taking the blame for something that the press—"

"Aided and abetted by one George Mott," Kay put in darkly.

Brice nodded. "That's right. Mott is at the root of this. He's got everyone stirred up about defense projects and job takeovers and machine societies."

"I see what you mean about misconceptions," Del said. "You've both pointed out some things I hadn't been aware of."

"You and all those other people who are screaming bloody murder out there," Kay said, and unconsciously made a fist. "There *must* be some way to reach them!"

It was Del's turn to take the floor. "Well, in fact," he said calmly, "there is."

Despite herself, she gave him a hopeful look. "Do you have any ideas?"

He laughed. "That's why I'm here."

Embarrassed at her slip, she said impatiently, "Well, would you mind sharing a few with us?"

"Not at all," he answered, sobering—but with a twinkle in his eye. "Now, given your opening remarks, I have a feeling you're not going to like this, but the fact is that the first thing I'd suggest is changing your company's image."

Kay stiffened. "Oh?"

He pretended not to notice her tone. "Obviously, part of the problem is that those of us who aren't directly involved in the science can't know all the details," he said. "For example, I think that most of society—and that includes me, I'm afraid—associates the word *robot* with a machine that is stronger than we are and smarter, not to mention immortal and indestructible, besides. Faced with all that, we humans can feel pretty puny."

Kay's expression showed her disdain. "Too many movies again," she said. "In other words, we're back to the unreasonable fear of robots."

"I don't think it's so unreasonable," Del persisted. "After all, we all fear what we don't understand."

"And you think it's *my* job to educate people?"

"If you want to get rid of those demonstrators outside, it is," he answered calmly. "And, after all, you're in the best position to do so, aren't you?"

"No, I'm not! I've got work to do here. I really can't take time to explain a very complicated science to every Tom, Dick or Harry who's got some hysterical fear that robots are going to take over the world!"

"I understand that it's not your choice—"

"It's not my *job!*"

"I understand that," Del said again, this time with a slight edge to his voice.

Kay could sense that he thought she was being obstinate. Well, fine, she thought; he could think what he liked. She was not going to start giving classes on the subject of robotics!

"I'm afraid," she said, her voice steely, "that you'll just have to think of another approach—if you can."

"Oh, I can," Del said, annoying her even further with his unshakable confidence. "That's *my* job."

"Well?" she challenged.

Unhesitatingly, he answered, "All right, another approach might be to...make robots seem less frightening and more...friendly."

"That's absurd!" She dismissed the notion with a wave of her hand. "Robots are neither friendly nor unfriendly. They just *are!*"

"And that's perhaps what makes them even more scary," Del shot back. "It's obvious to me that we have to figure out a way to make the concept less threatening to people—like you did a little while ago for me."

She wasn't going to be influenced, not by such a left-handed compliment—if that's what it had been intended to be. She wasn't sure just what he had intended; he could have meant anything. Meeting his glance, she demanded, "And how do you propose to do that?"

"By making you more familiar to people."

Not again! she thought, and said, "No. I've already told you—"

"Your company is the one under fire."

"That's true, but—"

"And you're the head of the company."

"Yes, but—"

"And so when people think of Stockwell Engineering, they're going to think of you. Wouldn't you like them to think positively about what you're doing?"

"I don't believe they have to think of me at all! What I do here isn't anyone's business but mine!"

"Not true," Del said. "Witness those protests."

She was silent. Somewhere there was a gap in his logic, but right now she couldn't find it.

"So, Del," Brice said quickly, before she could gather herself for another flurry, "what do you think we should do?"

Del held up his hand, intending to tick points off with his fingers. Kay hadn't noticed before, but he had square hands. Capable hands. Instead of admiring them, she became even more irritated than she already was. Why had she agreed to this absurd interview? Now all she could think was that if he was so capable, he wouldn't have chosen to make his living manipulating people. And that's exactly what he was trying to do to her, she decided. Why else was he looking at her like that, challenging her, intimating that she couldn't find the answer because *he'd* had it all this time?

"First," Del said, holding up his index finger, "we need to take advantage of what we have here. As I was going to say before, it's a plus that Ms. Stockwell is, number one, a woman... and number two, an attractive woman—"

She was outraged. "Now, wait just a minute! What sex I am and what I look like should have nothing to do with it!"

"That's true," Del agreed, "but it does. People tend to listen to someone who... er... looks like you."

Really annoyed, she flattened both hands on top of the desk and glared at him. "If that's true," she said evenly, "why haven't they listened to me before now?"

He shrugged. "Because you haven't been saying the right things."

"Oh?" she said acidly. "And what should I have said?"

He ignored the sarcasm. "You gave me some examples before. How about if I give you a few now?"

Gritting her teeth, she said, "Go ahead."

"Let me show you how important a choice of words or phrase can be. You can decide for yourself just how easily public opinion can be influenced in subtle ways. All right?"

Spacing her words deliberately, she said, "I'm listening."

"Okay.... You're fighting for citizenship. Would it be better to be called an undocumented worker or an illegal alien?"

She tightened her lips. Even she could see the trap in that particular example. "Well, when you put it like that—"

"Let's try another. You have to get about in a wheelchair. Do you want to be crippled or physically challenged?"

She glowered. "I'm not sure I'd want to be called either one."

"That's true, but if you *had* to be, which one would you prefer?"

"I don't know," she said stubbornly.

He was undeterred. "What about this? Are you liberal, which has taken on negative connotations, or progressive?"

She was still determined to be obstinate. "I don't see that it makes much difference."

"Depending on whose side you're on, indeed it does," he replied smoothly. "And how about these? Is the man who planted a bomb to free his people a freedom fighter or a terrorist? Do we raise taxes or implement revenue enhancements? I could go on, but I think you see what I mean."

"What I see is that your snappy little *buzzwords* or *sound bites*," Kay said the words with loathing, thinking of the increasingly popular technique of using thirty-second commercials to convey an idea, "add little or nothing to our understanding of the issues." She had an example of her own at hand. "For instance, the all-encompassing prodemocracy certainly doesn't spell out the differences between movements in China, East Germany and the Soviet Union, now, does it?"

Del flushed slightly, and she knew she had scored. It was a hollow victory, for Brice said quickly, "I see what you mean—both of you. But isn't the point—"

"The point," Kay interrupted curtly, "is that I'm not going to be a party to some clever little deception—a manipulation designed as a smoke screen to avoid the real issues! My company is in trouble, and I won't have our problems reduced to some catchphrase that's supposed to confound the issue and make everybody feel warm and cozy. I won't do it!"

For a moment there was silence. Kay knew she had overreacted. *Damn Adam!* she thought, and saw Brice's wounded expression. For his sake, she made herself apologize.

"I'm sorry," she said stiffly. "It's just . . . never mind. Go on."

Brice forgave her with a quick, reassuring smile before he turned to Del, saying, "I agree that as Stockwell's president Kay really is the best representative for the company. But since she is so opposed to these . . . er . . . newer tactics, can't we think of some other approach? How about a radio interview, or having her appear on one of the local television stations? Maybe she could even speak to a civic group or something. What do you think?" He turned to Kay. "How about you?"

She needed more time to think about it. "I don't know," she hedged. "It *might* work."

"I think so, too," Del said reluctantly, after he'd considered the idea for a moment.

He looked almost sorry that they might have reached a compromise, and Kay started to feel angry again. It hadn't been her idea that he come here; if he didn't like Brice's suggestion, he could just march right out again.

Brice saw her face just in time. "Good, good," he said heartily, before she could say what was on her mind. "I knew we could work something out!"

"Perhaps Mr. Rafferty needs a little more time to think about it, Brice," she said. "Maybe we should just table it for now."

Del's lips twitched slightly; he knew she was trying to extricate herself gracefully. "Not at all," he said. "In fact, I think Brice's suggestion has a great deal of merit. I'd need some time to work out the details, but I could get back to you—if you like."

Kay was certain she glimpsed a subtle challenge in that blue glance. Now she didn't know whether to tell him to leave or rashly agree to work with him. *Damn Brice!* she thought peevishly. If she hadn't listened to him, she wouldn't be in this awkward position.

She knew it wasn't going to work, even if she did want to try it—and she wasn't sure she did. Despite Del Rafferty's maddening confidence and her contempt of the business he was in, she could feel the pull of attraction, and she didn't like it. Not one bit.

Then she became even more annoyed. What was the matter with her? *Resisting* him wasn't the problem. No matter how attractive he was or how charismatic, what was really important here was the fact that she had contempt for everything he obviously believed in. He embraced all those loathsome image tactics like sound bites and buzzwords and spin doctors and God knew what else, while she dealt in digital electronics and electro-mechanical sensors and pneumatics. He didn't understand what she was about any more than she understood what drove him. They'd never get anything done, for she suspected that despite his courtesy today, once they started working together, they'd disagree about everything. Surely, there had to be some other solution!

But there wasn't. If there had been, she would have thought of it before now. Covertly, she glanced at him and was annoyed to see that his expression was almost amused, as though he sensed what a struggle she was having and was enjoying seeing her squirm. *Blast it all, anyway!* she thought, and said coolly, "I'd like to see what arrangements you intend to make before I commit myself. My schedule is very busy right now, but if you can come up with a workable plan, I would consider signing on with your agency."

Brice nearly groaned, but Del seemed only more amused. "Fine," he said, getting to his feet. "I'll put one of my people on it and give you a call by the end of next week. Is that acceptable?"

She wasn't sure. "You're not going to handle this yourself?"

He smiled. "As you say, I don't have the account yet. If we can work something out, then I'll decide."

Her eyes flashed, but before she could reply, Brice jumped in. "I'm sure that will be just fine," he said quickly, shooting Kay a quelling glance while he pumped Del's hand. Putting an arm around Del's shoulders, he began hustling him out.

Del stopped at the door to look at her. All she could see were those blue eyes. "I'll be in touch," he said.

It was just a saying, something everybody said. It didn't mean anything, certainly not from someone she'd just met. But absurdly, her heart gave a little leap. Annoyed with herself again, she gave him another cool smile. "Thank you for coming," she said.

"My pleasure," he replied, and left with Brice, who thanked him again for coming. Kay heard them laughing and talking out in the hall and frowned.

She should have said that she'd changed her mind, she thought; she should have told him that she wanted to handle things herself. She should have said *anything* but what she had. Now she'd gone halfway to committing herself, and why? Because Del Rafferty was a handsome, charismatic man who had—momentarily—charmed her into agreeing to give this a try.

Oh, what had she been thinking of? She didn't need another experience such as she had endured with Martin Winslow to prove that all image consultants were the same. Under that charm, behind the appeal, they were all alike—all surface and no substance, all form and no content. It was what they did, how they made their living. And if they all didn't believe it, why weren't they doing something else with their lives?

Damn it, this was a mistake, she thought; she'd known it the instant he'd come into the room. Putting her head in her hands, she cursed her quick temper and even quicker tongue. If he hadn't goaded her with that…that *look,* she never would have agreed to give the association a try. Now it was too late; she had practically committed herself.

FOR THE FIRST TIME since she'd come to live with him, Jennifer met her father at the door that night. He'd had a hell of a day and knew it showed. He'd been so tired coming home that he hadn't even had the energy to take off his tie; it was hanging askew, just like his state of mind. Even though every hour today had been filled with appointments and demands and command decisions—not to mention a quick meeting to sooth Chuck Turner's ruffled feelings—there was one interview he hadn't been able to get out of his head. He was still thinking about his appointment with Kay Stockwell when he turned into his driveway and Jennifer flung open the front door.

"Hi, Button," he said wearily as she joined him half-way up the walk. "How was school?"

"Never mind that!" Jennifer exclaimed. She took his briefcase from him, tossing it onto the hall table as they came in, practically dragging him into the living room. Pushing him down into his chair, she handed him the drink she'd made with a flourish.

Surprised at such solicitation, he gave the glass a cautious look. Except for the single ice cube floating around, it looked as if it were all bourbon.

"What's this?" he asked, stalling. He couldn't remember the last time he'd had a drink after work like this. He'd given that up long ago—when he realized some time after his divorce that the decanter was the first thing he reached for when he came home.

"I thought you might like one," Jennifer said eagerly. She dropped to the floor by his chair. "Now," she commanded. "Tell me all about Kay Stockwell. I know you had an appointment with her today, and I want to know every detail!"

Hoping he wouldn't choke, Del took a token sip of the drink before surreptitiously putting it aside. He was touched by Jennifer's gesture, but if he drank that much bourbon in one sitting, he wouldn't wake up until sometime next week.

"There's not much to tell," he said carefully. "We really didn't talk very long, and—"

"But what's she *like,* Dad?" Jennifer demanded.

He wasn't sure what to say. How could he admit to his daughter that he had felt totally off balance with Kay Stockwell from the moment he'd entered her office?

He'd known from the file that Stella had hastily prepared for him how old Kay was and what degrees she held. He had known what she looked like from newspaper pictures. But nothing had prepared him for the impact Kay had had on him. To say that she was beautiful and obviously very intelligent somehow didn't quite do her justice.

He'd been so overwhelmed, in fact, that he'd had a difficult time keeping his mind on business. Throughout the entire interview, he'd found his mind wandering, thinking at first how expressive her green eyes were, then how soft her skin looked. He'd been distracted by her hair, which was a beautiful color, sorrel shot with gold, and he kept wanting to reach out and touch her or catch another whiff of her tantalizing perfume.

"Dad!" Jennifer persisted. "What's she *like?* Is she as...as *valiant* as the papers claim?"

Del looked blankly at his daughter. *Valiant* was a good word for Kay Stockwell, he thought, remembering the fire in her eyes and her obvious struggle to put aside her own feelings for her company's sake. He wasn't sure just why she was so opposed to the concept of image enhancement; he would have to ask Brice if he had a clue. But her resistance to the idea was much stronger than he had expected, and he'd been surprised and dismayed by the sudden, inexplicable desire he'd felt to convince her that what he did had merit. He was wondering why he should care *what* she thought of him when Jennifer tugged impatiently at his sleeve.

"Dad! What did you *think?*"

He didn't know what to think at this point; he'd thought at first that he'd be happy to get the Stockwell account because it would be a bridge to communication with his daughter, but he was disturbed to realize that wasn't the only reason he was glad that Kay hadn't turned him down—yet, he amended. It was obvious she hadn't exactly been thrilled at the thought of their working together.

Well, he was just going to have to change her mind, he decided, and smiled at Jennifer. "I think," he said in a masterpiece of understatement, "that Kay Stockwell is quite a woman."

"I knew that!" Jennifer said with scorn. "Did you ask her the questions I gave you?"

That he could answer. He'd written down what Kay had said about women and engineering on the piece of paper Jennifer had given him, and he dug into his pocket and handed it across. Jennifer grabbed it and skimmed it.

"Oh, this is great!" she said. She stuffed the paper into her jeans and leaned forward again. "Do you think you can get more, Dad? Is she going to be your client? Will you—"

"Hey, hey," he said with a laugh, trying to stem the flow. "Nothing's been settled. We have to work out a few details yet."

"What details? When will you know? Will you see her soon?"

Feeling overwhelmed by the difficult and demanding females who seemed to have come into his life recently, he gave a helpless shake of his head. "I don't know yet, Button," he said. Even as he said the words, he was disturbed to realize just how much he wanted to see Kay Stockwell again.

CHAPTER FOUR

To Kay's surprise, Del Rafferty didn't wait until the end of the following week to get back to her, and he didn't assign someone in his office to phone her with the arrangements. On Wednesday, he called himself.

By then, however, she had become convinced that she'd never hear from him again—except, possibly, through a letter expressing regrets. He was too busy; he had so many other commitments, he'd say. She could imagine how polite and formal it would be, and she wouldn't blame him. She had acted like a witch. Who wouldn't have been put off?

Consequently, when Rachel buzzed through on Wednesday morning to tell her Del Rafferty was on the line, she was quite taken aback. And she was determined to be cautious. She hadn't liked it that she'd been unable to get his face out of her mind this past weekend, and as she reached for the receiver, she was dismayed at the little jolt of pleasure she felt at the thought of talking to him again.

"Kay Stockwell here," she said into the phone.

To her chagrin, he sounded amused at her clipped formality. "Del Rafferty, Ms. Stockwell," he replied equally formally. "I had a few minutes between appointments, so I thought I'd call to discuss what we talked about on Friday. Is this a bad time?"

Kay glanced at the mound of paperwork on her desk. Rachel had divided it into three piles: one stack was "Get to this now!"; the second was "Do immediately, if not sooner!"; and the third was "Can't wait!" Without a thought, she pushed all three away. This was more important, she told herself, and resolutely turned her back to the desk.

"Not at all," she said. "I'm between appointments myself." It wasn't true. Three people were waiting in the outer office for her, and she also had a stack of urgent phone calls to return. Deliberately putting those details out of her mind, she added, "What can I do for you?"

Sounding amused again, he said, "I thought the question was what I could do for you."

She didn't like the fact that he seemed to find her so humorous. Worse than that was the warmth she felt inside at hearing his deep voice. Curtly, she said, "You're right, of course. I had forgotten that Stockwell was being considered for your client list—and not that we were thinking of hiring you."

She could almost see him grin. "Touché," he said without a trace of apology. "Perhaps I didn't phrase that correctly."

"Perhaps."

Since her tone had cooled considerably, he obviously felt it was best to move on. "The reason I called was to tell you that I've worked out a tentative plan of attack," he said. "But before I go ahead, I'd really like to discuss the particulars with you."

"All right, go ahead."

"No, I don't mean over the phone. I'd hoped that we could meet in person, and that, if possible, I could get a sort of Cook's tour of the place. I need to know what exactly it is that you do at Stockwell, what goals you have in mind for the company—that sort of thing. Then I can start locking in potential appearances or speaking engagements for you. We need to start with places where the people are sympathetic—or at least open-minded—about your cause before we—"

She didn't know why, but she could feel herself getting irritated again—maybe because he was making so much sense. "I have no *cause,* Mr. Rafferty."

"Del, please. If we're going to be working together—"

"Are we going to do that? I thought you hadn't decided if you'd handle our account."

"No, as I said before, it's up to you."

He had ignored her sarcasm—had she meant to be sarcastic? At this moment, she wasn't quite sure. Did she want him to work for her or not? It should have been a simple decision. Why did it seem so fraught with peril?

Because she was attracted to him, that's why, she thought irritably. It was why she was being so hostile, a reaction that wasn't like her at all. Usually she bent over backward to be fair—or believed she did, anyway. But, aside from not being convinced that this approach was best for the company, she knew there was another reason she was so antagonistic. Certainly she resented the idea that one of her former employees could say or do what he liked, while *she* had to redefine her position—as well as her company's image. But she knew her distraction right now was mostly due to this very inconvenient attraction she was feeling toward the man who might be able to help.

"Well, I haven't decided yet," she said, avoiding the issue.

"Understandable," he replied smoothly, "since I haven't given you anything to decide *about*. That's why I wanted to meet."

She wanted to meet him, too, and that made her even more upset with herself. The last thing she needed right now was to have these feelings surfacing. It wasn't that she had dramatically sworn off all men after her doomed love affair, or because the company was her life—although these days it *was*. She did want to meet someone—if only to prove to herself that not all men were swine.

The problem was that she had promised herself after her experience with Martin Winslow she would never get involved with another image consultant, no matter *how* attractive he was. She wasn't so foolish or naive as to think that all people in Del's profession were as opportunistic and self-serving as Marty had been; there were probably some nice consultants around...somewhere. She just hadn't wanted to devote any time or energy to finding one.

But now one had found her, and much as she would have liked to tell him politely that she'd changed her mind, after all, the thought of the rock-throwing incident prevented her from doing so. There had been no repeat, thank heaven; the demonstrators had even backed off for a few days, showing up again only this morning, but not as loud and belligerent as they had been before. But there was no guarantee that it wouldn't happen again. Right now, Del Rafferty seemed her best hope to stop this before it got even more out of hand, and as for getting involved...well, she just wouldn't.

Oh, no? a nagging little voice asked.

No, she told it firmly. She had worked with handsome, attractive men before and hadn't made a fool of

herself by falling for them. She could do it again. And if
Del could actually do what he'd said and defuse the situation so she could concentrate on her work, it would be
worth a little...personal inconvenience. It was the long
run that mattered, and she had exciting long-term plans
for the company.

"Ms. Stockwell?"

Del's voice brought her abruptly back to the present.
She realized she had been silent too long. "Please call me
Kay," she said. "And, after thinking about it, I believe
you're right. We should talk about strategy, and if you
think it would be helpful for you to see what we're doing
here, I'll arrange a tour. Just tell me what time and day
would be convenient."

If he was surprised at her capitulation, he didn't show
it. He knew that she had never offered anyone else a tour
of the place before; ever since Mott had stirred up the
press, every journalist in the state, it seemed, had clam-
ored for an inspection of the facilities, but she had flatly
refused every request.

"Thank you," he said. "I know how much heat you've
taken on this, and I appreciate your trust."

She was surprised into saying, "Well, if you're going
to help, it makes sense for you to know what we're aiming for here."

"My thoughts, exactly. I think we should get started
right away. I'd like to work up a proposal before things
get worse, so if it's okay with you, I can clear some time
this afternoon for a quick run-through. I could be there
at—how about three? Would that suit you?"

Kay had no need to look at her schedule; every working hour for the next month was filled. Resolutely trying
not to think of the disaster this would be to her calendar,
she said, "Three will be fine. See you then."

As soon as she put the phone down, she buzzed for her secretary. "Cancel my three o'clock appointment," she said when Rachel appeared. "Del Rafferty is coming for a meeting and a tour of the plant."

Rachel's eyes widened. She was a small, thin young woman with brown hair in a frizzy halo around her head and big, square tortoiseshell-framed eyeglasses magnifying her blue eyes. "A *tour?*" she echoed, knowing Kay's stand on allowing outsiders into the plant. Then she saw the boss's expression and nodded hastily. "Okay, whatever you say. But your three o'clock is—"

"I know who it is," Kay said, wondering if she was out of her mind. She had been scheduled to meet Vernon MacAffee, a venture capitalist who had expressed an interest in robotics. This afternoon, she had hoped to convince him that he'd be even more interested if he invested several of his millions in Stockwell Engineering. "Tell him something...unavoidable...came up," she said, mentally crossing her fingers. "He'll understand."

"Okay," Rachel said, moving toward the door. But she cast a worried look over her shoulder at Kay as she went back to her desk, and when she sat down to place the call, she still looked doubtful.

ACROSS TOWN, Del was having a similar conversation with *his* secretary, who was less understanding than Rachel.

"You want me to *cancel* everything after three today?" Stella repeated incredulously after Del had called her in. "But you were scheduled to fly to—"

"I know what I was supposed to do," Del growled, wondering if he'd gone around the bend. He was supposed to meet with a *very* important client this afternoon in Atlanta to start developing a congressional campaign. "But this is more important," he said, avoiding Stella's eyes. "Arthur will just have to understand."

"Oh . . . right," Stella said significantly. She paused. "Anything else, boss? A cup of hemlock, maybe? A call to the guys in the little white coats?"

Glowering, he said, "Just do it, okay, Stella?"

"You're the boss," she said. But he didn't miss the pitying glance she tossed him when she went out, and she was still shaking her head as she went back to her desk.

Del couldn't blame her for being confused; his actions were inexplicable, even to himself. But he'd gone too far to back down now, and just before three that afternoon, he found himself approaching the gates at Stockwell Engineering for the second time in less than a week. Although it seemed there weren't quite as many demonstrators milling around this day, and those who were here appeared more subdued than before, the content of the signs they were carrying was the same. Del suspected that it wouldn't be too long before they rallied once more.

Or are stirred up again, he thought, waiting while the guard at the gate checked his name against a clipboard. When the guard finally waved him through, he put the thought of the protesters out of his mind and headed toward the three-story square brick building that housed Stockwell Engineering. But as he pulled into a parking space in front, he realized that he was really looking forward to this meeting, and he frowned. He didn't like this . . . this sense of anticipation he felt, and he couldn't understand why the thought of seeing Kay again made him feel this way.

Deciding that he didn't want to examine this sensation too closely, he reached for his briefcase and got out of the car. He adjusted his tie and just barely resisted the temptation to check his appearance in the mirror bolted to the door. Feeling foolish and adolescent, he slammed the car door shut and strode quickly up the cement walk.

The front doors opened onto a small tile foyer, where, since the trouble with George Mott and the press, a reception desk had been installed. A big, burly man in uniform was sitting behind the desk. Unwelcome visitors would have to be foolhardy to try to get past this man, Del thought, for when the guard smiled and stood, he easily topped Del's own six-foot-two height and probably outweighed him by about thirty pounds.

"You're Mr. Rafferty," the man said.

"I am," Del agreed. "I'm here to see—"

"I know—Ms. Stockwell. She was going to meet you in her office, but there's been a little emergency, so she told me to send you down to the teaching lab. Just take the elevator to the basement and turn left. You can't miss it."

"Why, because of all the smoke?" Del said, trying a joke. The guard looked at him expressionlessly, and he shrugged and shook his head. "Never mind. Where are the elevators?"

Still with that same lack of expression, the big man pointed to the silver doors behind Del. "Press B," he said. "And turn left."

"Thanks," Del said, wondering if possibly the guard was some kind of robot prototype. He looked real enough, but maybe around here, you couldn't be sure.

With a whoosh, the elevator took him to the basement. It wasn't a long trip, and when the doors opened again, Del stepped out cautiously. The guard hadn't told him what *kind* of emergency Kay was involved in, and he wasn't sure whether any minute he'd hear sirens or bells going off or be pushed out of the way by a renegade runaway robot. Smiling to himself at the ridiculous notion, he was just turning to the left as he'd been told, when he nearly collided with a waist-high cylinder on wheels that was rolling quickly toward him. Startled, he leaped back, trying to get out of the way, but just then someone shouted, "Don't move! Stay right there!"

At the sound, Del looked up—a little wildly, he had to admit. A man in a lab coat had appeared in a doorway down the hall to yell at him, and he looked quickly down at the metal can again. He'd thought he was being funny with his visions of runaway robots, but now it seemed he'd—literally—run into one, and he wasn't sure what it might do. Was it dangerous? Would it attack? Just then the cylinder stopped, and to his relief, Kay appeared from the same doorway as the man who had shouted at him. They were both coming down the hall quickly after it, the edges of their white lab coats billowing behind them. The man, whose head barely came to Kay's shoulder, shouted again, "Don't *move!*"

Wondering what was going on, Del did as he was told. Not sure whether to be afraid—would the thing release a cloud of poison gas or cut him in half with a laser?—he just stood there like an idiot until Kay and her companion reached him.

"Kay, what . . . ?" he started to say.

"Shh!" she commanded without looking at him. She was intent on the cylinder, as was the little man with her. They were both staring at it with such engrossed absorption that Del looked back down again, too. The thing hadn't moved—and continued to stay as motionless as the three humans surrounding it. Del wasn't sure what they were all waiting for, but he stood there like everyone else, gazing raptly at the thing until finally, after about two minutes of motionless silence, Kay sighed.

"I guess that's it, then," she said.

The man with her looked even more unhappy. "I'm sorry, Kay. I really thought we had it this time."

"Me, too," she said, and suddenly seemed to realize Del was still standing there. "Oh..." she said uncertainly. "Hi."

"Hi," Del said, still watching the cylinder with one wary eye. "Can I move now?"

"Might as well," she said, "since obviously it isn't going to."

Hoping this was true, Del cautiously started to step out of the way. As soon as he moved, the little cylinder went into motion again. Thinking he was about to be attacked, after all, Del jumped hastily back against the elevator doors, which, fortunately, were shut. As he watched, the rolling robot, or whatever the hell it was, began tooling merrily down the hall, Kay's lab-coated companion in hot pursuit.

"Great," Kay muttered. "*Now* it moves!"

Deciding he'd like to know what was going on, Del relaxed his tight grip on his briefcase and turned to Kay, who was still watching the chase. "What was all that about?" he asked. "Was that thing about to attack, or what?"

"Attack?" she repeated, her attention still taken up with the drama being enacted down the hall. Then she seemed to realize what he'd said, for she looked away from the runaway cylinder and its hotfooted companion and back to Del's face. "Attack?" she repeated, her eyes beginning to crinkle with laughter. Trying to hide her amusement, she put her hand over her mouth, but it was too late. Laughter burst from her as Del stood there, glaring, and she seemed to find his indignant expression even more humorous. "I'm sorry, but I—" The cough with which she attempted to cover up her laughter turned into another burst of mirth.

Somewhat embarrassed, Del tugged at his tie. "I'm glad you think it's funny," he said stiffly.

Seeing his expression, Kay managed to get herself under control. "I'm sorry," she said again, hiding her smile with an effort. "It's just—" She started to laugh again, caught herself, and said more somberly, "It's really not funny."

"No, it isn't," he agreed. "Now, would you mind telling me what the hell's going on? Why did that man yell at me to stop like that? Or do you treat all your visitors this way?"

She was completely serious now. "We don't have any visitors—"

"Yes, well, I can see why. You'd probably scare the life out of them."

She looked at him curiously. "You weren't really *scared,* were you?"

He didn't know what he'd felt. He just knew that for a tense few seconds there, every robot he'd ever seen in every science fiction movie he'd ever watched had flashed menacingly before his eyes. But with Kay's green eyes looking at him like that, he couldn't admit it. "Of course not. But when that man shouted like that, I didn't know what was supposed to happen. Can you blame me? The guard upstairs said there was some kind of emergency—"

She was trying to laugh again. "And you thought it was a runaway robot?" she asked, her lips twitching.

"I didn't know what to think," he retorted. "He told me not to move, and I didn't. That's all I know."

Merriment had turned her eyes very green. "Well, you did just fine," she said reassuringly. Del had the impression that if they'd known each other a little better, she would have given him a little congratulatory pat on the arm. Then she glanced down the hallway. The little man in the lab coat was returning, pushing the metal cylinder before him.

"Mort, I'd like to introduce Del Rafferty," she said, drawing the man near. "Del, this is Mort Lachlan, my chief engineer."

Aware of the robot beside him and hoping it didn't think it was a guard dog, Del warily held out his hand. "Pleased to meet you."

"Likewise," Mort murmured, clearly distracted. He returned the handshake, then looked at Kay glumly. "This is really disappointing."

Kay nodded. "I guess it's back to the drawing board. Maybe we'll have better luck on the next run."

"I hope so," Mort said, and then waved them both goodbye. Del noticed that the robot didn't say anything but just trundled away with the engineer, complacent as could be. As the odd couple disappeared through the doorway some distance down the hall, Kay turned back to Del again.

"I'm sorry. Now, where were we?"

Beginning to wonder if he'd taken a short elevator ride into the twilight zone, Del hardly knew where to begin. "I'm not sure," he said. "Is it safe to move now?"

Kay laughed. "Absolutely. The next runaway robot isn't scheduled for an hour, so we have plenty of time to make it to the lab. Come on. It's this way."

They went in the direction the others had gone, and as they passed an open door, Del glanced in warily. Mort was busy with the metal cylinder, which he had placed on a long, narrow table cluttered with wires, gadgets, tools, circuit boards and other complicated looking things. He was so immersed in what he was doing that he didn't even look up as Del and Kay went by. The next door led into a similar laboratory, this one much bigger and partitioned off in giant areas—one of which was bare except for a long, three-sectioned complicated tubelike affair, with wheels at each juncture to make it mobile. When Kay saw him staring, she explained.

"That's what we call a robot arm," she said. "It's one of hundreds of different kinds in the industry, and this type is about half the size of the one used by the space shuttle to carry satellites out of its cargo hold and into space. We're experimenting with changing the design so it's smaller but stronger and even more flexible."

"It looks strong enough to me," Del said, staring at the massive thing as they edged by. "It could probably pick up this entire building."

"It'll be even stronger when we get through with it," Kay said with a smile, and gestured him toward a tiny cubicle at the end of the vast room. Obviously an office, the cubicle had a desk, two chairs and a computer terminal. The desk was littered with schematics, charts and blueprints of some kind, with a couple of coffee cups perched atop the whole mess. With a grimace, Kay took the cups and moved them aside. Then she scooped up a stack of paper from one of the chairs and put it on the floor. She indicated for Del to sit while she took a chair behind the desk.

"I'm sorry I had to meet you here," she said, "but I guess it doesn't matter, anyway. You've seen my office, and you did want a tour of the robotics section, so…here we are. Where would you like to start?"

Del hadn't the faintest idea. "I don't know," he said, glancing around. The pegboard walls of the cubicle were covered with drawings, designs of circuit boards, computer printouts and pages filled with what looked like hieroglyphics to him. Wondering if this had been such a good idea, after all, he turned back to Kay and said, "Maybe we should start with what happened in the hall."

"Oh, that," she said, her smile disappearing into instant gloom. "Well, that was an experiment that we obviously haven't perfected yet." She gave him a keen look. "How technical do you want to get?"

He glanced at the nearest thing to him—a page of calculations with symbols that meant nothing to him. "Layman's terms will do just fine."

Despite her depression about the experiment that had gone wrong, she smiled again. And, as distracted as he was, Del couldn't help thinking how lovely her smile was. She had a beautiful mouth with white, even teeth and an enticing way of biting her lip just slightly before she smiled, as though she were reluctant to let someone else in on her amusement. He also liked the way she threw her head back a little when she laughed, so that...

Hastily, he dragged his thoughts back to the task at hand. Kay was already explaining. "Without getting really involved, the experiment Mort was working on just now was designed to see if the robot could adjust its program to an unexpected obstacle in its path. It did just fine in simple trial runs in here, and we had planned on putting something out in the hall, but then you came out of the elevator, and—"

"I get it," he said. "When Mort yelled for me to stop, you were waiting to see if it could figure out a way to get around me."

Pleased, she nodded. "Exactly. But as you saw, it couldn't process that data, and so it...locked up."

"And once the obstacle—me—was removed—"

"It was able to carry on," Kay finished. She gave him another one of those intent looks. "Now you understand what I meant last week when I said that even the most advanced robots are rather... dim."

Del was beginning to understand. The problem was too many people didn't. If that robot hadn't been able to figure out a simple way around him, it was obvious there was a long way to go before intelligent machines took over the world.

"It must be discouraging," he ventured.

"It can be," she agreed. "But it can also be immensely rewarding, too. After all, we have come a long way since a man named Charles Babbage invented the first mechanical computer in the 1820s."

"That long ago?" Del couldn't hide his astonishment.

Kay smiled at his expression. "You're surprised, but one of the first machines ever to be controlled by a stored program—an idea central to modern digital computers, of course—was a loom designed to weave patterned silk—what we all call jacquard. It was invented by a man named Joseph Jacquard, in fact, in 1801, no less. His program was stored on cards with holes punched in them, so that even unskilled weavers could produce cloth that had once required great skill and patience to produce. Now, of course, punched cards, punched tapes and, presently, magnetic tapes and disks are used to control machines. But without that technology, today's robots wouldn't be possible."

"So it's truly a matter of programming?"

"Essentially—that, and feedback."

"Feedback?"

She thought a moment for an example. "Try drawing a picture with your eyes closed," she said. "You'll find it nearly impossible. That's because you need to see what your hand is doing in order to control it properly. In other words, information about the position of your hand must be fed back through the eyes to the brain. In turn, the correct control signals are sent back to the muscles that move the hand—feedback. In the same way, robots must have some method of monitoring their own behavior before they can perform even simple tasks, like picking up an object. The same strengths and forces aren't required, for example, to pick up a two-ton cement slab and to take an egg out of a carton. That's where feedback comes in—to help the robot differentiate."

"And how do you...er...feed in feedback?" Del asked, fascinated.

"There are so many ways I hardly know how to answer." And she launched into a monologue about things like hydraulics, pneumatics, electric motors, solenoids, pulleys, levers, gears and drive shafts.

"Is that *all*?" he asked.

She laughed. "Not quite. I could spend a couple of hours discussing the topic. I haven't even mentioned all the progress that has been made in the field. In the forties, for example, a single computer could fill an entire room. Now the invention of the silicon chip, which can fit on the head of a matchstick, makes hand-held computers much more powerful than their earlier cousins."

Del noticed a change come over Kay as she talked of the field she obviously loved. He was sure that if she could speak to the public this way, most of her problems with the media and the protesters would be resolved. When she explained things so naturally and simply but with obvious devotion and clear competence in the field, she was like a different person. A person he would like to know better himself. Blocking out this last thought, he said hastily, "How do you...uh... teach robots feedback?"

She cocked her head. "Are you sure you want to get into this?"

"Absolutely," he said, and then quickly qualified, "as long as you make it simple enough even for me to understand."

A smile touched her eyes, giving them that deep green glow that was beginning to fascinate him more and more. "I don't think you're as simple as you'd like me to believe," she said. "But as far as feedback is concerned, there are four basic ways to achieve it with robots, each more complicated than the last. The first is called walkthrough teaching. Let's say we want to teach a robot to open a door. With walk-through, we'd hold its hand and move it through all the steps necessary—reaching out, taking hold of the handle, turning the handle, pushing the door open, letting go of the handle and bringing its hand back. The robot would record every movement that each of its joints made while it was being taught, and then, when we gave it the signal, it would play back the movements exactly as it had recorded. This kind of walkthrough teaching is especially useful for teaching skills like paint spraying and welding."

Intrigued as much by the play of expression on her face as she explained as by what she was saying, Del murmured, "Okay, I can understand that. What's the second method?"

Kay smiled that transforming smile. "The second way to teach a robot is by using a remote control device called a teaching pendant. We have someone doing that right now. Come on, I'll show you."

With Del following willingly, she led the way to one of the partitioned off sections in the great underground laboratory. A young woman was working there when they arrived, holding a box with switches and watching another robot arm attached to a giant clamp-type affair that was bolted to the floor. The arm, which was constructed with numerous lines, pulleys and clamps, swiveled and swooped over the woman's head as she worked the switches. She glanced at them, but when Kay shook her head, she kept working.

"That's Jessie Zinzer, one of our programming experts," Kay said quietly to Del. "What's she's doing now is using the teaching pendant. The box she's holding is attached to the robot's computer, and those switches operate the motors in each of the robot's joints. Using the switches, the arm is moved to each position for the job it's being taught, and then a record button is pressed so that it will remember that position. When it's learned every position, the robot can run through them all in the right sequence to get the job done."

Del was fascinated by the procedure. They watched a few more minutes, then Kay waved at the young woman and they went to another section of the big lab, where a man was working with a much smaller arm.

"This is a much more complicated way of teaching," Kay explained, while they observed the man working with the arm and a special kind of keyboard on which he continually punched instructions. "What this programmer is doing is writing a computer program in a special language to tell the arm how to move each of its parts. One language, called LOGO, is especially designed to control simple mobile robots, like the one we call the turtle, but for industrial robots like this one, we use much more complicated languages."

They moved on, ending the fascinating tour with Mort and the metal cylinder Del had met out in the hall. The engineer was so absorbed in what he was doing that he barely looked up, and as Del glanced at all the complicated circuitry on the worktable, Kay explained.

"This is the fourth method I was telling you about. In this last way of teaching, we ask robots to learn by working a problem out for themselves." She grimaced. "As you saw today, it's not easy to do. Very few robots have been built that are smart enough to learn like this, and those that have succeeded have been experimental devices that needed enormous computer power. One of the most famous of the early experiments along these lines was a robot built by Stanford Research Institute in the 1960s. It could find its way around a room by avoiding obstacles it could see with a TV camera, and it could even find an electric socket and recharge itself. But even today, while we have made giant strides, that sort of machine intelligence is still very hard to achieve. In fact, we're still at the stage in many areas where even a robot that has been taught to pick up parts from a conveyer belt and put them into boxes will just as happily go through the motions if the conveyer belt breaks down and no parts are arriving. It will also continue dropping parts onto the floor if the box to put them in isn't where it should be." She smiled wryly. "As you can see, we have a *long* way to go."

Leaving Mort still absorbed in his task, they went back to the little cubicle from which they had begun the tour. When they were seated again, Kay sat back with a sigh. "There's so much information, I don't know what to give you. I can see your eyes glazing over with what I've already said, and yet I've only scratched the surface on what we're doing here. I don't know how I'm going to get it all across to . . . those people out there."

"Now that I've seen some of what you're doing, let me worry about that," Del said. "In fact, I was just thinking that it might help if you came to *my* office, so I could show you some of what *we* do there. Then we'll both have a better idea how to go ahead."

She had begun to look wary the instant he suggested coming to him. "Do you think that's really . . . necessary?" she asked. "I mean, I thought you were just going to arrange a radio interview or two."

"I had planned on doing a little more than that," he said dryly. "After all, if you just wanted to go on the radio, you could arrange that yourself, couldn't you?"

"Well, yes," she said reluctantly. "I suppose so."

"Well, then?"

As he had seen her do before, she made up her mind quickly. She obviously didn't care much for the idea, but she said, "All right, if you think that's best, I'll come. What time?"

"Make it easy on yourself, Kay. I know how busy you are."

Now that she'd agreed to come, she obviously wanted to get it over with as soon as possible. "I've got an appointment in your part of town early afternoon tomorrow. I could be at your office by about three, if that's all right."

Resolutely not thinking of what his secretary was going to say about having to rearrange his schedule again at the last minute, Del smiled. "That'll be just fine."

Still looking uncertain, Kay stood. Del stood with her. "Is there . . . anything else you'd like to see or go over before you leave?" she asked.

There were a thousand things he wanted to talk to this intriguing woman about—not one of them having to do with robots or robotics or the demonstrations outside the company gate. But with those green eyes of hers on his face, he couldn't seem to think straight. What was she doing to him? he wondered. He couldn't remember the last time a woman had been able to make him feel so off balance, almost gauche, and yet Kay Stockwell seemed able to do it without even trying. Deciding that maybe he should leave while the leaving was good, he said, "No, no, I've taken enough of your time."

To his disappointment, she didn't argue. "Well, if you're sure...." she said, and walked him to the elevator, where she stopped. "I'd show you out," she said apologetically, "but Mort is probably ready for another test on that robot by now, so if you don't mind..."

"Not at all," Del said, punching the elevator button. "It's simple enough, but if I can't find the way, I'm sure Goliath will probably be able to point me to the parking lot."

"Goliath...?" she repeated, a tiny frown furrowing her brow. Then she smiled. "Oh, you mean Jerry, the guard," she said with a laugh. "Isn't he something?"

"He is," Del agreed as the elevator came. "I'm just not sure what. Did you hire him away from the Chicago Bears, or is he a prototype?"

Kay laughed, a silvery little laugh that made Del feel a little hot. "Of what?" she teased. "One of those androids you're fond of talking about?"

"And you said they didn't exist," Del answered, glad he had to leave. The longer he stayed with Kay, the more reluctant he was to go. "Well, I'll see you tomorrow afternoon, then."

"I'll be there," she promised.

Mercifully, the elevator doors swooshed closed just then, saving him from making a fool of himself by telling her that he'd thought of a few more questions for her, after all.

TO HIS ANNOYANCE, Del was still thinking about Kay when he got home that night. He had gone back to the office after his tour, but he hadn't been able to concentrate, so he had finally just stuffed the work he'd been supposed to be doing into his briefcase and left. On arriving home, he was relieved for once to see that Jennifer was barricaded in her room again. He tossed his heavy attaché onto the hall table and went into the living room, where he collapsed into his favorite chair, only to get up again two seconds later and head into the kitchen to see what Mrs. Nivens had left for dinner. He wasn't really hungry, but he thought that maybe food would take his mind off this woman he'd just met. He felt ridiculous— the situation was ridiculous—but even as he lifted the lid of the Crock-Pot casserole on the counter and bent to take an appreciative whiff of the stew the housekeeper had fixed for them, he was still thinking about Kay— about what a beautiful smile she had and how animated and knowledgeable she had been when she was showing him around that incredible robot laboratory. She hadn't talked down to him—engineer to layman—and yet she had explained some very complicated procedures in simple terms. As someone who had helped shape others into successful politicians, company presidents and high-powered executives, he appreciated a talent like that, and even as he thought about how rich a color Kay's hair was or how soft her skin looked, he was thinking how best to use that talent of hers to advantage.

Or, at least, that's what he *thought* he was thinking about. When he realized that he was still standing there like an idiot with the Crock-Pot lid in his hand, he banged it down again and went to call Jennifer for dinner.

CHAPTER FIVE

KAY WOKE UP the next morning feeling as though she were being attacked by a giant washcloth. When she sat up, sputtering, she realized that Duffy, her black-and-white part Border collie, was energetically licking her face. "Duffy, stop!" she cried, trying to push him away. He thought it was a signal to play and began bouncing all over her and the bed.

She groaned, overwhelmed by all this vibrancy so early in the morning. Then she glanced at the clock. When she saw what time it was, she knew why the dog was so eager. It was after six. Either she'd forgotten to set the alarm or it hadn't gone off. If she didn't hurry, she wouldn't have time to take Duffy for his morning walk, which would constitute a major breach of promise.

Muttering to herself, she pushed her hair out of her eyes. In the beginning, the early-morning walk had seemed a good idea: a little fresh air, a little exercise before work.... But now, if she didn't feel like going or if something came up, Duffy sulked as though she'd let him down. He expected to go, she had taught him to expect it, and that was that. If waking her up himself didn't work, he'd disappear downstairs and a few minutes later she'd hear the ominous thud that meant he was into the living room wastebasket again and was happily scattering paper from one end of the room to the other. It was his only bad habit—and one that she could *not* break.

Whenever he was left alone—or felt she had reneged on a promise—he'd attack that wastebasket. She'd spent a lot of time collecting bits and scraps of paper he'd scattered around before she got the hint. Now when she was at work or out, he stayed in the backyard with his own doghouse and bed and toys, where he couldn't do any harm.

"Okay, okay," she muttered when he began pawing at her arm to make sure she wouldn't go back to sleep again. Then she saw the leash he'd brought in and dropped on the bed, and she had to laugh. "*Okay,* I get the hint. Do you mind if I get dressed first?"

Duffy barked, then leaped down to the floor while Kay tried to untangle herself from the blankets. She hadn't had a good night's sleep. Unable to get Del Rafferty out of her mind, she'd tossed and turned half the night. So this morning she felt out of sorts and already tired as she made the bed.

"I must have been out of my mind to agree to meet him today," she muttered, pulling the bedspread up and tucking the ends under the pillow. She didn't have a spare minute to herself for weeks ahead, and yet she had blithely told him she would see him sometime around three. She gave a brief, impatient shake of her head. She couldn't understand it; it wasn't like her to be impulsive, much less to ignore her responsibilities. When she got to the office, she would call and . . .

Then her shoulders sagged. She would have slumped down on the bed again if Duffy hadn't been giving her that soulful look. She wouldn't cancel the appointment, and she knew it. She wanted to see Del again, especially in his own environment. She was hoping that when he gave her the tour of his office, her feelings of attraction would vanish. Once she saw the computers that collated all those useless market surveys, the rooms where they made the thirty-second commercials that were supposed to mean something significant, the people who gathered all that information for him and then shaped the data to suit their own purposes—surely she'd feel differently. Whatever appeal he had for her would dissipate in the reality of what he did for a living, and then it wouldn't matter how good-looking or charismatic he was. No amount of charm could survive that, she thought.

Then why do I find Del Rafferty so intriguing?

"Because he listens to me," she muttered as she went to get dressed. She took out a pair of jeans. "Because he seems to understand why I feel so strongly about robotics," she went on, getting out a sweater. She pulled on a pair of socks and her underwear. "Because he's going to help."

But then she felt even more impatient at such rationalization. Why shouldn't he help? she wondered indignantly. She was going to hire him; that was his *job*.

"Oh, nuts," she muttered, shoving her feet into running shoes, then reaching for her comb.

Downstairs in the hallway, with Duffy waiting anxiously by the front door, Kay stopped long enough to grab a coat and snap the lead onto the dog's collar. When Duffy pulled eagerly on the leash, she came out to the front porch and closed the door behind her. It was nearly the end of September now, and the leaves on the big, old trees on her quiet street were wearing their autumn colors. The sun wasn't fully up yet, but the sky was already streaked with mauve and gold, and the chill in the air made her pull the collar of her coat up around her ears. It looked as if it were going to be a beautiful day, but as Illinois natives always said, "If you don't like the weather, wait a few minutes, and it'll change for you."

Thinking that she should have remembered a hat, she debated about going back inside to look for one, but Duffy was so anxious that she didn't have the heart to delay their walk. She started off, the dog leaping ahead of her as far as the leash would allow, while she looked back for a moment to appreciate her house.

She was proud of her home, which she'd bought last year, although with its high, pitched roof and deep eaves and long front porch it was really more a cottage than a house. It perched like a contented little hen under two old maple trees, all white clapboard with green trim. Inside, it had two bedrooms upstairs, an old-fashioned bath with a claw-foot tub that was perfect for soaking, a modern little kitchen downstairs and a good-size living room. But it was the backyard that had convinced her to buy, for the grassy space encircled by a tall wood fence was perfect for Duffy.

The dog strained harder at the leash just then, practically pulling her off her feet, and she muttered in fond exasperation as she hurried after him. She'd found Duffy huddled one rainy night next to her car, not long after she'd come to Springfield. Because she had still been feeling bruised and battered by her affair with Adam, and because the dog had looked just as forlorn and lonely as she'd felt herself, she couldn't just leave him. Duffy had repaid her kindness with undying devotion. He was always waiting when she came home, his long, plumed tail wagging so furiously that if he'd been a helicopter, he would have taken right off. Aside from his maddening propensity to get into wastepaper baskets, he was a perfect gentleman. With one ear tipped up and one flopping down, he was always ready to listen to her and seemed to understand what she was saying. At night he slept at the foot of her bed. She couldn't imagine life without Duffy, not even when he persisted in dragging her out before dawn to enjoy each new day.

But, she reminded herself, it was getting late. Wishing she could take Duffy to the lake, or at least out to the farm today instead of going in to work, she whistled reluctantly to him, and they headed back home. An hour later, dressed in a business suit, Kay was on her way to work, leaving Duffy behind in his doghouse in the backyard, snug with an old blanket and a new soup bone. Resolutely trying not to think of her appointment with Del at three o'clock that afternoon, she planned to sit down at her desk and not look up until noon.

SHORTLY BEFORE THREE, across town in room 105 at a private school called O'Leary High, Jennifer Rafferty sat as close to the back of the classroom as possible and stared out the window. It was her last class of the day, and normally she enjoyed science. But the teacher, Mrs. Polehemus, was talking about the upcoming Science Fair, and since Jennifer had no intention of participating in that event, she wasn't paying attention. She was thinking about the Milk Duds candy in her purse and wondering if she could sneak a few out of the box without making any noise. Eating or chewing gum in class was absolutely forbidden, but she hadn't had anything to eat since lunch, and she was starving. She was just reaching surreptitiously for her purse on the floor when the teacher turned in her direction.

"Jennifer Rafferty, what are you doing?"

Guilty as sin, Jennifer jumped in fright. She knew she had turned bright red, and that made her even more upset. Cursing her fair skin that flushed crimson at the least opportunity, she peeped toward the front of the classroom. Mrs. Polehemus, all five foot two of her, was looking questioningly down the row of desks, and she had no choice but to drag herself ponderously to her feet. In this school, students did not address the teachers while lolling in their seats.

"I'm sorry, Mrs. Polehemus?" she said. She felt hot, and there were black spots floating before her eyes. She *hated* to be singled out in class; it seemed to make everything so much worse. Trying desperately to ignore all the eyes turned toward her, she concentrated on a space above the teacher's head. Swallowing over the growing lump in her throat, she made herself say, "What was the question?"

There was a giggle from someone to the right of her and a guffaw from one of the boys toward the front. Wishing the floor would open or the roof fall in, Jennifer looked at the teacher, who, miraculously, took pity just this once. Almost kindly, Mrs. Polehemus said, "I asked you, Jennifer, what you were doing for the Science Fair."

"Oh...I...uh...gee, Mrs. Polehemus," Jennifer said, her voice strangled. "I...uh, hadn't really thought about it."

There was another burst of giggles, quickly stifled when the teacher threw a severe glance in the culprit's direction. "Well, then, Jennifer," Mrs. Polehemus said, "perhaps it's time you did."

"Yes, ma'am," Jennifer said quickly, and began to sit down, mightily relieved that she'd been let off the hook so easily. But her ordeal was just beginning, for the teacher, looking thoughtful in that dreaded way teachers had that meant that some poor student was going to regret it, gestured.

"Just a minute, Jennifer," Mrs. Polehemus said, looking more thoughtful by the minute. "Since you haven't signed up for any of the committees, why don't I just put you in charge of giving the opening address that day." She paused. "Perhaps that would induce you to devote a little more time to your science studies, do you think? All right, then. Now—"

Jennifer was so horrified that she couldn't speak until the teacher turned toward the blackboard again. But when she realized Mrs. Polehemus thought the matter was already settled and was going on to something else, she managed to break free of her trance. Give the opening address? she thought in complete panic. She'd never be able to do it. She'd die of fright or faint or, worse, throw up. No, no, she couldn't do it! She wouldn't! She'd... she'd run away first!

"I... I can't!" she said shrilly. She was so upset that she didn't even care what the other students thought. "Oh, please, Mrs. Polehemus, anything but that! I... I wouldn't know what to say!"

The teacher turned with a piece of chalk in her hand. "I beg your pardon?"

"I said, I can't do it!" Jennifer cried. She looked around at all the curious, shocked and—in one case— jealous faces that were turned her way and jerked her eyes up to the teacher again. "Please!" she begged. "Don't make me!"

Mrs. Polehemus frowned. "Jennifer, you're making a fuss about nothing."

But to Jennifer, it wasn't nothing—not at all. Even if by some miracle she didn't become completely paralyzed speaking before all those people, she could just imagine the whispers, snickers and cruel jokes that would come her way that day.

There's the fat girl. Do you think she'll make it up to the podium?

If she can't, we'll just make a ramp and roll *her up! No problem.*

Just thinking about it made her cringe. She couldn't do it. She'd die a million deaths—or worse, she'd make a complete fool of herself. . . and live to tell about it.

"Mrs. Polehemus, please, there must be someone else!" she said urgently, stridently. Frantically, her eyes searched the classroom and settled—miraculously—on Betty Jo Quinn, the owner of the jealous face she'd glimpsed earlier. Betty Jo was the best in drama class—she said so herself. Jennifer knew that she'd *love* to give the opening address, and she said desperately, "How about Betty Jo? She could do it much better than me!"

"Than I," Mrs. Polehemus corrected automatically. She glanced at the other girl, who sat forward eagerly in her seat. Jennifer held her breath, hoping the teacher would rethink the idea. But Mrs. Polehemus shook her head.

"No, I don't think so," the ruler of Jennifer's fate said, to the intense disappointment of both girls. Betty Jo glared in Jennifer's direction and flounced around, pointedly folding her arms across her waist.

"Now, then," Mrs. Polehemus said, turning once again to the blackboard. "Let's move—"

"Wait!" Jennifer cried, committing the unpardonable sin of interrupting—again. She was too unnerved to notice. "I've got another idea!"

Slowly, Mrs. Polehemus turned around again. Her expression was turning frosty. "I'm sorry, Jennifer. The matter has already been decided."

"What if I could get someone. . . someone really important to give the opening address?" Jennifer blurted before she had time to think. She didn't know how she was ever going to accomplish what had just popped into her head, but she'd think about that later. Right now, she could only concentrate on getting out of this mess. She had to convince the teacher; she *had* to! She just couldn't get up there; she'd kill herself first! It was bad enough that she hadn't made any friends since she'd come; the thought of making a fool of herself in front of the entire school terrified her so she was willing to risk even the teacher's wrath.

"Wouldn't that be better, Mrs. Polehemus?" she babbled. "Wouldn't it? Someone important, who really had something to say?"

The teacher's voice cooled considerably. "Whom did you have in mind, Jennifer?"

"Kay Stockwell," Jennifer said in desperation, seizing on the name that had been floating half in, half out of her subconscious.

Mrs. Polehemus frowned. "Kay Stockwell—of Stockwell Engineering?"

"Yes, yes," Jennifer said eagerly. "She'd be perfect, I know it!"

Mrs. Polehemus seemed even more doubtful. "You know her?"

"She's a client of my dad's," Jennifer explained quickly, rushing on before any objections could be raised. "I could ask her. If she says yes, will it be okay?"

"Well, I don't know...."

"She could talk to everyone about robotics," Jennifer said, feverishly willing the teacher to say yes. "Maybe she could even bring some—I don't know. But we'd get to listen firsthand to someone talk about one of the most important developments in science and engineering in the future. And since we've studied a little about it here in class, I know it—"

"All right, all right, Jennifer," Mrs. Polehemus said, holding up a hand to stem the frantic flow. When Jennifer reluctantly subsided, she went on, "Let's leave it like this. You ask her. If she says yes, we'll be pleased to hear her speak. In fact, it might be good to hear what she has to say, given the publicity currently surrounding her company. If she agrees, I'll consider it your contribution to the fair. But if she has other commitments, that will mean that you—"

"Oh, she'll do it, she'll do it, I'm sure!" Jennifer cried, so relieved she was almost in tears. She didn't dare think how she was going to make all this come to pass, but if she didn't, she'd just disappear. Head off to Greenland, or someplace, where neither her father nor any of her teachers could ever find her.

"All right, then, we'll leave that up to you," Mrs. Polehemus said. But it was obvious she was still skeptical. She started to say something else, but just then the bell rang, and she dismissed the class. Jennifer started out, but to her astonishment, she was suddenly surrounded by classmates.

"Do you really think you can get Kay Stockwell to speak?" one of the girls asked. "My dad says—"

"Who's Kay Stockwell?" a boy asked.

Before Jennifer could answer, another boy piped up with, "Oh, she's some broad—"

Jennifer turned fiercely in his direction. "How dare you say that? Kay Stockwell is no *broad!*"

"Jennifer's right," the girl said, raking the offender up and down with an indignant glance. "What a *disgusting* thing to say!"

"Honestly," another girl muttered. "Sometimes I think guys still live in caves!"

The boy who had made the remark, a tall redhead who Jennifer thought was named Eddie, flushed. "Hey, I just—"

"Well, don't," a third girl said. She tossed her head, startling Jennifer by linking arms. "Don't pay any attention to them," she counseled wisely. "They're just *ignorant.*"

Jennifer was feeling a little ignorant herself. She couldn't imagine why these girls had come to her defense, but she was too grateful—and too surprised—to question the sudden championing. Shyly, she said, "Thanks."

The first girl, a pretty blue-eyed blonde named Susan, smiled back. "Hey, that's okay. We females have to stick together, right? Besides, I thought it was neat the way you got out of giving that opening address old Mrs. Pole Stack was trying to rope you into."

"Me, too," the third girl, the brunette named Trudy, said with a sigh. "*I'm* supposed to be doing an experiment demonstrating that force is equal to mass times acceleration. With Perry *Alden,* if you can imagine that!"

Perry Alden was the smartest boy in class, the quintessential science buff: a gangly, bespectacled youth who either had his eyes on his slide rule—no calculator for him—or his nose in a book. Jennifer, who suspected that Perry was just shy, like herself, felt brave enough to say, "Well, at least working with Perry, you'll get an A."

Trudy looked at her for a minute, then she laughed. "You're right. I hadn't thought of it like that," she said in delight as the other girls drifted away. "Say, do you want to go get a soda, or something?"

Basking in the sudden, unexpected glow of being included, Jennifer wanted that more than anything. But just as she was about to accept, she saw Mrs. Polehemus leaving the classroom by the other door, and she was instantly and painfully reminded of her perilous position. If she didn't want to give that opening address, she'd better go see her dad and beg for his help. Hoping she wasn't risking what might be a newfound friendship, she said, "I...uh...I'd love to, but I can't. Can we make it another time?"

"Sure," Trudy said easily, and then grimaced. "I've got to meet Perry in the science lab, anyway. See ya later, okay?"

"Okay," Jennifer said, and stared happily for a moment after Trudy as the girl started down the hall. Then, remembering her errand, her smile disappeared, replaced by a sinking feeling of dread. Her expression grim, she turned the other way and hurried off.

The closer she got to her father's office downtown the more nervous Jennifer got. By the time the bus arrived at the building, she was in a panic, and only the thought of being forced to make the Science Fair opening address herself propelled her through the front doors of the office tower and up to her father's floor. Oh, why had she ever said anything? Why had the teacher singled her out? She didn't know what she was going to say now that she was here, and when she thought how awful things were at home and how she and her father hadn't been getting along at *all*, she wanted to turn around and run right out again. How could she ask him to ask Kay Stockwell to speak? He'd want to know why, and she'd have to confess that she'd gotten herself into this mess because she hadn't volunteered for any of the science committees. And why was that? he'd be sure to ask. Because she hated her school and everything and everyone in it, she'd have to answer—with the possible exception of Trudy Diller, maybe, she thought suddenly, and a couple of the other girls who had come to her defense. And maybe that Eddie, who, despite his obvious insensitivity where *women* were concerned, was still kind of cute....

No, no, she was getting off the track. She was here to ask her father a giant favor, not to think about boys, no matter how cute they were. Besides, it didn't make any difference. A boy like Eddie would *never* give a blimp like her a second glance. Maybe, before she'd gained all this weight...

No, she didn't want to think about that, either. She hated how fat she'd become, even if it wasn't really her fault. If she hadn't had to leave New York and her old school and all her friends behind, she wouldn't have gained all this weight. So it was really her father who was to blame—her father, whom she had come to ask for something she just knew he was going to refuse. Oh, why hadn't she just been run over by a bus?

With all these thoughts flying around her head, Jennifer was so upset when she reached the third floor, where her father's offices were, that she just burst right in. Her father's secretary, a *skinny,* stylish young woman with long fingernails—Jennifer had bitten hers to the quick—looked up, startled at her sudden entrance.

"Is my dad here?" Jennifer asked quickly, practically slamming the door behind her in her nervousness.

"Yes, he's here," Stella said. "But you—"

Jennifer couldn't wait. She knew that if she didn't go in there right this *instant,* she'd lose what little courage she had and run off to join a convent, where she'd never be seen again.

"Thanks," she said, breathing hard—both from exertion and the anxiety that was building up and making her feel faint. "I'll just be a minute."

"Wait!" Stella cried, but Jennifer was already heading toward the door. Before she could think about it, she flung it open.

"Dad, I've got to talk to you," she blurted, seeing Del at his desk. He was standing, facing a part of the room that was hidden from her, but she was suddenly so paralyzed with fright that she couldn't make herself come all the way inside. Clutching the doorknob as though it were a lifeline, she held her schoolbooks close to her chest with the other arm. All she could think about was how much she wanted to get this over with—ask her Dad her favor and run out again. She was so nervous he'd refuse. Perhaps if she spoke very fast, in such a hurry that he didn't have time to think, he'd agree before he realized what he was doing.

"I know you're busy," she said, her words practically running into each other, "but this can't wait, honest. Oh, Dad, I need a favor! You *have* to ask Kay Stockwell if she'll speak at our Science Fair this month! I promised the teacher you'd ask, and if you don't, I'll be in real trouble. Please, Dad! If you do this for me, I promise I'll never ask you for anything again—ever! I'll keep my room clean, and I'll help with the dishes—whatever you want, but please, please, *please* ask her! I'll never be able to face anyone in that school ever again if you don't! My life will be over, and I don't know what I'll do then! This is a real emergency, and I—"

"Whoa!" Del said, trying not to laugh. "I can't understand a word you're saying!"

"Dad!" she cried, beside herself. "This isn't a time to joke! I need you to ask Kay Stockwell to speak at our Science Fair! She is a client of yours. Will you ask her? Oh, please! If you don't, I'll—"

Still trying not to laugh, Del gestured. "Why don't you ask her yourself?"

"Dad, *please!*" Jennifer cried. Then she realized what he'd said. "I...what?" she stammered, and felt her heart thud to her feet as she followed his glance and peered around the door. When she saw Kay Stockwell sitting on the couch next to the wall, she almost died. She knew it was Kay; she had seen her picture in the paper; she had been following her story for weeks now, for journalism class. Oh, she couldn't believe this. How could she have done such a stupid thing? How could she have made such a complete, miserable, *fat* fool of herself?

"Kay, I'd like you to meet my daughter, Jennifer," Del said, his lips still twitching with his effort not to laugh. "Jennifer, please come in and say hello to Kay Stockwell."

Somehow, Jennifer wasn't sure how, she managed to come the rest of the way into the room as Kay Stockwell stood. On feet that felt like big tubs of sand, she dragged herself across the carpet and stopped in front of this beautiful, smart, sophisticated woman in the cinnamon-colored business suit with the cream-colored silk blouse and matching high heels, her shining hair just touching her collar, her green eyes hiding, Jennifer was sure, her complete scorn for what was obviously a walrus with no brains in her head.

"Hello, Jennifer," she said. Her voice was low and husky, like Kathleen Turner's or Lauren Bacall's, making Jennifer feel even more inadequate. She wasn't only beautiful and smart, Jennifer thought miserably, she had a sexy voice, as well.

"Hello," she mumbled, sure that Kay was just being kind. She had never felt so fat, ugly, stupid and...and *short* in her life. But, knowing her father would expect it, she held out her hand, forcing herself to add, "It's so nice to meet you."

"My pleasure," Kay said, giving her fingers a quick, brisk shake. She smiled a smile that would have made a model envious. "What was that about a Science Fair?"

Jennifer wanted to die right there. She couldn't ask this gorgeous woman a favor; she just couldn't! "Uh...it wasn't important," she muttered, and looked quickly at her father, mutely begging him to rescue her.

But to her surprise, her father seemed just as bemused as she felt in Kay's presence. As unnerved as she was, Jennifer was still able to note that he didn't seem himself—not at all. He was looking at Kay like...like Roy Andershot looked at Tammy Blakely at school, Jennifer thought suddenly. Roy and Tammy were seniors, and Roy was the captain of the football team, while Tammy was—what else?—head cheerleader. Jennifer had followed their romance from afar, swooning like the rest of the girls whenever Roy strode down the hall in his letterman's jacket. She had seen the way Roy looked at Tammy as they stood by her locker, and to her astonishment, her father was looking at Kay Stockwell just like that now.

Oh, man, she thought. *He's too* old *for that!*

"Jennifer?" Kay said.

With an effort, Del jerked his eyes away from Kay, to his daughter. "Er...yes, Jennifer, what were you saying?"

All she wanted to do was get out of here. Not only did she feel like a third wheel, but she was sure she had interrupted something...special.

"Uh...it wasn't important, Dad," she said, beginning to back toward the door. "I...uh...I'm sorry I interrupted. I'll see you later, okay?"

She had almost reached the door—and escaped—when the death grip she had on her books slipped. Her palms were wet with nervous perspiration, and suddenly her history books and one of her English texts began to slip from her grasp. She made a frantic effort to catch them, succeeded only in loosening her hold on the others, and, like a pack of cards that had been fanned, they all seemed to explode in the air at once before raining down around her feet.

"Oh, no!" she cried, blushing furiously and wishing she could disappear. Quickly, trying to hide her red face, she bent down.

"Here, let me—" Del said, reaching down to help.

Father and daughter cracked heads and yelped.

"*Dad!*" Jennifer cried.

"I'm sorry, Button!" Del said, reaching for her to see if she was all right.

She wasn't. She was positive now that she was going to die of complete mortification right here. Oh, how could he have called her by that...that *juvenile* nickname? She wanted to whirl around and run out, but all her books were sprawled at her feet. With a helpless glance at Kay, who, to her horror was bending to help, she cried, "I can get them! I can get them! Please—"

But Kay was already calmly gathering the spilled texts into a neat stack. "Here," she said with that dazzling smile, holding them out. "It used to happen to me all the time...."

Her face practically purple, Jennifer silently took the books. But as upset as she was, she still noticed that Kay had stacked them the easiest way to carry—the long, thick ones on the bottom, the other arranged side by side on top.

"Thanks," she muttered, "but I doubt that."

"No, it's true," Kay assured her. "Now, what's this about a Science Fair?"

By now, Jennifer had decided that her father wasn't going to be any help at all. Telling herself that she'd just have to do it, she explained as quickly as she could, ending with, "But you don't have to do it, Ms. Stockwell. I'll just tell my teacher that I asked and that you said you couldn't. It'll be all right, honest."

Kay smiled that smile again. Jennifer knew that when she got home, she was going to practice that same smile herself in front of the mirror—her own mirror, in the absolute, locked privacy of her bathroom upstairs.

"What day is the fair?" Kay asked.

Jennifer stopped thinking about Kay's looks. Wide-eyed, she glanced up. "You'd...you'd really think of doing it?"

"Of course? Why not?"

Jennifer knew she had turned crimson again. Now that she'd finally gotten up the courage to make her request, it seemed so...so *brazen* to ask a woman of Kay Stockwell's stature to take time out from her busy schedule to speak to a few kids at a local high school on the day of their stupid Science Fair.

"Well, well...because..." she stammered. "I know how important your work is and how much trouble you're having, and I—"

"Do you think my work is important?" Kay asked curiously.

Jennifer looked at her in surprise. "Sure I do." Then, because Kay seemed to be encouraging her to go on, she felt courageous enough to add, "And I think you've been getting a bum rap in the paper, too. If more people knew—or tried to understand—what you're trying to do with robotics, you wouldn't have half as much trouble!" She cast a quick glance in her father's direction, not quite sure how he'd feel about what she was going to say next. Then she decided just to say it. He could only ground her for the rest of her life, and since she never went anywhere, anyway, it didn't matter, did it? Defiantly she added, "And you wouldn't be having this much trouble if this place and the people here weren't so... so *provincial!*"

"Now, Jennifer," Del immediately protested. "I realize this isn't New York, but as I was just saying to Ms. Stockwell, the community needs to be educated—"

"And how better to accomplish that than by talking to the people who are going to be working with robotics in the future?" Kay said with a wink in Jennifer's direction. "You've been trying to convince me to make a few speaking appearances, Del, and now I think you're right. I'll start by speaking to the high school."

Jennifer looked at her in astonishment. "You will? You really will?"

"Now, Kay," Del said as he had said to his daughter. "Do you realize—"

But Kay had already decided. It was obvious to Jennifer that once she made up her mind, the deed was as good as done. Politely dismissing the father's objections with a lift of her hand, she turned to his goggling daughter. "What time and day?" she asked. "Just tell me, and I'll be there. Oh, and would you like me to bring some robots, to demonstrate?"

Jennifer felt as though she'd died and gone to heaven. "That would be wonderful, Ms. Stockwell," she said fervently, telling her the time and date. She felt like sinking to her knees and giving thanks. Now, not only would she *not* have to make a fool of herself by trying to give a speech, but maybe the kids in her science class, at least, would look at her differently. "Thank you so much...."

She left a few minutes later, sailing out with a beatific smile.

When the door closed behind her and the adults were alone again, Kay turned to Del. "You have a lovely daughter."

He looked wry. "Thank you. But she's changed a lot recently, I'm afraid. I don't know whether it was leaving New York to come and live with me for a year or just turning fifteen. Sometimes I think I don't know her at all anymore."

Kay laughed. "You probably don't. My own father used to say that about me when I was Jennifer's age. But we got through it, somehow."

"How?"

He looked so bleak that she decided to tease him. "I turned twenty-one."

"I have to wait that long?" He seemed horrified at the thought.

She hid her smile. "Well, you could always send her away to college. That's what my father did."

"He sounds like a wise man. How did he wait until then?"

She laughed. "He had to. My grandfather—his father—wouldn't allow him to pack me off to boarding school."

He looked at her curiously. "What about your mother?"

"My mother died when I was very young, so they—my father and my grandfather Emmett—had to be both parents to me."

"That must have been . . . difficult."

She shrugged. "Maybe for them, but not for me. They were both so good to me and tried so hard that I really didn't miss a mother's presence. I don't think I did, anyway." She smiled again. "How could I, when my father took me shopping for Easter dresses and Granddad volunteered to be den mother when I wanted to become a Girl Scout?"

Admiringly, Del shook his head. "Well, they obviously did a good job."

Kay's cheeks turned pink. "Thank you," she said. "But so will you. It's obvious that your daughter loves you."

Del turned glum again. "Is it? She was on her best behavior today because she wanted something, but you can see that even that leaves a lot to be desired. And you should see her at home."

"Perhaps this thing with the Science Fair will help."

"I hope so. But I wanted to talk to you about that. I know Jennifer put you on the spot, but you really don't have to—"

"Oh, but I want to. You and Brice have both been telling me how important it is to educate the public about robotics, and I'm beginning to think you're right. So, what better place to start than with the generation that is going to have to deal with that science? And I really don't mind," she added with a wicked grin. "Isn't a high school the best place to recruit?"

LONG AFTER KAY HAD GONE and the rest of his staff had left for home that night, Del sat alone in his office, brooding. He couldn't get that scene with Kay and Jennifer out of his mind, and the more he thought about it, the more wistful he felt. He hadn't seen that side of Jennifer in longer than he could remember, and for a few

minutes there, despite her awkwardness and embarrassment, she had been the young girl he missed so much instead of the difficult, taciturn teenager she had become.
Kay was responsible for that, he knew; not only had she
kindly consented to speak at Jennifer's Science Fair, but
she had seemed genuinely interested in what his daughter had to say. Watching them, he had started to wonder...

But there was no percentage in *that* line of thought, he
told himself hastily. As attractive as Kay Stockwell was—
as interesting and intriguing and intelligent and beautiful—she was still his client, and he had to remember that.
He had an ironclad rule around here, and that was *never*
to get involved with his clients. He'd seen that happen to
other colleagues, and he knew that it meant nothing but
trouble. When a man was involved, no matter to what
extent, he couldn't keep his mind on business, and that
wasn't good either for him *or* the person he was repre-
senting. Kay had hired him to help her change her company's image, and that's all he was going to do. He
couldn't afford to get sidetracked with side issues, no
matter how attractive they might be.

Besides, he thought, he had enough problems at the
moment. One woman in his life at a time was sufficient,
and as had already been amply demonstrated, his
daughter was all he could handle right now.

On that thought, he reached over and switched off the
desk lamp and went home.

KAY WAS THOUGHTFUL, too, when she went home that
night. All through greeting Duffy and getting his dinner
and then fixing something to eat herself, she thought
about meeting Jennifer and being with Del that day. Even
though Jennifer had been embarrassed and almost un-

bearably shy, Kay had immediately identified and sympathized, for she'd once felt exactly like that herself. And, having experienced those feelings, she could see beyond the bashfulness and teenage clumsiness to the young woman Jennifer was in the process of becoming, and she couldn't help thinking how lucky Del was, despite his current problems with this difficult teenage stage, to be the father of such a beautiful young girl. They looked so much alike, Kay thought, with their thick, curly black hair and those deep blue eyes. Jennifer was truly a feminine version of Del, and when Kay found herself wondering what it would be like to be part of that family, she quickly rinsed off her dinner dishes and surprised Duffy by taking him for a brisk evening walk.

The ruse worked. By the time they came home again, she was so tired she took her shower and fell into bed. It had been a long day and she'd done too much thinking.

CHAPTER SIX

KAY WAS A SMASH at the Science Fair. Whether it was curiosity about the strange contraptions she had brought with her as exhibits or the notoriety she'd gained from all the media publicity that aroused such interest, five minutes before she was scheduled to begin her speech, the auditorium at O'Leary High was jammed. As she peered out from side stage and saw every seat taken, her sense of humor surfaced. Maybe neither curiosity nor notoriety had played a part; maybe it had been a simple decree from the principal of the school that all the students attend.

"Nervous?" asked someone behind her.

She turned, and there was Del, looking handsome as always, today in a dark suit with a striped tie. Despite her objections, he had insisted on bringing someone to film her speech today, and behind him stood a man with a TV camera on his shoulder. When the cameraman smiled and gave her a thumbs-up, she smiled, too. It wasn't *his* fault that Del hadn't listened to her protests, so she couldn't blame him. But she still thought the whole idea was ridiculous. Who could possibly be interested in a speech she was giving to a high school?

She didn't have time to wonder about it, for just then she and Del were joined by Jennifer's science teacher, Althea Polehemus, whom Kay had met earlier, and by

Jennifer herself, who was scheduled to introduce her. Jennifer looked pale and ready to faint.

"Are you all right?" Kay asked in concern.

Jennifer gave her a mute, helpless look. Then, retching, she said, "I think I'm going to be sick," and rushed off, presumably to the bathroom.

"Oh, dear, I was afraid of this," Mrs. Polehemus said worriedly. "Maybe I should just go ahead and introduce you myself."

But Kay knew how Jennifer felt. She'd once been practically paralyzed with stage fright herself. Having to be in the limelight with Adam while he was running for the Senate had cured her of that. Being able to speak naturally in public was probably the one good thing to come out of that relationship.

"No, she'll be okay," she told everyone confidently. "I'll go talk to her."

Mrs. Polehemus glanced anxiously at her watch. They could hear the restless and increasing noise of teenagers who had been sitting too long. "Are you sure?" the teacher asked. "We don't have much time."

"Maybe I should talk to her," Del suggested.

"No, let me," Kay said, and hurried off.

As she had suspected, she found Jennifer leaning weakly against one of the sinks in the women's bathroom. Beads of sweat glistened on the girl's forehead, and tendrils of hair clung to her pasty face. Kay knew at a glance that she'd been sick, and she quickly pulled a paper towel from the dispenser and wet it. As she dabbed at Jennifer's cheeks, she smiled encouragingly.

"You're going to do just fine," she said.

Jennifer looked as if she were going to be sick all over again. "I can't go out there," she said, desperately clutching Kay's hand. "I just *can't!*"

"Sure you can," Kay said cheerfully. "All you have to—"

"No, I can't! I can't!" Jennifer moaned. "I just know I'll do something *awful*—like fall down in a faint, or worse, get sick all over the podium!"

Kay wet the towel again. "Everybody thinks that at first," she soothed. "But you'll be fine. Remember, these are your schoolmates out there, your friends—"

"They're *not* my friends!" Jennifer said miserably. Then she reconsidered. Weakly, she added, "Well, not *all* of them. Trudy, maybe...."

"Well, then, when you go out there, just look at Trudy and concentrate on her," Kay said. "Forget everybody else, and just talk to her as though you were chatting after class. Do you think you could do that?"

Jennifer shuddered. "I...I don't know. Maybe...."

Seeing that she was making headway, Kay went on, "And I'll be right there. If you get stuck or can't remember what you wanted to say, all you have to do is look at me. Just tell everybody who I am and why I'm here, and I'll do the rest, okay?"

"Well..."

Kay threw the towel away. "It'll be easy, you'll see," she said. "And after it's done, you'll wonder why you were ever nervous."

"I'm not so sure about *that,*" Jennifer said weakly, but she followed as Kay led the way out of the bathroom and back to their place at the side of the stage.

"You okay, Button?" Del said when he saw how pale she was.

Jennifer looked mournfully at her father. "I don't know," she said, and then saw the podium out on center stage. Her eyes widened. It looked very lonely sitting there under the floodlights, and she started to shake.

"I think," Kay said hurriedly to Mrs. Polehemus, who was going to give a brief introduction opening the Science Fair, "that we'd better get started, don't you?"

The teacher glanced at Jennifer, who was getting more white-faced by the second, and nodded. Calmly, she walked out onstage directly to the podium and quieted everyone down. Kay hardly paid attention to what the woman said; she was too preoccupied with Jennifer.

"You're going to do just fine," she whispered as Mrs. Polehemus came to the end of her speech.

Jennifer turned in terror to Kay as the teacher introduced her. "Come out with me! Oh, please, come out with me! I can't go out there alone!"

It wasn't planned that Kay accompany Jennifer out onstage while she was being introduced, but she didn't hesitate. "All right," she agreed, and quickly turned to Del. "You're going to have to help me by sending the robots out when I give the cue," she said. "Do you think you can do that?"

"Me?" For an instant, Del looked as panic-stricken as his daughter. He shot a quick glance at the machines Kay had brought with her to demonstrate. "I don't even know—"

With Mrs. Polehemus waiting and Jennifer looking at any second as though she might turn tail and run, Kay quickly explained what she wanted him to do and then took Jennifer's arm. "You ready?" she said confidently. "Then, let's go...."

Before Jennifer knew it, they were out onstage. The hot spotlights hit them as soon as they reached the podium. Under cover of the applause that greeted their appearance, Kay whispered. "You can do it, honey. Just grab that mike...."

Looking as though she were in a trance, Jennifer obeyed. But as she grabbed the microphone with her sweaty hand, a shrill whine went up from the equipment. Everyone in the audience groaned and put their hands over their ears, and she looked in panic at Kay.

"You're doing fine," Kay said calmly. "Go ahead."

Jerkily, Jennifer turned her head. Blinking in the harsh glare of the lights, she lowered her death grip on the microphone and said so quickly that all the words ran together, "This-is-Kay-Stockwell-she's-here-to-talk-to-us-about-robots-thank-you-goodbye." Then she turned and ran off the stage, leaving Kay alone.

As though it had been planned like that, Kay stepped serenely up to the mike. "Hi," she said easily. "As Jennifer just told you, my name is Kay Stockwell, and I'm here to talk to you about robots and robotics...."

At this point, she surreptitiously gestured to Del, praying that he remembered what to do next while she went on with her text. "Now, the first question we have to ask ourselves is, What is a robot? Well, there are many kinds. Some do heavy lifting and stacking jobs in factories, some use tools like welding torches and paint sprayers, others guide weapons or work forklifts or drive buses. There are even robots to shear sheep and count chocolate chips in cookies...."

As she spoke, what looked like a small, rectangular box came out from side stage and began scuttling across the stage. When it reached the podium, it made a quick detour and finished its journey by disappearing off the other side. When the kids saw it, they laughed and pointed, and Kay smiled. "There are even robots that look like lunch boxes," she said, "although I'm afraid they don't carry the kinds of sandwiches everyone wants to trade...."

Another laugh and applause, and Kay was on her way. She told the assemblage that robots range in size from the "turtle" they had just seen and small desktop arms for light assembly work, to large floor-mounted arms that can easily lift a truck or a car. Then, with another covert gesture to Del, she could see the audience visibly tense when, from side stage, a walking robot appeared. It looked like a tall, complicated tin can with six jointed, spidery legs, and with Kay pretending not to notice, it started walking toward her. As the kids began to ooh and aah and look very impressed, Kay unconcernedly went on with her talk, saying that robots could vary greatly in appearance.

"A robot may look like a truck, a multijointed metal arm, a six-legged metal spider, a snake or even a person," she said, ignoring the machine as it advanced, science-fiction-like, complete with clanks and bangs and other assorted ominous noises, upon her. "But what they all have in common is the fact that they are machines, capable of being programmed or taught to do various useful tasks...."

Some of the younger kids in the audience were getting nervous. The walking robot was getting closer to Kay, until it seemed to loom right over her. She still pretended not to know it was there, until finally, some of the students couldn't stand it.

"Look out!" several cried. "Look out! Look out!"

Kay feigned not being able to hear the clanking machine behind her. "What?" she said. "I didn't hear that—"

"Look out! Look behind you!" came more shouts— some amused, others sounding anxious.

At last Kay elected to understand. She turned around just as the big machine, topping her by almost two feet, came to a stop directly behind her.

"Down boy," she said, and as if on command, but actually having been carefully preprogrammed by Mort, who had spent hours on the sequence, the big machine folded its spidery legs and slowly sank down, just like a dog coming to heel. There was an amazed silence from the audience, and then, suddenly, the auditorium erupted with wild applause.

Kay turned back to her audience. She waited a moment, then she said calmly, "Any questions?"

There were, more than she could possibly answer in the time allotted. One of the first, from a bespectacled boy in the front row, was, "Do you think that robots are ever going to take the place of humans?"

"That's a good question," Kay said. "And the answer is, no, I don't. In the past few years, those of us involved in the science have been rethinking what robots should do and how they should look. In the beginning, we tried to make them do everything people do and look as much like people as possible, but the more we tried to build humanlike machines, the more problems we ran into. Humans are *very* complicated and complex creatures, you know, and the problems turned out to be much more difficult than we expected. So now we're looking for new ways to have robots serve as assistants to humans, rather than as their replacements. And as you can see from the one behind me, they don't need to look like humans at all."

"What about in medicine?" another boy asked.

"Remember that movie where some people are shrunk to the size of microbes and they cruise around someone's body? Well, we all know that we can't really shrink *people,* but scientists at Tokyo University are going after something that could have been cribbed right from that film—an ultraminiature submarine that can be launched into a person's bloodstream. Building it will require gears and other parts much smaller than anything yet made from metal, so they're employing a new technology called micromachining. The sub would also have to be equipped with very tiny devices for inspecting tissue and relaying the findings to doctors, who could then direct the little robot to cut out or treat any diseased parts. As you can imagine, if the team can pull the technology together, this will change the entire field of medicine.''

Another question came from a girl to Kay's right. ''If we're interested in a career in robotics, what should we do?''

''Start planning now,'' Kay said promptly. ''The field of robotics is a complex one, and with continuing advances, in the future it probably won't be possible for one person to possess all the knowledge needed to assemble increasingly complicated robots. At Stockwell Engineering now, we have teams of people who work together, each sharing skills. Some work on robot bodies and others work on the brains, or the computers that drive them. If you're working with the computer mind of the robot, you will need training in computer science, of course. A knowledge of how computers work is essential, as is learning how to develop software. You'll also have to study linguistics, or the science of language, so that you can make your robot understand and respond to commands. And—I know some of you won't like to hear this, but mathematics is very important, and physics, too.''

"Aw, gee," another student groaned, from somewhere in front. "All that math and science. It sounds so *complicated!*"

Kay smiled sympathetically. "It is. But one of the other things you can study that will be equally important is something called cognitive psychology, which is a fancy term for the study of how people think. Another course of study might be ethics, which is the study of what humans consider right and wrong. And sociology will play a part, too, because we need to know how humans act as a society and how that society will interact with machines. So you see, you have a whole spectrum of study from which to choose. It's not *all* science and math."

Mrs. Polehemus came back out onstage at that point, warily skirting the walking robot, which still sat unmoving behind Kay. "I'm afraid we only have time for one more question before we break for lunch, people. Anyone?"

A tall redheaded boy in the back row stood. "We've all heard that someday robots might rise up and take over the world, but how close are we to developing a real artificial intelligence, Ms. Stockwell? Can you answer that?"

"I can try," Kay said, "although the answer depends on interested young men and women like yourselves, who are going to develop the next generations of robots. Right now, for all our advances, robots still can't match science fiction." She turned and gestured to the big, silent robot behind her. "As you have seen, working robots rarely turn out to look anything like their movie counterparts. Still, researchers at the University of Utah have succeeded in creating a dexterous four-fingered hand capable of picking a flower without crushing the stem. The key to making robots smarter lies in computer power that can enhance their intelligence, but even at Carnegie-Mellon, which has one of the premier robotics research divisions in the country, researchers say that some of the service robots they're working on still have only reached the intelligence quotient of a worm.'' She smiled, ending her speech. ''So I don't think we have to worry yet about robots taking over the world. Right now, it'll be a big day when a robot learns how to tie a shoelace by itself.''

Kay left the stage to thunderous applause, shrieks of approval, whistles and the rising din of stamping feet. The kids wanted her to come out and take a bow, which she did, activating the walking robot again with a hidden movement of her hand, so that it rose and accompanied her off the stage for the second and final time. The kids loved it, and even more encouraging to Kay than the wild applause were the snatches of comments she heard as the horde streamed out of the auditorium.

''Wow, did you believe . . . ?''

''Who would have ever thought . . . ?''

''I think I'm going to sign up for calculus next semester.''

''Do you think I can get into physics this late?''

Grinning to herself, Kay turned to accept the congratulations of Mrs. Polehemus and the school's principal, Edgar Tarrey. Both were generous with their praise, but it was Jennifer she wanted to talk to, and when she saw her standing with her father, Kay excused herself and went over.

''You were wonderful, Jennifer,'' she said as she came up to father and daughter. ''I know how scared you were, but you did it, and you can really be proud.''

''I was just telling her the same thing,'' Del said, smiling at his daughter's flushed face. Jennifer's eyes were shining—with pride and relief—but it was Kay she was looking at and not him. He gave a wry shrug and glanced at Kay. "Somehow, I think it carries more weight from you."

"That's not true, Dad," Jennifer said, blushing. "But thank you, Ms. Stockwell. I appreciate what you just said, but I wasn't nearly as good as you. You were great!"

Kay smiled. "Why don't you call me Kay? Now that we've had our trial by fire together, I think we can be less formal, don't you?"

Jennifer smiled shyly. "I'd like that . . . Kay."

Before they could say anything else, two teenagers came up, a dark-haired girl and the tall redheaded boy Kay remembered from the assembly. When Jennifer saw them, she looked even more flustered. "Hi, you guys...."

The girl came forward with a big grin. "You were fantastic, Jennifer! I couldn't have done what you did in a million years. I bet Mrs. Polehemus gives you an A now!"

Jennifer gave a shudder of remembrance. "I hope so, 'cause going out there deserves it." Then she seemed to remember the two adults and turned to Kay and Del to introduce them to her friends.

"Dad, Kay, this is Trudy and Eddie. You guys, this is Kay Stockwell, and my father, Del Rafferty."

Eddie was almost as tall as Kay, a good-looking boy who grinned appreciatively. "That was a good talk you gave, Ms. Stockwell," he said. "I really enjoyed it."

"Me, too," Trudy piped up. "I'll bet you had half the kids thinking about a career in robotics—even me, and I can't add two and two!"

Kay laughed. "I'm glad you enjoyed it. I hope you learned something."

"I did," Trudy said mischievously. "And that's to stay away from those walking robots. Did you ever do any work for the movies? I'm sure I saw that big spider-thing in *Alien*."

"Well, it wasn't Stockwell Engineering that was responsible, but robots play a big part in entertainment today," Kay said. "For instance, did you know that the robotics that power Disneyland's audio-animatronics were invented by U.S. scientists developing the Polaris missile system?"

Eddie looked impressed. "No kidding!"

"No kidding," Kay said.

"Wow."

Kay suddenly became aware of Del's cameraman hovering in the background, still filming. She had graciously agreed to spend the day at the school, where the Science Fair continued, in case any of the students had questions; she had even brought an exhibit to set up. In her booth was a video showing various robots and robotic arms at work, and two of her people were there right now, demonstrating the walking robot and the turtle, along with a hand and an arm. From the crowd that surrounded the exhibit, it was obvious that it was one of the most popular, but Kay wasn't thinking about that as she began to tour the school with Jennifer and Del. She couldn't understand why the cameraman was still with them, and when she got a chance, she pulled Del to one side and asked him.

"Why is that guy still following us around?" she whispered as Jennifer and her friends ran off.

Del glanced over his shoulder. "Oh, you mean Vince? He's here to film you today—you know that."

"Yes, but I thought he'd be finished after my speech. How am I going to talk to the kids and answer questions with a camera in my face?"

"The same way everyone else does—by ignoring it."

"I *can't* ignore it. Every time I look up, he's...*there.*"

Del smiled. "That's his job. And, I might add, he's good at it. That's why he's here with me today. So just pretend he's invisible."

"This is impossible. I can't..."

But just then, a knot of students came shyly up. They had obviously elected a spokesman, for someone was pushed to the front, where he gulped and said, "Ms. Stockwell? Can I ask you a question?"

"Sure," Kay said, putting aside her own problems at the moment to make the nervous lad at ease. "What is it?"

"Well, you know, when you were talking about robots just now? Well, we were just wondering... I mean, how expensive are they? Could we buy one of those walking robots you brought?"

Kay hid a smile. "It depends on how big your allowance is. That particular model costs about two hundred and fifty thousand dollars."

Everyone looked shocked. "Gee, that much?"

She tried not to laugh. "That's not too much when you consider that some robots can cost about two hundred *million*—in part because of highly complex software. But they do come cheaper. For example, some security robots cost around a hundred thousand per unit, while others that we call assistant robots, at use in hospitals and such, are a steal at only twenty-five thousand."

One of the girls in the group nudged someone else with her elbow. "See?" she hissed. "I *told* you."

"Thanks," the spokesman said, and the knot of teen-agers drifted off. As they walked away, Kay heard the speaker of the group say, "Well, how did I know? I just wanted to set it loose in the mall. Can you imagine all the adults it would have *scared?*"

She was shaking her head in amusement when she happened to glance up. The camera was still whirring busily, and that reminded her that she still hadn't settled this with Del. Turning back to him, she said, "Don't you think enough is enough?"

Smiling, he shook his head. "No, we're going to do this all day."

"But why?" she persisted. "It doesn't make sense!"

"It makes perfect sense," he countered. "We need to analyze your gestures, the way you smile, your body language, everything about you for your upcoming talks."

"I thought I was going to do radio spots. What difference does it make what my *smile* is like, for heaven's sake?"

"You'd be surprised, even for radio," he said. "But it does make a difference for television."

Kay stopped abruptly. "You didn't have any television appearances penciled in on that schedule you gave me—I'm sure of it."

"I know, but I changed my mind."

She looked at him suspiciously. "Why?"

"Because when I saw you today, I realized we should pursue that area. You're a natural."

"I was talking to *kids.*"

"The hardest audience," he said complacently. "You can't fool 'em, can't convince 'em, can *so* easily bore 'em. But from what I saw, they were all on the edge of their seats—"

"That's because I had the robots. I knew teenagers would be impressed and intrigued, but I'd never pull that stunt with adults. They'd either be scared out of their wits or think I'd lost my mind."

"That reminds me. How *did* you get that robot to sit on command?"

"Easy," she said, deciding to teach him a lesson. "There's a real little person inside working levers like a madman."

Del smiled. "I'm serious."

Kay didn't have time to answer, for just then another group of students came up, and then another, and before she knew it, she and Del were separated. As he had been instructed, Vince stuck like glue all through lunch, which she ate sitting in the middle of a big group of teenagers, answering questions that sometimes didn't have anything to do with engineering or robotics. Once, she looked up and saw Del watching her, and the look on his face made her so flustered that she flubbed an answer and had to backtrack, red-faced with embarrassment.

Why was he looking at her like that? she wondered, as she answered a question from someone about what it had been like to work for NASA. And then, feeling even more distracted, she wondered why she had felt that little thrill when she'd looked up and realized he was watching her.

Oh, no, she thought, *it can't be happening again!* She'd been so sure she had her emotions under control, but now she remembered feeling this way when she first realized she was attracted to Adam. He'd seemed just as handsome to her then as Del did now....

But it wasn't only Del's looks that attracted her, she thought bemusedly, as she answered another question about what it was like to be a woman in engineering. No, it was something about his expression, something about the way he smiled, the gestures he made... even his walk that made her heart beat a little faster despite herself. And even when he was being his most exasperating—as he had been earlier in his insistence that Vince follow her around all day—she still felt something stir inside her. Just looking at him made her feel strange, and when he smiled at her from across the quadrangle, where they were all having lunch, she quickly turned away.

This won't do, she told herself sternly, and forced herself to pay more attention to the eager kids who surrounded her. By a fierce effort of will, she managed to forget Del for an hour or so, but when she realized that it was getting late and that the fair would be winding up soon, she began to look around for him. She saw Jennifer at the center of a group of kids, and despite her preoccupation with Jennifer's father, felt satisfied. She knew how unhappy Jennifer had been at school, because the girl had told her, but now it seemed as though she had finally broken through one barrier. Kay hoped so, anyway; she remembered her own first years in high school and sympathized.

She, too, had been shy—and too interested in science and math to pay attention to social skills. Although she had assured Del during their conversation about her mother that she hadn't really missed a maternal influence at home while she was growing up, she had long ago realized that the lack had definitely been there. Her father had made her feel that there wasn't anything she couldn't do to compete in a so-called man's world, and she was grateful to him for that. But she had missed the subtle feminine things a mother would have helped with; choosing clothes, makeup, hairstyles—what to say to boys. She had been a senior in high school before she realized how much she had missed, so reticent that she wasn't really sure how to catch up. Her first date had been to the senior prom, and it had been an agony until she and her escort discovered a mutual fascination with wave mechanics. Then the night had sped by.

She laughed to think about it now, but it was a relief that things had changed by the time she reached college. By then, she had discovered fashion magazines along with technical journals, and when she had finally shed her braces, she had gone to a professional hairdresser for the first time in her life. But those early years had been difficult, and as she covertly watched Jennifer, who was part of the group without actually being *in* yet, her heart ached.

Still, Jennifer was a beautiful, intelligent young girl, Kay thought, and she had a father who obviously doted on her. Thinking of how loving her own father had been, she was sure that once they got through this awkward stage, things would be all right between the Raffertys, too.

Reminded of Del, she began looking around again. It was almost time to leave, and she didn't want to go without saying goodbye. But where was he? Had he already gone?

Then she spotted him near the exhibit she'd set up, and she smiled to herself. Surreptitiously, he was examining the walking robot, looking under and around it, trying to peer inside the big body of the thing—looking, Kay thought in amusement, as curious as the kids had been. Deciding to tease him a little, she went to join him.

"Hi," she said, coming up behind him, the ever-faithful Vince trailing along with his camera. "What are you looking for?"

His face reddening, Del straightened. "Nothing," he said too quickly. "In fact, I—"

But he was interrupted just then by Jennifer, who rushed up. "Dad, can I go down to Albert's with Trudy and some of the others?"

Albert's was the latest local teenage hangout, and as Del hesitated, his glance met Kay's. Something he saw in her face must have reassured him, for he nodded and said, "All right, but be home in time for dinner, okay?"

"Okay!" Jennifer said happily, turning to give Trudy a thumbs-up sign. Then she looked at Kay, suddenly shy. "Thank you for giving the talk today," she said. "It was wonderful, and I . . . I appreciate you getting me out of a jam."

"No problem," Kay said, not wanting to make a big deal out of it. "Anytime."

Jennifer flushed. "Thanks . . . and thanks again. You really were super."

Kay smiled. "You weren't so bad yourself. Have a good time."

"Thanks, I will," Jennifer said, and ran off.

A bemused expression on his face, Del watched his daughter go. "This has done her good," he murmured. Then he glanced at Kay, "It's done you both good. I think you really made some points here today, Kay."

"I hope so," Kay said with a glance around. The fair was ending, kids departing hurriedly so they wouldn't have to help with cleanup; resigned teachers lending a hand to take down exhibits and return materials and tools to classrooms. Kay's own people were dismantling Stockwell Engineering's booth, and as she watched them taking down the video setup, she added, "The kids seemed to enjoy it, anyway."

"They were impressed, all right," Del agreed. "And so was I. So impressed, in fact, that I called my office and had them contact *Good Morning, Springfield*—that local talk show that's so popular. You're scheduled to appear later this week."

Slowly, Kay turned to look at him. "You set that up without asking me?"

He looked surprised at her tone. "You said you'd do some television appearances."

"Yes, but not *talk* shows!"

"Why not?" he said in that reasonable tone she was already beginning to distrust. "Look how much good you did today. It's obvious that these kids—and the teachers, too—all came away from that speech of yours with a completely different idea about robots and robotics than they had before. Think of how many more people you can reach through television."

"Yes, but when I agreed to that, I thought I'd be appearing on a *serious* program!" she protested.

"Ah, some scientific thing that only scientists watch, right? But you don't need to convince those people, Kay—they're already on your side. You need to reach John and Joan Q. Public. They're the ones you have to influence."

There was a flaw in his logic, but at the moment, she couldn't see where. Feeling boxed in, she had to agree. But she did so reluctantly and without much good grace.

"All right," she said. "I'll do it." Then she frowned at him. "But you'd better tell those people at the station that I'm not going to do some little piece of...of fluff!"

Amusement gleamed in Del's eyes. "I'll tell them," he said solemnly. "In fact, if you like, I'll have them sign a contract stating that no one on the program will be permitted to laugh."

He was mocking her, and she decided to teach him a lesson. "Fine," she said, and then smiled wickedly as she gestured to the walking robot. "And by the way, if you were looking for the little man inside, he isn't there. He did such a good job earlier when I needed him that I told him he could go home for the day."

And with that, she waved and left.

CHAPTER SEVEN

WHEN KAY ARRIVED at the local television station, she discovered that the hostess for the show *Good Morning, Springfield* was every telemarketer's dream. Blond and blue-eyed, the woman had a willowy figure, a perfect manicure, carefully coiffed hair, artful makeup and a smile that seemed painted on her face. Her name was Georgette MacGuire, and even before they were introduced, Kay was having second thoughts. She and Georgette met briefly in the Green Room five minutes before the show was due to start, and when the hostess earnestly assured her that she just *loved* that darling little robot—What was his name? R2D2?—in *Star Wars*, it was clear to Kay that she was in big trouble.

But despite her urge to turn and run, it was too late to say she'd changed her mind, and after submitting to a makeup girl who made her feel as though she had donned a mask of clay, she heard her name called, and suddenly she was on the set.

Georgette, her blue silk skirt carefully fanned around her, was already sitting out there, perched cozily on one of the two oatmeal-colored tweed chairs that had been placed on the dais. Between the chairs was a fake lamp on a cardboard table, and as Kay took her seat, she thought that she should have known. If the show didn't even have a real lamp, how much could she count on for substance? she wondered, and tried to brace herself.

Georgette gave her a sunny smile as the director started the five-second countdown. Then the camera light blinked red, and right on cue, the hostess said brightly into the big round lens, "Today, we're honored to have with us one of Springfield's own, Miss Kay Stockwell of Stockwell Engineering, the company that's been in the papers quite a little bit lately." Perkily, she turned to her guest. "Kay... Is it all right if I call you Kay?"

"Yes, of course," Kay said politely.

Her smile in place, Georgette turned back to the camera. "Now, then, Kay," she said breathlessly, "can you tell us a little bit about what you do out there with those robots at that big old engineering plant of yours?"

Wondering where to start, Kay said, "Perhaps it would be helpful if we defined what a robot *is* first."

Georgette looked delighted. "Yes, that would be nice," she agreed, and turned to the camera again. "I'm sure many in our audience out there have never even *seen* a robot except in movies, and I don't think that counts, do you?"

Kay managed a stiff smile. "No, I don't think so. Robots in movies are light-years away from where the state of robotics is now, but regardless, a robot still is a machine much like any other. It's made of metal and plastic and is driven by motors and pistons."

"Like a car, you mean?" Georgette asked.

"Well, not exactly. Two things distinguish a robot from other kinds of machines." Warming to her subject, Kay ignored Georgette, the set and the cameramen as she explained exactly what robots could and could not do. She tried to keep everything in layman's terms, but after a few sentences Kay could see that Georgette didn't have the faintest idea what she was talking about or what to say next. Realizing they couldn't just sit there in silence, Kay plowed on.

"Unfortunately, as I said, the robots we've all seen in the movies haven't been built yet—except on Hollywood soundstages. Most robots look..."

But before she could explain further, someone behind a camera made a motion with his hand, and Georgette interrupted with a practiced smile and a restraining hand on Kay's arm. "Well, isn't that interesting!" she chirped brightly. "But unfortunately, we're running out of time. Before you go, I know our audience is dying to know a few things about *you*. Would you mind if I asked you a few personal questions?"

Warily, Kay said, "I don't know. What are they?"

Looking conspiratorial, Georgette leaned closer to her. The camera moved in. "You know, I've been looking at you during this marvelous, informative interview and thinking that you *must* be an autumn. Are you? Have you ever had your colors done? You must have, because that suit you're wearing is perfect for your coloring. Where did you get it, anyway? It's just divine. I've had my colors done, of course, and as you've probably guessed, I'm a summer myself. But with that hair and those eyes, I'm sure you must be a fall."

Kay couldn't have said what she was thinking if she'd tried. Fortunately, she didn't have to, for just then the relieved producer made a stabbing motion, and they went to commercial. Wondering how things could have disintegrated so quickly and completely, Kay stood and turned to her hostess to choke out a stilted but polite thank-you. Before she could say anything, a half-dozen people rushed onto the dais, almost pushing her out of the way. Georgette was instantly surrounded, but she managed to reach out a long, crimson-nailed hand.

"You were marvelous, Kay," she said from behind the barrage of hair and makeup people who were fussing around her. "Thank you so much. One of these days, we'll have to do lunch...."

Shuddering at the thought, Kay muttered something and escaped. As she left the set, she passed by Georgette's next guest, a woman in her sixties carrying a pink poodle. The dog had ribbons pinned to its ears that were a perfect match to the bows the woman had in her hair, and when Kay saw that both poodle and owner also wore matching jeweled collars, all she could think of was getting out of there. What was she doing in this place? When she saw Del, she was going to give him a piece of her mind. He had promised her no fluff!

She was still irate when she got back to Stockwell Engineering and immediately had Rachel place a call to Rafferty Associates. But Del wasn't in his office; his secretary told hers that he was out with other clients until late that afternoon. Politely, she added that if Ms. Stockwell wished, he could call her as soon as he returned.

Ms. Stockwell wished, Kay told Rachel stiffly, and was still agitated when Brice knocked a few minutes later. He looked surprised at her surprise and reminded her that they had a meeting scheduled at noon.

"Damn. I forgot all about it," she muttered. After the morning's fiasco, the last thing she wanted to do was sit down with a group of investors and try to convince them to back her newest robotics research. If any of them had seen Georgette's program, Kay was sure they would never take her seriously. An *autumn,* she thought, and wondered if she could wait until that afternoon to tell Del just what she thought.

Then she realized that, as tempting as it was, she couldn't blame Del entirely. After all, the responsibility was hers. She was an adult, capable of making her own decisions, and since she had agreed to do the show, she had only herself to blame that it hadn't turned out the way she wanted it to. If she'd had any doubts, she should have looked into it more completely before agreeing to go on.

"I saw the show this morning," Brice said just then.

She gave him a black look. "I'd rather not talk about that, if you don't mind."

"I don't know why. I thought it went pretty well."

"Oh, really? Which part?" she said sarcastically. "The one where Georgette was trying to decide which season I was, or when we were comparing wardrobe notes?"

He tried not to smile. "The part where you were explaining what a robot is."

"Or trying to," she said, and then erupted. "I'm not going to do this anymore, Brice! I said I'd try, and I did. But not even you can think appearing on programs like that is going to do the company any good. No one there was interested in robotics! If they were, I would have been allowed to talk about that instead of discussing where I buy my clothes!"

He was accustomed to her quick temper, and he started to say, "I admit that—" Then he saw her expression and amended hastily, "All right, but it wasn't a *total* loss."

She lifted a scornful eyebrow. "Oh no?"

"No," he persisted. "It wasn't. You got some much-needed exposure—"

"Oh, great. Just the kind I needed. I looked like a complete idiot!"

"You've never done that, Kay," he said severely. "And I won't have you talking that way. So this didn't work out. Del will just try something else."

"Oh, no, he won't! I told you—"

"Before you say anything, I think you should know that George Mott has been on the move again."

That stopped her in her tracks. She'd been pacing back and forth before the desk; now she halted and looked at him. "And?" she said warily.

"And the word is that he's going to sue you—and the company—for firing him."

"What!" She was so outraged that for a few seconds she couldn't think of a response. Her paralysis didn't last long. "He can't do that!" she stated angrily. And then, her voice lower, she said, "Can he?"

"I don't know. I've got our legal department working on it in case he carries out his threat. So far he hasn't actually filed suit, but if he does..."

Slowly, she sank onto the edge of the desk. "If he does," she said bitterly, "it will mean more ugly publicity."

"In which case, no matter how well within your rights you were to fire him, we're going to look like the heartless industrial company squashing the little guy."

"Oh, great," she muttered. "What else?"

She'd meant the question rhetorically, but Brice apparently hadn't finished delivering the bad news. "Er...Mort wanted me to tell you that they've run into another snag on the QSA-46 system. They're going to have to reprogram part of the sequence."

Kay wanted to groan. The QSA—an acronym for Quadrilateral System Aid—was Stockwell's big project, mostly hush-hush because Kay didn't want it publicized. She and Brice had had arguments about it before, Brice insisting that some of the heat of the negative publicity would be cooled if she would come out and explain what they were *really* trying to do here; she equally insistent that the project remain shrouded in secrecy. She had invested a lot of the talent and most of the research money she'd been granted into the QSA, which was a voice controlled robotic system designed to help the physically impaired. So far, even the most advanced systems of its kind were able to perform only a dozen or so specific tasks, and for Kay, it hadn't been nearly enough. To her way of thinking, a quadriplegic who depended on a robot arm to help him or her needed it to do more than provide a drink, lift a fork, brush teeth or offer a shave.

But competition, especially in voice controlled robotics technology, was fierce, and as much as Kay wanted to help people, she also had to be realistic. Industrial spies were everywhere, and as long as the public believed Stockwell was concentrating on service or defense robots, attention would be deflected from what they were really trying to do here. She knew she couldn't keep it a secret for long; she just hoped that it would be long enough for Stockwell to take the patent on the new system.

But they couldn't do that if it wasn't working, and when she looked at Brice, her eyes flashed a warning. "I know what you're thinking, and—"

He held up a hand. "No, we've discussed it before. I know you don't want the QSA publicized."

"I don't."

"All right, but if that's so, I think it's even more important to counter whatever new mischief Mott is planning, don't you?"

She had to agree, but that didn't mean she had to like it. "Thank God I fired him before we got the R & D money for the QSA," she muttered. "Can you imagine where we'd be if Mott knew what we were developing here?"

"I hate to think. It's bad enough now," Brice said, shuddering. Then he looked at her again. "Still, we have to be practical, Kay. You can't allow the public to think that we're solely concerned with developing defense contracts here. And you're going to have to tell Del—"

"Oh, no, I'm not," she said quickly. "Things are fine as they are right now."

"But he could do so much more if he knew the truth. This way, he's working in the dark."

Kay's expression turned even more grim. "Isn't that where image consultants like to be?"

"Now, Kay, that isn't fair."

"Well, it wasn't fair of him to book me on a show like *Good Morning, Springfield!*"

"Fine," Brice said calmly. "Tell him that."

She glared at him. "You can be sure I will!"

"And after you tell him off, will you give him another chance?"

"No," she said, and then saw his expression and felt ashamed of herself. "Well, maybe!" she said grudgingly, but as he started to smile, she shook her finger at him. "But he's going to have to do a lot better than this morning or, as the kids say, I'm outta here."

Now that she had conceded him the point, Brice grinned. "Speaking of kids, I hear you did a great job at that Science Fair. You had them all eating out of your hand."

Remembering how pleased Mort had been when she'd told him how well the walking robot had performed, Kay smiled in spite of herself. "I wouldn't say that, but it did go well, I think," she said. Then her smile faded. "I just wish adults were as easy to convince."

"Don't be so hard on yourself, Kay. You're doing fine."

Am I? Sometimes she wondered.

AS HIS SECRETARY had promised, Del called late that afternoon. Actually, it was nearly six o'clock, but Kay hadn't noticed the time until she picked up the phone. He sounded so wary that she had to smile, and once she did, she couldn't be angry with him anymore. It was obvious that he already knew what had happened on the show this morning, and when she heard a note in his voice that sounded like a white flag waving, she decided to teach him a little lesson.

"Hi," he said, trying to sound casual. "I got your message. Sorry I didn't call until now, but I've had appointments stacked up from here to Pittsburgh."

"I see," she said. And that was all.

He obviously wanted to get it over with. "Look, about the show this morning—"

"Oh, you saw it?"

"Yes, I just saw the video we recorded. Now, Kay, I know what you're going to say.—"

"You do?"

"Yes, I do. But you have to realize that *Good Morning, Springfield* was only a first step in a very complicated process."

"Yes, so you've told me."

"And we can't—" He stopped abruptly. "You're angry, aren't you?"

"Angry?" she repeated. "Now, why would I be angry? Because I thought I was going to get a chance to educate people about robotics, when what you had in mind was having me do a piece of fluff? Because my hostess was more interested in what season I was than what research my company is engaged in?"

There was a silence. "I'm sorry, Kay. But when I booked you on that show, you were supposed to be interviewed by someone else."

She wasn't ready to let him off the hook. "A pity you didn't warn me before I made a fool of myself."

"You didn't do that," he said quickly. "In fact, your ratings tested quite high."

"My...ratings?" she said. "My *ratings?*" she repeated, her voice rising despite herself. Whatever zest she'd had for taking him to task about this abruptly vanished. Reminded that that had been one of Martin Winslow's favorite words, she said, "What are you talking about?"

"Uh...it's a little complicated to go into over the phone. Why don't we have dinner, and I'll explain."

"Dinner!" She sounded as if she'd never heard of such a thing.

Obviously realizing that he was in the doghouse, Del was at his most persuasive. "Yes, you do have to eat, don't you? So do I. I thought tonight we could do it together."

"Tonight?"

"It's as good a time as any, don't you think?"

She didn't know what to think. Did she want to see him outside the office, even to discuss business? The more she thought about it, the more convinced she became that it wasn't a good idea. Not a good idea at all. "Well, I don't know," she said, stalling while she tried to think of an excuse.

"I'll bring Jennifer, if you like."

She was silent. How fraught with danger could a simple dinner be, especially when Del's fifteen-year-old daughter tagged along? she asked herself, and realized she was relenting even as she tried a last-ditch attempt at escape. "Well, I don't know. I have a few things to take care of at home...."

"We could meet."

"Where?" she said warily.

"How about Malarkey's on Green Street? About... eight?"

Now that she'd gone this far, she couldn't refuse or she *would* look like a fool. But she was still reluctant when she said, "I guess eight will be okay."

"Great. See you then."

"Yes...." she murmured, and then rushed home to change.

Duffy met her at the back door, wagging his helicopter tail, so delighted to see her that she felt guilty about leaving him again to go out.

"It'll be an early evening," she promised him, after she had fed him his supper and was upstairs trying to decide what to wear. He came with her, sitting on the rag rug by the side of the bed, where he started to sleep every night, only to end up cuddled up on top of the bed, keeping Kay's feet warm. As always, he watched her with his head cocked as she padded back and forth muttering to herself—and him—as though he could understand every word she said.

She went to and from the closet, rejecting one thing after another. A business suit seemed too...businesslike, but were pants and a sweater too casual? Maybe she should wear a dress. No, that was too formal, she thought; it would give a...a stamp to the evening that she didn't want it to have. Finally, she settled on white flannel slacks with a long-sleeved emerald-green silk blouse and a gold necklace of heavy links. Flats completed her casual ensemble, and after brushing her hair and redoing her makeup, she was ready to go.

"Sorry, boy," she told Duffy, putting him outside again with a rawhide bone for company. Then she got into the car and drove back downtown.

She had been to Malarkey's before; it was a bright little restaurant housed in a brick building, with wooden tables and pegged floors and red-checked tablecloths all around. The menu was printed on paddleboards, one to each table, and when Kay walked in, the delicious aroma of homemade soup wafted over to greet her. She saw that Del and his daughter had arrived before her, and as she made her way to where they were sitting at a table by the window, Del got up to hold a chair for her.

"Thank you," she murmured as she sat down. She smiled at the teenager. "Hi, Jennifer."

"Hi," the girl said shyly, and reached for the basket of bread that had been placed on the table. After searching through for the biggest piece, she buttered it lavishly, and when she popped it into her mouth, Del gave her a glance but didn't say anything. Instead, he turned to Kay.

"Thank you for coming," he said, his voice low. "And I am sorry about this morning. Can I make it up by ordering you a drink?"

Ordinarily, Kay didn't drink, but for some reason, even with Jennifer here, she was beginning to feel nervous again. She'd ignored her trepidation coming here; while driving into town, she had concentrated on what she was going to tell him about the interview with Georgette MacGuire. Now she knew how ridiculous she was being. In addition to the fact that she could hardly start a quarrel in front of his daughter, she wasn't in a position to berate Del about anything. Brice had been right, she thought bleakly; with George Mott threatening to sue the company, she needed Del's expertise even more.

But she wasn't going to agree to appear on any more shows like *Good Morning, Springfield,* she decided, and suddenly realized why she'd had that bad feeling about the whole business from the moment she'd met Georgette MacGuire. She hadn't thought of it before now, but Georgette had been wearing *that* shade of blue. Kay should have walked out the moment she'd noticed.

Reminded of the whole unpleasant experience, she changed her mind again and said, "Yes, I'll have a glass of white wine."

But as Del turned to signal the waitress, she felt annoyed again. Why did she need false courage? she asked herself. Could the answer be sitting right across from her? Her irritation with Del about the television booking had stayed with her all day, but now that they were face-to-face, she was finding it difficult to sustain her pique. Naturally he looked even more handsome tonight than he usually did. Dressed casually in loafers and slacks and a thick fisherman's knit sweater, with the collar of a white sport shirt just showing above the crew neck, he looked suave and assured and *very* good-looking. She could almost feel the sexual pull and was suddenly glad she had ordered the wine. Feeling a little flushed, she needed something to distract her.

"So, how are things at school, Jennifer?" she asked, after the waitress had come and gone with their order.

Jennifer reached for another piece of bread. Bashfully, she said, "Better. I thought I was *never* going to make friends, but now I have Trudy, and . . . well, things are starting to be pretty okay."

Kay smiled. "I'm glad to hear that. I know how difficult school can be."

Jennifer paused with the buttered bread halfway to her mouth. "Oh, no, not you. I bet you were the most popular girl in the school."

Kay laughed. "Hardly! I didn't date at all until I was a senior, and then it was only because I asked the last boy in the class who didn't have a date if he'd go with me to the senior prom. Since he was just as big a—what's the word now...nerd...geek as I was, we spent the night talking physics."

Jennifer's mouth dropped open. "You're kidding me."

Kay shook her head. "I swear."

"But...but you're so beautiful!"

Kay laughed again. "Thank you, but I've changed a lot since then—I hope. When I was in high school, I was always the tallest girl and the skinniest, and I wore braces and had hair as straight as a board. I was so shy I never spoke to anyone but a teacher—and then only if I was called on. And I went around with my head stuck in a book because I didn't have any friends."

Slowly, Jennifer put down the bread. "What...what happened to make you different?"

Kay shrugged. "I grew up, I guess. I got interested in something other than how left out I always felt." She grinned wickedly. "I discovered robotics."

Del, who had been listening with a fascinated expression, watching the play of emotions on Kay's face, leaned forward. "What *did* spark your interest in robotics?" he asked curiously.

Kay's smile turned sad and reminiscent at the same time. She wasn't sure they wanted to hear this, but she said, "I went to college with a girl who'd had polio as a child and was paralyzed because of it. Her name was

Bernadette—Bennie, we called her—and she was an engineering student like I was, except she was studying robotics because she believed the science could help people like her.'' When she saw that both Del and his daughter seemed interested, she went on, emotion coloring her voice. ''We all had such respect for her. There she was, going to college, taking all those tough classes and writing with her toes. She had to be plugged into a respirator every night, and—''

''Wait a minute,'' Jennifer said. ''She wrote with her toes? I thought you said she was paralyzed.''

''She was,'' Kay said. ''But her paralysis was in the upper torso. Bennie couldn't use her arms, so she learned to write with her feet.''

Jennifer sat back, looking awed. ''Wow. And I thought *I* had problems!''

Del glanced approvingly at his daughter, then at Kay. ''She certainly sounds like someone to be admired. Do you still keep in touch?''

Kay shook her head sadly. ''No, Bennie died soon after graduation of a respiratory infection,'' she said, and then, because she didn't want to cast a pall over the evening, smiled. ''But I've never forgotten her, and knowing her piqued my interest in robotics.'' She glanced at Jennifer, who still seemed thoughtful. ''You see, Jennifer, knowing Bennie helped me to see things differently. When you go to school with a girl who writes with her toes and wears a plug in her throat, it sort of puts things into perspective. Suddenly, I didn't feel quite so ugly and shy and tall. I was just glad to be healthy.''

There was a silence while Del and his daughter digested what she'd said. Then the waitress came with their orders, and Kay decided she'd talked long enough about herself. She glanced at Del over her bowl of soup.

"I've told you how I got into my field—how about you?" she asked.

"Oh, that's easy," Jennifer said, speaking up before Del could answer the question himself. Over her plate of hamburger and fries, she grinned in her father's direction, and her tone took on a singsong quality as though she were quoting something that Del had often said. "In a visual society such as ours, the people who have the real power are those who can provoke the most vivid images."

"Ah," Kay said, looking at Del. "So you're after power, is that it?"

Carefully, Del cut a piece of his steak. "It depends on how you interpret that," he said, meeting her eyes. "I could just be the person who makes sure that the right people attain the necessary image to gain power themselves."

"Well, that was convoluted enough to confuse anyone," Kay said, only half in jest. "But if you really believe that, why are you in Springfield? Why not Washington or New York or L.A.?"

"I've worked in big cities," he said with a shrug. "In fact, until last year, my company was based in Houston. But I like small towns better, and with instant communication these days, it doesn't really matter where I am. As they say, all I have to do is reach out to touch someone."

Kay couldn't argue with that, but she still felt there were more reasons than he let on. The conversation drifted to other things after that, and when she happened to mention something about spending summers on her grandfather's farm, Jennifer looked up from her dessert of chocolate cake with surprise.

"You grew up on a farm?" she squeaked in disbelief.

With a teasing glance in Del's direction, Kay laughed and said to Jennifer, "You know, with the way you're so surprised at my background, I wonder what image I really do have here! Yes, my grandfather has a farm outside town, and when I was growing up, I spent every summer there helping out."

Jennifer's eyes widened. "You mean with...cows and pigs and chickens and everything?"

"Even a horse or two," Kay said, amused. "Although Granddad's horses weren't the fiery steeds I longed for when I was a girl. They were fat old Belgians who couldn't be coaxed out of a walk no matter what I tried. Granddad used them for plowing when the tractor broke down."

An amazed expression on her face, Jennifer sat back. "Wow," she said. "I've never known anyone who lived on a farm!"

"Coming from New York City, I guess not," Kay said, smiling. "Maybe we can go out there sometime. It isn't that far, and Granddad always likes company."

Her eyes shining, Jennifer turned to her father. "Could we, Dad? Could we?"

Del had been watching Kay; with an effort, he jerked his glance from her face and looked at his daughter. "We'll see, Button," he said, reaching for his wallet. "But for now, I think we'd better say good-night and get you home. You've got school tomorrow, and it's getting late."

"Aw, Dad! You're acting like I'm a child! It's early yet!"

"Not for me," Kay said. "I've got a big day myself tomorrow, so I've got to get some sleep." She grinned at Jennifer. "I'm not as young as I used to be."

Jennifer gave her a worshipful look. "You look fine to me!"

"Me, too," Del murmured as he stood up to help Kay with her coat. Just for an instant, his hands rested on her shoulders, and she was dismayed and surprised at the thrill she felt at his touch.

"Thanks," she said hastily, and glanced down at the bills he'd left for the waitress. "And for dinner, too. Next time, it's my treat."

Del's eyes met hers. "Will there be a next time?"

The words were out before she knew it. Appalled, she heard herself say, "Well, you could both come to dinner at my house next Saturday night—if you don't have other plans, that is."

"Gee, we'd love to!" Jennifer exclaimed before her father could say anything. Eagerly, she turned to him. "Wouldn't we, Dad?"

Del hesitated just an instant. It was obvious that he was wondering—as Kay herself was frantically doing at the moment—if this was such a good idea. But then he saw the enthusiastic expression on his daughter's face and knew he couldn't refuse. "Yes," he said, turning to Kay. "We'd like that very much."

"Good," she replied, trying not to think that she could get lost in that deep blue gaze. "Then I'll expect you at . . . seven?"

"Fine," he answered, still holding her eyes. Something seemed to have zinged to life between them, making them both feel a little breathless. "Can we bring anything?"

A shield and a suit of armor for me, Kay thought, and quickly shook her head, wondering where that thought had come from. "Just yourselves," she answered, and said good-night before she could do any more damage to her equilibrium.

In the car on the way home, she wondered what had possessed her. She *never* mixed business with pleasure; it was one of her ironclad rules. She hadn't known she was even *thinking* about inviting Del and his daughter to dinner until the words were out, and then it was too late to retract. Was it because she unconsciously identified with Jennifer? she wondered. As dearly as she loved her father and grandfather, she had been lonely as a girl and just as shy and insecure as Del's daughter seemed to be. Was that why she'd invited them?

Or was it because she hadn't had any real kind of social life since breaking up with Adam? She had enjoyed going out tonight; she'd had a good time with both Raffertys, father and daughter. Then another thought occurred to her, and she squirmed. Maybe *too* good a time with the father, eh?

Even though she was alone, she could feel her face getting red. She could make as many excuses as she liked, but wasn't the truth that, as much as she liked Jennifer, as deeply as she identified with that shy loneliness of hers, it wasn't so much the daughter who drew her as it was her attraction to the father? Oh, why not admit it? she asked herself. Wasn't the real reason she had invited them to dinner next week because she wanted to see Del outside the office again?

Cheeks burning, Kay pulled into her driveway.

JENNIFER WAS SILENT in the car on the way home. At first Del thought it was because she had fallen asleep, but when he glanced over and saw that she was staring out the window, he had to ask.

"Did you have a good time tonight?"

She turned her head to look at him. Her eyes shone in the darkness. "Oh, yes, the best!" she said, and then sighed. "Isn't she beautiful, Dad? Isn't she the most beautiful woman you've ever seen?"

Hastily, Del returned his attention to his driving. "Yes, she's very attractive," he muttered.

Jennifer bolted upright on the seat. "Attractive! At*tractive*! Oh, Dad, only you could say that! She's gorgeous! And so smart, too! And so nice, and so—"

"Whoa!" He had to laugh. "I take it you like her."

"*Like* her! Oh, if I could be like that . . . !"

"Now, wait a minute. I like you just the way you are. I don't want you to ch—"

"Oh, Dad, you know what I mean!"

He wasn't sure he did—or wanted to—especially when she abruptly turned to him and gave him a considering look. "Why haven't you ever married again?" she asked.

Now he was certain he didn't like the direction of the conversation. "Because I never wanted to," he said. "Because I didn't have time. Because—"

"Because you never found someone other than Mom that you fell in love with?"

"Exactly," he said, increasingly uncomfortable. "Now, can we drop th—"

"You could love Kay, couldn't you?" she interrupted.

He could feel himself getting hot—flushed, not angry. "I think anyone could love Kay," he said as lightly as he could. "Now, do you mind if we drop this? I'm glad you had a good time tonight, Button, but—"

"I'm going on a diet," she announced suddenly.

Wondering if all men felt as though they were dealing with a whirlwind where women were concerned, he looked at her in surprise. "A diet?" he said warily. "Why?"

Jennifer bounced back against the car seat again. "Because if I'm going to fit into my good pants by next Saturday, I have to lose some weight," she said. "You want me to look nice when we go over to Kay's, don't you?"

Feeling more helpless by the minute, Del said. "You always look nice, Button."

"Oh, Dad...." Another heavy sigh, this one accompanied by a doleful shake of the head at the ignorance of fathers. "You know what I mean!"

"Well, I—"

She bounced up again. "And you should get a haircut before Saturday, all right?"

He couldn't prevent a quick glance in the rearview mirror. He thought he looked just fine. "A haircut?" he repeated. "Why?"

"*Dad,* don't you want to look *nice?*"

"I *do* look nice," he protested. "I suppose you want me to get a new suit, too!"

She looked immediately thoughtful. "That's not a bad idea. Kay said we should be casual, but you *do* look pretty good in a suit. You could—"

Now he could see where this was going. "Jennifer..." he said warningly.

"Okay, okay, it was just an idea, all right?" she said as they pulled into the driveway. But as she opened the car door and started to get out, she grinned at him. "But you do look good in a suit, Dad," she said. "You really should think about it."

She was at the front door before he could reply. As he put the key into the lock, Del tried to be amused. But as he passed the hall mirror, he paused. The same old Del looked back at him, and as he stared at his reflection, he wondered for the first time what Kay saw when she looked at him. Unconsciously, he straightened, pulling his shoulders back, then peering forward. *Did* he need a haircut? Maybe it was a little long over the ears....

Then he realized what he was doing and felt like an idiot. Turning away from the mirror, he went into the living room to fetch his briefcase. He didn't notice Jennifer watching him from the head of the stairs, one hand covering her mouth, her eyes crinkled up in an effort to hold back a delighted laugh.

CHAPTER EIGHT

ONCE SHE RESIGNED herself to breaking her own rule about not mixing her professional life with her personal one, Kay began to look forward to having Del and his daughter for dinner. Although she rarely went to any trouble just for herself, she was a good cook, and after recognizing her complete lack of social life since breaking up with Adam, she knew it was time to end her self-imposed isolation. And, because nothing could possibly happen between her and Del with Jennifer present, she felt fairly secure. Or as secure as she was ever going to feel where Del was concerned.

She was truly fond of Jennifer Rafferty, she thought, and then realized that the troubled teenager was tugging at her heart, as well. Kay had never really thought much about having children; she assumed it was something that would happen in the far distant future when her career and her work were under control—and, of course, a potential husband and father had entered the picture, she thought wryly. Once she had "blossomed" in college, she'd had relationships, but none were really serious until Adam came along. He had been the first man she had ever considered marrying. But then Adam had changed. Now he was where he'd always wanted to be—legislating from Washington.

Well, good luck to him, Kay thought, trying not to be bitter. Still, she couldn't ignore the march of time much longer; as they said, the dreaded clock was ticking away, and before long it might be too late. The thought was a little scary, so she wondered whimsically if she should start with an existing child and work down to an infant later. She'd heard it said a teenager tested one's parental and maternal instincts more than any other age, so if she could survive Jennifer, she would be prepared for anything.

Wondering just how serious she was, Kay told herself it was too soon to decide anything more profound than what she was going to have for dinner when the Raffertys came on Saturday. Then, after planning her menu, she embarked on a flurry of housework, cleaning the entire house from top to bottom. Even Duffy's reproachful stare didn't save him; he got a bath, too, forced to stand still in the tub while she soaped even his ears. He retaliated when she was finished by leaping out and shaking his coat as hard as he could, spraying Kay and the entire bathroom in the process. Then, looking pleased—if a little drippingly bedraggled—he stalked out. She had her revenge later, when she collared him and went over him with the hair dryer. After that, they considered themselves even.

At last, everything—including the dog—was ready. Dressed in green slacks and a rust-colored sweater, with an apron tied around her waist, Kay was just checking the pot roast again when the doorbell rang. Immediately, Duffy, who was watching the cooking proceedings avidly, leaped up and ran into the living room, barking.

"I'll be right there!" Kay called over the noise. Carefully, she shut the oven door and then stood where she was for a moment, wondering why she suddenly felt so nervous. To calm herself, she glanced around. Everything was in order, from the table set with her mother's

china and silver, to the centerpiece of flowers she'd had
made up. A cheerful fire crackled in the living room fireplace, and the house looked—even she had to admit it—
inviting. Quickly untying the apron, she hurried out to
answer the door.

"Oh, you have a dog!" Jennifer exclaimed the instant
Kay opened the door. She and her father were both
armed with packages, but Jennifer thrust hers into her
father's already-overburdened arms and dropped down
immediately to reach eagerly for Duffy. When the dog
backed suspiciously away, she gave Kay an anxious look.
"Can I touch him? Will he bite?"

"He won't bite, but he's a little leery of strangers at
first, honey," Kay said. "His name's Duffy. Just hold
out your hand and let him come to you. It'll be all right,
you'll see."

Jennifer did as she was bid, holding out her hand to the
dog and pleading, "I won't hurt you. Come on,
Duffy...come on, now...."

Once Duffy decided to become friends, he could be a
little overpowering. After an initial wary sniff and then
a quick look in Kay's direction, the dog apparently decided that Jennifer passed muster. His tail began to wag,
and then, with a sharp bark, he launched himself into her
arms, licking her face. Laughing, Jennifer hugged him
close.

"Oh, he's wonderful!" she cried, sputtering as Duffy
plied his tongue again. "Where did you get him?"

"He got me, I'm afraid," Kay said with a laugh, and
then realized that Del was still standing out on the porch.
With Jennifer squatting in front of the doorway and the
dog jumping all over her, he couldn't get by, and when his
and Kay's eyes met, he looked at her meaningfully.

"Mind if I come in, too?" he asked.

Embarrassed, Kay quickly called the dog while Jennifer hauled herself to her feet. Belatedly, the girl remembered that she was supposed to give something to Kay. She grabbed her package back from her father and thrust it out.

"Why, thank you, Jennifer, but what's this? I said you didn't have to bring anything."

"I know," the girl said, shy again now that she didn't have the dog to distract her. "But Dad said we shouldn't come empty-handed, so we brought this."

"And these," Del said, allowed to enter at last while Kay shut the door behind him. Jennifer had already given her wine, but he sheepishly held out what he was carrying—a bottle of champagne and a big bouquet of flowers wrapped in protective paper.

"Why... how nice!" Kay said, touched and embarrassed at the same time.

Jennifer shrugged out of her car coat. "We were going to bring candy, too," she said mischievously, "but I thought that'd be a little much."

Kay grinned back. "Much too much," she agreed, glancing at Del. "Can I take your coat? Then I'd better put these in water." She peeked into the wrapping and saw the carnations in a riot of rainbow colors. Her glance met Del's again. "Carnations," she murmured. "They're my favorite flower...."

"I thought they might be," he said, reddening a little himself. "But I didn't know what color—"

"They're perfect," she replied, and then realized abruptly that they were still standing in the hallway. Hurriedly collecting her guests' coats, she gestured toward the living room, and with Duffy bounding beside them, they went in. Kay left them for a moment to put the flowers in water and check on the dinner, and when she came back in, Jennifer was sitting happily by the fireplace, Duffy close beside her. Del's attention had been caught by the few framed photographs she had scattered among the shelves of one floor-to-ceiling bookcase.

"Jennifer, did you see this?" he said. "It's a picture of Kay at the space center with the astronauts."

"No kidding! Really?" Intrigued, Jennifer jumped up and went to look. "Wow. Do you think she really knew these guys?"

"I don't know," Del said, glancing at Kay. "Why don't we ask her?"

Since they were obviously interested, Kay went over to explain. "That was taken when I was working on a consulting basis for NASA," she said, indicating the photo of her and four of the astronauts—two men and two women. The crew were wearing uniforms and looked very official, even when laughing into the camera. They were all obviously enjoying themselves.

"Gee, they look like they're having fun," Jennifer said.

Kay smiled in remembrance. "They were a foursome, all right. I went down there to help them work with the big robotic arm the shuttle uses in space. It was really an experience."

Jennifer's eyes widened. "Did you get to sit inside a spaceship?"

Kay laughed. "Well, they don't call it that, you know. But yes, I did. But the most interesting thing I did while I was there—apart from my work, that is—was experience weightlessness. It's like flying, but not quite."

"Wow," Jennifer said, immediately looking wistful. "I'd give *anything* to be weightless, even for a minute!"

"It's not all it's cracked up to be, I assure you," Kay told her.

"You can say that—you're so slim! But me—" Abruptly, Jennifer broke off.

Quietly, Kay said, "I think you look lovely tonight, Jennifer. Are those new pants?"

Jennifer turned pink with pleasure. "No, not exactly. But it's been a long time since I've been able to wear them." She hesitated, then added shyly, "I lost some weight this week."

Kay smiled. "Well, don't lose too much. You *can* be too thin, you know."

"Oh, I don't know about *that*," Jennifer said, sighing. "For instance, I wish I looked just like you."

Kay smiled, accepting the compliment but deflecting its importance. "Well, isn't it good that you don't? Think how boring it would be if we all looked alike."

"It wouldn't be, if we all looked like you."

On impulse, Kay gave her a hug. "You know, I think I'm going to keep you around," she said lightly. "You're certainly good for the ego." Then she turned to Del, who had been silently watching during this exchange. "Would you like some of that wine you brought—or the champagne? Dinner won't be for about a half hour, so we have time."

Looking a little bemused, he said, "I brought those for you, but . . . wine would be nice."

Noting his expression and wondering what he was really thinking, Kay nodded and then looked at Jennifer. "I have some sparkling cider, if you like, or a soft drink."

"I'll have some wine, too," Jennifer said, and then saw her father's expression. "Or, maybe I'd better have a cola."

Kay started off to get the drinks, but just then Jennifer put her finger on another of the small, framed pictures. "Is this your grandfather, the one you told us about, who has the farm?"

Kay looked at the photo Jennifer indicated. The man in the photo was wearing jeans, a checked shirt and a baseball cap. He was leaning against a tractor and had a straw sticking out of his mouth. Weathered though his skin might be, with silver hair peeking out from under the cap, he still looked young and vigorous, and Kay smiled with genuine affection. "Yes, that's Granddad," she said. "And don't let that pose fool you. He *never* chews on straw, and he's rarely been that motionless in his entire life."

"He's a handsome man," Del commented, and glanced at the picture beside it, of a man in a business suit. "And this must be your father. The resemblance between them is undeniable."

"Yes, it is—was," Kay said softly. She still found it difficult to talk about her father.

Del seemed to sense her disquiet, for he touched the photo of the astronauts again. "Very impressive," he commented.

"Yes, well, that was a long time ago," she said, and, because she felt a little embarrassed by his obvious admiration, pointed to another small photo, one neither Jennifer nor he had noticed before. It was one of Kay in a laboratory, wearing a wrinkled white lab coat that had obviously seen better days, with two pencils stuck in her hair and another in her mouth. As though that weren't unflattering enough, she was surrounded by computer printouts in disheveled stacks, a jumble of electronic parts scattered on a table in front of her and had a streak of black down one cheek. Her hair was in wild disorder, and whoever had taken the picture had caught her just as she looked up, an expression of panicked dismay on her face. She looked—there was no other way to say it—like the mad scientist. Seeing Del's expression, she smiled.

"That's the real me," she said. "Trying to figure out what went wrong with yet another experiment." Her expression turned just a little wistful. "It was one of my father's favorite pictures. That's why I still keep it around."

And before he could respond, she went out to the kitchen to get the drinks. When she came back with the tray, Del took his glass and lifted it up. "I'd like to make a toast," he said, holding Kay's eyes. "To success."

"Success," Kay murmured, but her glance told him that they still had to talk about that. She hadn't forgotten last week's fiasco, and she wasn't going to have a repeat.

Dinner was ready soon after that, and when they all sat down to pot roast and potatoes, green peas flavored with dill and fresh rolls, Jennifer was lavish with praise.

"I'm afraid I can't take credit for the rolls," Kay said with a laugh. "I can bake bread when I have time, but these days it seems about all I can do is go down to Jensen's bakery and pick them up ready-made."

"Did your mother teach you how to cook?" Jennifer asked eagerly.

Kay didn't know why she was so interested, but she gently shook her head. "No, I'm afraid not, Jennifer. My mother died when I was very young. I . . . I never really knew her."

Looking shocked, Jennifer sat back in her chair. "Gee . . . I'm sorry. I didn't know."

"How could you?" Kay said lightly, then she smiled. "But it's all right. As I've told you, my grandfather is a man of many talents. He's the one who taught me to cook—all the staples, anyway. My father was the one who taught me to make bread."

"No kidding." Jennifer seemed impressed. Then, with a mischievous glance in her own father's direction, she added innocently, "I didn't know men could cook. Dad can't even boil water."

"How do you manage, then?" Kay couldn't help asking. "Do you do the cooking?"

"Oh, no."

"We have a housekeeper," Del said, reddening slightly. He looked reprovingly at his daughter before adding, "And I'm not totally helpless. On Mrs. Nivens's nights off, I usually scrape together something edible."

Jennifer giggled. "Oh, Dad! Bacon and eggs? Tuna sandwiches?"

Kay hid a smile. "Well, at least he tries, Jennifer. Some men never do, you know. They grow up thinking they'll never have to cook."

"Dad grew up in Chicago," Jennifer said helpfully. "But he never talks about it."

"Oh?" When Kay glanced at Del, she saw something in his eyes that warned her this was a subject best left alone. When she looked at Jennifer again, she saw the girl gazing longingly at the meat platter.

Seeing her glance, Kay asked, "You're welcome to more, but save room for dessert, too. *That* I did make—apple pie, if that's all right."

Jennifer's eyes lit up. "Apple pie! Homemade?"

"About as homemade as you can get. The only thing I didn't do is grow the apples myself."

"Wow!" Jennifer exclaimed, and then added enviously, "I wish I could cook."

"What do you mean?" Del said. "You can cook. You used to help your mother all the time."

GET 4 BOOKS

FREE

Return this card, and we'll send you 4 brand-new Harlequin Superromance® novels, absolutely *FREE!* We'll even pay the postage both ways!

We're making you this offer to introduce you to the benefits of the Harlequin Reader Service®: free home delivery of brand-new romance novels, **AND** at a saving of 33¢ apiece compared to the cover price!

Accepting these 4 free books places you under no obligation to continue. You may cancel at any time, even just after receiving your free shipment. If you do not cancel, every month, we'll send 4 more Harlequin Superromance® novels and bill you just $2.96* apiece—that's all!

Yes! Please send me my 4 free Harlequin Superromance® novels, as explained above.

Name

Address   Apt.

City   State   Zip

134 CIH ADGR (U-H-SR-11/91)

*Terms and prices subject to change without notice. Offer limited to one per household and not valid to current Harlequin Superromance® subscribers.

Sales tax applicable in NY.
© 1990 Harlequin Enterprises Limited.
PRINTED IN CANADA

DETACH ALONG DOTTED LINE AND MAIL TODAY! – DETACH ALONG DOTTED LINE AND MAIL TODAY! – DETACH ALONG DOTTED LINE AND MAIL TODAY!

Get 4 Books FREE

SEE BACK OF CARD FOR DETAILS

DETACH ALONG DOTTED LINE AND MAIL TODAY! – DETACH ALONG DOTTED LINE AND MAIL TODAY! – DETACH ALONG DOTTED LINE AND MAIL TODAY!

FREE MYSTERY GIFT

We will be happy to send you a free bonus gift! To request it, please check here, and mail this reply card promptly!

Thank you!

BUSINESS REPLY CARD

FIRST CLASS MAIL   PERMIT NO. 717   BUFFALO, NY

POSTAGE WILL BE PAID BY ADDRESSEE

HARLEQUIN READER SERVICE®

3010 WALDEN AVE
P O BOX 1867
BUFFALO NY 14240-9952

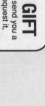

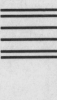

NO POSTAGE
NECESSARY
IF MAILED
IN THE
UNITED STATES

Jennifer's eyes dropped. "Yeah, well...that was a long time ago. Mom doesn't cook much these days. It's easier to go out or catch a burger or something."

Del stiffened. "You mean your mother doesn't fix meals anymore?" he demanded. "Since when?"

"Since...I don't know when," Jennifer said, turning sulky. "Besides, why do you care? You told me you did that yourself."

"Yes, but I didn't have a child at home to take care of," Del said, and then seemed to remember that they were guests in Kay's home. "Never mind," he muttered. "We'll discuss this later."

"I don't know why we have to discuss it at all," Jennifer said rebelliously. "You won't let me live with Mom right now, so what does it matter?"

Despite Del's efforts, Kay could see the beginnings of an argument. Since that was the last thing she wanted to be in the middle of, she said hastily, "Why don't we wait awhile for dessert? Del, would you like some coffee?"

Looking relieved that an altercation had been avoided, Del nodded. "Yes, that would be fine. Would you like some help?"

"Oh, no, I can manage."

At a look from her father, Jennifer pushed away from the table. "I'll help clear," she muttered, obviously not relishing the task.

Kay took pity on her. "No, let's leave it for now. I hate to have guests traipsing back and forth to the kitchen carrying dirty plates. I'll get it in the morning. In the meantime, would you like to take Duffy for a walk? He and I usually go out about this time—if you wouldn't mind."

Jennifer's eyes lit up again. "Mind! I'd love it! Where's his leash?"

A few minutes later, when Jennifer was bundled up in her coat and Duffy was jumping around on the end of his lead, Kay saw the two out the front door. Laughing and waving, she watched until they hit the end of the front walk, then she closed the door. When she turned, Del was standing there watching her. He had such a strange expression on his face that she paused.

"What is it?"

He shook his head. "Nothing, really," he said, sounding resigned. "It's just that sometimes I think everybody in the world handles her better than I do."

Kay couldn't help smiling. "You're her father. She's a teenager. You're not supposed to get along at this particular time in your lives."

He sighed. "You're just saying that to make me feel better."

This time she laughed. Heading toward the kitchen so she could get the coffee, she said, "It'll pass. Trust me."

He followed her through the swinging door. Looking bleak, he said, "When? When I'm too old to notice... or care?"

Smiling again, she reached for the cups and saucers she'd already laid out on the counter. The coffee was ready, and she poured them both a cup. "You love her, it's obvious. And she adores you. That's obvious, too. It'll work out."

He couldn't have looked more skeptical. "Obvious? To whom, I'd like to know. On her *good* days she treats me like I'm beneath contempt or some lower form of life, and on the bad days... Well, we won't even talk about that. If you only knew what it's been like since she came to live with me—"

He broke off, sounding so bitter that Kay was surprised into asking, "You didn't want her to come and live with you?"

He leaned against the counter, rubbing his temples. Suddenly he looked so tired and worn that Kay felt an impulse to put her arms around him and comfort him. Dismayed by her feelings, she stayed safely where she was, on the other side of the counter, as he said, his voice low, "Yes, I wanted her. I've wanted her ever since the divorce eight years ago. But her mother fought me for custody, and, well... you know how these things go. We had holidays and a few weeks in summer, but... well, it wasn't enough."

Kay stared down into her coffee cup. "No, I suppose not," she said.

Del went on. "But then Maxine—that's my ex-wife—got married again this year—" his lip curled slightly in contempt "—to some tennis bum who attaches himself to every tournament in sight. I don't know how they manage, and I don't really care. But I wasn't going to let Jennifer be dragged willy-nilly all over Europe just to satisfy one of Maxine's whims, so I insisted that she allow Jennifer to come and live with me."

"And now you're the villain," Kay said in understanding. "You're not only responsible for making her miss out on such an exciting opportunity, but you've taken her away from her home and her friends and everything she knows."

"You got it," he said, and looked, if possible, even more bleak. "She's changed so much, Kay. You wouldn't believe she was the same girl. And this weight gain! I know it's a symbol of how unhappy she is, but I don't know what to do about it."

She wanted to put her hand on his arm, but she didn't dare. She didn't trust herself to touch him, for she was feeling swamped with feelings she really didn't want to deal with.

"She just needs time to adjust, Del," she said, trying to be comforting. But even she could hear how weak it sounded, and she shook her head. "Fifteen is such a difficult age...."

"So is forty—especially when you're trying to be a good father," he said unhappily. Then he made a determined effort to lighten the conversation. "Well, if you have any suggestions, I'd be happy to hear them. Anything short of stringing her up from a yardarm will be seriously considered, I promise you. And maybe I'll eventually have to resort to that."

Kay laughed. "I doubt you'll have to do anything so drastic," she said, and then had a sudden idea. "Does she have a pet? She responded so positively to Duffy that maybe if she had a puppy or a kitten of her own—"

Del groaned. "Oh, that's all I need, an animal around the house! Cat or dog hairs flying around, footprints on the couch, my housekeeper up in arms! Can't you think of anything else?"

Kay grinned wickedly. "You could always get her a horse."

He looked appalled. "Now that I think about it, the cat or dog idea isn't half-bad," he said. "Er...where did you get Duffy?"

"Duffy got me," she said. "I found him by my car one night in a rainstorm, right after—" She stopped abruptly, not sure she wanted to tell him.

Before he saw the indecision on her face, Del prodded, "Right after...?" Then he saw her expression and said, "If you don't want to talk about it, I understand."

She stood there uncertainly. Although Del had been honest with her about Jennifer, she was still not sure how much—if anything—she wanted to tell him about herself. She began hesitantly. "It was right after I came back to Springfield. I had been engaged to be married, but we broke off the relationship, and I...I came home to work for my father." She forced herself to meet his eyes. "It was a very unhappy time for me. The reason Adam and I broke up was because he wanted to run for political office, and the consultant he hired didn't think I was the right...material for a politician's wife." She made herself say it all. "Adam apparently agreed."

"Obviously a mistake on Adam's part," Del said quietly. His admiring glance told her he would never have made that same error.

"And mine," she said. "I should have realized what kind of man he was—that he could be so easily swayed." She smiled slightly, bitterly. "Not an auspicious sign of character for his constituents, is it?"

"I think I'm beginning to understand why you have such an aversion to consultants, Kay," he said. "Why didn't you tell me in the beginning?"

"Are you kidding? What was I going to say? That I'd already gone a few rounds with someone in your profession and come away bruised, if not the definite loser?"

He shook his head angrily. "That's not the way it's supposed to be," he muttered. "No wonder you feel the way you do."

"Well, maybe you can make me change my mind," she suggested.

"From that outright hostility you showed when we first met?"

"How can you say that? Brice had me on my best behavior that day."

"If that was your best behavior," he said with a mock shudder, "then I'm glad I didn't get you on a bad day. You could be as formidable as my daughter."

She laughed, equilibrium restored—or so she thought. But as she walked toward the sink, Del reached out and put a hand on her arm. She was so startled at the gesture that she nearly jumped.

"I'm sorry you had a bad experience with one consultant," Del said seriously. "But that doesn't mean we're all like that. Believe me, Kay."

And as she gazed into his eyes, she realized that for the first time she *was* starting to believe him. It was a strange feeling, for she had harbored such deep resentment for Marty Winslow and everyone like him for so long that she hadn't realized she'd begun to change.

"I'd like to believe that," she said, unable to look away. "But we'll see."

Again, she started toward the sink, but he didn't release her arm. "I don't want to change you, Kay," he said softly. "I like you just the way you are."

This time when she turned back to look at him, he was so close she brushed against him. The intimate contact sent shock waves zinging through her. She was wondering why she felt this way, when she realized that he was going to kiss her.

"Del . . ." she said. That was all she could say. Suddenly, it was as if she couldn't breathe, and as she stared at him helplessly, he put his arms around her and gently pulled her close. He began to lower his head toward hers, pulling her body even closer to him—so close that the scent of his cologne filled her nostrils even as those marvelous eyes of his filled her vision. She had time for only a fleeting thought. How well they seemed to fit together: thigh against thigh, his chest pressing against her breasts, his arms around her waist and the small of her back. Dazedly, she thought it was as though they'd been made to order. . . .

Then he kissed her.

His lips were warm and smooth, gentle at first, then, when she responded by reaching up and cradling the back of his head with her hands, more demanding. Their mouths opened and their tongues met, and as the kiss deepened, Kay felt as though she were being swept away to someplace she'd never been before. She could feel desire emanating from him, feel it in the tensing of his body, the tightening of his arms around her, hear it in the quickening of his breathing. It had been so long since she had kissed and been kissed that she wanted it to go on forever. As though in a dream, she could feel herself melting into him, feel the trembling begin in her legs, feel that warmth spreading through her body, demanding more.

"Oh, Del . . . !" she murmured, and pressed against him.

He made a sound in his throat—she never knew what. For just when she felt as though she were being swept away utterly, she heard the front door open and then slam again, followed by a sudden quick brush of outside air. Without warning, Duffy came barging into the kitchen, closely followed by a red-cheeked and flushed Jennifer, who looked at them in sheer delight as they sprang guiltily apart.

"We're back!" Jennifer announced, giggling.

Del didn't seem to know where to look. Avoiding both Kay's and his daughter's eyes, he muttered, "I can see that."

Kay pulled herself together. "Did you have a nice walk?"

"Yeah, it was great," Jennifer said, her eyes sparkling as she looked from one to the other. Then she giggled again. "But I can see that it wasn't long enough! Are we ready for dessert yet, or do you two want to carry on?"

Weakly, avoiding Del's flushed face, knowing her own color was just as high, Kay went to cut the pie.

CHAPTER NINE

TWO DAYS AFTER her dinner party with Del and his daughter, Kay was still trying to decide how she felt about that kiss. She'd spent all Sunday in a daze, so confused about her feelings for Del that she didn't know whether to be glad or not that Jennifer had interrupted. Remembering her response, she felt hot all over again. She didn't like the fact that she'd lost control—or seemed about to lose it—to such an extent. She hated to think what she would have done if Jennifer hadn't come in.

It was obvious, she told herself as she got dressed for work on Monday morning, that somehow she had to regain her composure. After all, as she had reiterated over and over again all day yesterday, she wasn't looking for a relationship at this critical time in her life, and even if she was, it certainly wouldn't be with a business associate—and emphatically not one in Del's despicable line of work.

Del might have assured her that he wasn't like Martin Winslow—and even she could see now that he wasn't—but she still couldn't forget the fact that the two men shared the same profession. No matter how attractive Del was, no matter how attracted she was to him, he believed in image over substance—an idea that she would never accept.

*But if that's so, why don't you just fire him and get on
with it? How can you work with a man whose profession you despise?*

Oh, she was getting to hate that insidious little voice
that nagged her at the most inconvenient times. She
didn't *know* why she didn't fire him; she was no longer
sure how she could work with someone in his profession. At this point, she couldn't be certain of anything.

Except talk shows, she thought, clinging to one fact
about which she was absolutely positive. Never again! she
thought with a shudder. She was hard at work when Del
called to tell her he'd booked her on another one.

"What?" she cried when she took the call and he told
her about the new arrangements. "Del, you can't be serious! You *know* how I feel about this!"

He was at his most soothing, persuasive best. "Yes,
but this show is different."

"It can't be! They're all the same!"

"No, they're not. Will you listen?"

"No!" she said, but she did—with growing alarm—as
he explained about the *Amanda May Crosby Show.* It
was based in Chicago, but unlike *Good Morning,
Springfield,* this was no local show. It was seen across the
nation. Proudly, he told her that the spot was so popular
that guests were lined up months in advance, but he'd
pulled a few strings and called in a couple of favors to get
her booked in one week. For some reason she didn't feel
especially grateful.

"No," she said firmly. She wasn't going to be talked
into this, no matter how persuasive he was. "It's out of
the question. I don't care if it's the caliber of *Face The
Nation*—I won't do it. As you might trouble yourself to
recall, the last one was a disaster."

"No, it wasn't," he said with that assurance she had admired, but which now set her teeth on edge. "You got exposure—"

"Oh, yes, right," she said sarcastically. "And just the kind I needed to put the company—not to mention myself—in *such* a good light."

He ignored the thrust. "Regardless of what you feel, Kay, the fact is that it was a good experience. We were able to see how you look on camera, how you handle yourself, how you come across—everything we need to know to make your next appearance even better. So this is what I want you to do—"

"You're not listening to me," she interrupted. "I've said I won't do it."

There was a silence. Then in that tone she was beginning to know all too well, he said, "Well, that's up to you, of course. I thought we had agreed that you'd give it a try."

"I never agreed to another talk show!" she said stubbornly.

He was silent again, letting her think about it, which she did, all too clearly. With George Mott's lawsuit hanging over her head, she couldn't afford the luxury of being childish, and she just couldn't face Brice and tell him she'd reneged on her promise so soon. He knew that, and he knew *she* knew it. Feeling boxed in and annoyed because he was right, she finally said, as ungraciously as she could, "All right. I'll try it one more time. But this one better work, Del, or—"

"Don't worry, trust me."

"I never trust a man who tells me to trust him. They're usually the most untrustworthy of all."

She could hear the smile in his voice. "All right, don't trust me then. Will you listen, instead?"

"Reluctantly. What is it?"

"This is what I want you to do...."

He wanted her to come to his office and put herself in the hands of his capable staff, who would—

"They're not going to try and change me, are they?" she interrupted again, halfway into his explanation.

He sounded shocked at the very idea. "Of course not! They're just here to advise you."

She was still suspicious. "On what?"

"Oh...things like diction, elocution, presentation, makeup, wardrobe—"

"They want to change me," she said irately. "I knew it!"

"No, that's not true," he insisted. "You'll see. Can you be here this afternoon about two?"

"I don't know," she said peevishly. "I've got more to do than prepare for some stupid talk show, you know."

"Well, fine," he said equably. "I just thought it would be good preparation for your appearance before that Senate subcommittee."

It was her turn to be silent. Finally, she said, "How did you know about that?"

"Brice told me," he said. Then, "Why? It wasn't a secret, was it?"

Kay hesitated. Her appearance before the Senate sub-committee wasn't exactly top secret, but she didn't want it generally known, and she especially didn't want the press to get hold of it just yet. It was an important event for her. If she succeeded in convincing the committee that the work they were doing here was worthy of a grant, it would be a giant step forward for the company. In addition to the venture capital she was about to acquire, she would have government backing—a crucial springboard for success. Work in robotics was enormously expensive, especially the kind she was doing here, and to put it bluntly, she needed all the money she could get.

She tightened her lips. That's why this business with George Mott was so infuriating and untimely. With so much riding on her Washington appearance several months hence, she couldn't afford all the negative publicity—especially if it was complicated by a wrongful firing suit. People in the nation's capital might be used to dealing with scandal at times, but that didn't mean they'd overlook it when someone came before them, hat in hand. And with the latest setback in Stockwell's biggest project—the QSA program for the physically impaired—getting that grant was more important than ever. Kay couldn't afford to fail, not when the company had come so far.

"No, it wasn't a secret," she said finally. "I just don't want the press to get hold of it yet. I've got enough problems without trying to field questions about that."

"Agreed. That's why I think our plans from here on should be formulated with your Washington appearance in mind," he said, and hesitated before he added, "Kay, I know how important this to you. I also know what I'm doing. Can you trust me on this?"

When he put it like that, she could hardly refuse. But was Amanda May really necessary? she wondered mournfully, even as she agreed to at least give it a try.

"And if today at two isn't convenient," he went on persuasively, "why don't you name a time?"

"All right, I will. Two is too early—I'll never get done here in time. Four would be better for me."

"Four is fine."

She really hated it when he was so agreeable, she thought, and said irritably, "All right, but I'm warning you, Del..."

"What's that?"

Her eyes narrowed. "I won't wear blue!"

She'd never told him about that particular fiasco with Martin Winslow, so why was he chuckling as he said goodbye?

THE LAST TIME Kay had come to Del's offices, he hadn't had an opportunity to show her around. Del had intended to give her the grand tour, but before they could get to it, Jennifer had burst in on them with her Science Fair dilemma, and after that, it had been too late. All Kay had seen was a hallway full of office doors, and as she parked behind the building that afternoon exactly at four, she could feel herself getting tense. Was it because she remembered all too well Martin Winslow's offices in Phoenix, where scores of people sat plugged into computers and video screens, analyzing all the data coming in over millions of lines? Or was it because she still wasn't sure how to react to Del after their dinner party Saturday night? Speaking on the phone was one thing; seeing him face-to-face after their kiss was another.

But now that she was here, she couldn't just change her mind and go away, so she left the car and went inside. Before she knew it, the big double doors of Rafferty Associates were right in front of her, and she paused a moment to take a deep breath. Then, hoping she looked more composed than she felt, she went in.

As before, a secretary was sitting at the desk when she entered, typing away furiously, a pair of headphones clamped to her head. The young woman looked up as Kay came in and immediately switched off the Dictaphone machine. Smiling, she stood.

"Good afternoon, Ms. Stockwell," she said. "I'll tell Del you're here."

As she disappeared in the direction of Del's office, Kay tried to relax. All she had to do was be businesslike, she told herself, and thought she was prepared when the secretary, whose name she remembered to be Stella, reappeared. Right behind her was Del. When her heart gave a lurch and she suddenly felt a little breathless again, she realized with dismay that she wasn't prepared at all.

"Hi," she said, willing herself to appear poised and in charge of things. "I hope I'm not late."

"No, you're right on time," he said, and to her astonishment, immediately took her arm, practically propelling her ahead of him. Over his shoulder, he told his secretary, "I'm going to show Ms. Stockwell around, so take care of things for a few minutes, will you, Stella? I'll be back . . . in a while."

"Certainly, Mr. Rafferty," the secretary said primly. But Kay was sure she saw a knowing look in the young woman's eyes as Del hustled her out of the reception area and down the hallway.

Kay extricated herself from his grasp. Since she was already feeling so off balance, she was a little sharper than she intended. "For heaven's sake, Del, what's the rush?"

"Well, I know how busy you are, and I thought you'd want to get started right away."

"Yes, but—" She realized then that he was just as nervous and felt just as awkward about this meeting as she did. Thinking how silly it was for them to be dancing around the obvious when they were both adults, she stopped and looked at him. Fortunately, for the moment, they were alone in the hallway. "Del, I—"

"Now, Kay, I know what you're going to say—"

They spoke at the same time, and she was amused. "You do?" she said. "Well, that's interesting, because I haven't the faintest idea myself."

"You . . . don't?"

He looked so confused that she almost laughed. But she was feeling increasingly tense herself, and she just wanted to get it over with. "Look, what happened Saturday night was—"

"A mistake," he said, and saw her face. Looking chagrined, he changed it to, "An aberration?"

She couldn't help it; she smiled. "I don't know what it was, to tell you the truth," she said. "Let's just say it was . . . unexpected."

He looked relieved. "Then you aren't angry?"

"Angry? Of course not. What made you think that?"

"Well, you sounded so . . . so formal this morning when I called. I thought you were upset."

"Not about that," she said, reminded all over again. "If anything, I was reluctant at the idea of having to do this talk show of yours. Del, are you *sure* it's really necessary?"

She must have looked agitated, for he said, "I'm not going to force you to do something you don't want to do. If you really have strong feelings about this, then we'll just have to think of something else."

Now she felt silly and foolish. "No, no, it's not that," she said, and then sighed. "I hate it when you don't argue. How am I supposed to fight that?"

"You're not supposed to," he said with a relieved smile. "But it won't be so bad," he went on to promise. "And you *are* turning things around, you know. You got high marks from the press for doing the Science Fair at the high school, and despite what you might think of Georgette MacGuire, you did get your message across.

Haven't you noticed that the press isn't nearly so negative now?''

Thinking of George Mott's latest salvo, she said gloomily, ''It's just a lull. If Mott really does sue, things are bound to start up all over again.''

''Yes, but by then we'll have the upper hand. Once you go live on *Amanda May* and then do the promos I've planned for the media and we send out the print ads—''

''Wait a minute. You never told me anything about those. What do you mean, promos? I never agreed to do any television ads!''

''Why don't you just wait and see what we've got on the drawing board?'' he said soothingly. ''After all, that's why you're here, and it is what you're paying us for, remember? Come on, let me show you.''

But before they could start, one of the office doors opened, and a young man stepped out into the hallway, a sheaf of papers in his hand. When he saw them standing there, he stopped in surprise.

''Del, I was just coming to see you. I didn't know you had . . . someone here.''

Del gestured the young man forward. ''Kay, I'd like you to meet one of my assistants, Hugh Marsh. Hugh, this is Kay Stockwell, of—''

''I know,'' the young man said with a grin. ''Stockwell Engineering. I hear you're doing some pretty fancy stuff out there.''

Smiling, Kay held out her hand. ''Not as fancy as some of the things you do here, I think.''

Hugh grinned again and turned back to Del. ''I wanted to talk to you about the trial lawyers' campaign, but it can wait.''

''What's the problem?''

Hugh shrugged. "The initiative. I don't know the best way to attack it."

Del was all-business. With his hand still on Kay's arm to show he hadn't forgotten her, he spoke briskly to his assistant. "Remember, there are five basic points to attack an initiative. One, it will cost money. Two, it will result in unintentional negative consequences. Three, it will serve special interests rather than the common good. Four, it will increase bureaucracy. And five—"

Hugh grinned again. "It has a fatal flaw in design. But which attack should we concentrate on?"

"You decide, then get back to me," Del said, and gestured for Kay to proceed while the young man went back to his office, frowning in deep thought.

Kay looked at Del curiously before they approached the next office. "Do you give all your people that kind of latitude, or is he someone special?"

Del smiled. "My protégé, you mean? No, he's just an extremely competent young man who needs a little confidence building, that's all. I like to give everybody a lot of elbowroom. I find they think better that way. Don't you?"

She had to admit she did. Then she sighed. "But sometimes it's a fine line, isn't it?" she asked. She shook her head. "If I'd known that when I took over as president of Stockwell, I—"

"You would have done it, anyway," Del said confidently, and then laughed at her expression. Shrugging, he said, "It's the mark of a born leader. You've got it written all over you."

And before she could reply to that, he opened a door and gestured her inside. Three people—two women and a man—were huddled around one of the many cluttered desks in the room. When they saw Del, they all straightened, and after introductions had been performed, one of the women, with an apologetic smile at Kay, said to Del, "I know you're busy, but we've got a problem. We can't come up with a good caption for the bank scandal spot."

"What have you got so far?"

With a fascinated Kay looking over his shoulder, they showed Del a montage of photographs. All were of investments the bank had made that had gone sour. Del picked one out of the stack—a deserted building that epitomized poor investment. The windows were smashed and knocked out, and graffiti covered the stone-block walls.

"How about using this," he said, "with a caption that says, 'Now we *all* have a piece of the rock.'"

They left the office on a chorus of approval. With Kay silently following, glancing every now and then at Del as though she were getting a completely different picture of him, he showed her some of the other offices, starting with the computer analysis room, which was filled with all the expected computer equipment, the monitors and printers and fax machines and copiers.

Already impressed, Kay was even more dazzled when they toured the photography studio, the video display and editing room and the graphic arts office—a complex in itself, with typesetting equipment and more computers that were set up to do the newest in desktop publishing. The tour ended in a totally self-contained miniature television studio.

"My goodness," Kay said, awed. "I didn't realize—"

Del grinned. "How much goes into this business of image? Well, you've seen the whole setup. What do you think now?"

"I'm not sure," Kay said, looking around. "If I didn't know better, I'd think I was in a real television station."

"You are," he said. "This is where we're going to make you a star."

And before she could respond to *that,* he left her with other members of his staff, who had been instructed to advise her on presentation, diction, appearance, voice, posture—you name it, Kay thought, her head spinning. By the time she left at six, she didn't know whether she was coming or going.

"Definitely an autumn," one of the staffers said when they were first introduced. Her name was Persis, and she was there to advise on what colors and styles Kay should wear. With a conspiratorial smile, she added, "But Georgette told you that already, right?"

The way she said it made Kay laugh at the memory despite herself, and after that, she just put herself into the staff's capable hands. After more advice on hair and makeup and how to sit and what gestures to make and which to avoid, she was handed a script to memorize, then she had to practice in front of the camera. She wasn't aware that the session was being recorded until she was taken to another room so everybody could analyze her performance. Then she had to do it again and again until everyone—including Kay—was satisfied. By the time it was over, even she had to admit that she not only looked and sounded better, but she seemed more confident, more assured and more forceful without coming off as superior and aggressive.

"Definitely a no-no," her voice coach had said. "You want people to agree with you, sometimes without even knowing why. The last thing you want to do is alienate them. So speak more from your *chest,* like this...." He proceeded to demonstrate, sounding like a cross between Orson Welles and Laurence Olivier. "And *round* your vowels, like this...."

Kay wasn't sure she'd ever get it right, but at last the man seemed satisfied. At least, he smiled for the first time and even patted her arm. "You'll do just fine. All you have to do is go home and practice. And remember, you *speak* from your *diaphragm,* so your words *roll* like *waves*...."

Wafted out on a tide of good wishes, Kay stopped in to say good-night to Del, who was deeply involved in another production meeting. He started to excuse himself so he could talk to her, but she was exhausted by that time, and she just waved at him and mouthed goodbye.

ONE WEEK LATER, to the accompaniment of headlines in the paper stating that George Mott was considering filing a multimillion-dollar suit against Stockwell Engineering for wrongful firing, and the dismaying news that a rival robotics company had made a breakthrough on a project similar to Kay's QSA, Kay and Del left for Chicago and the taping of the *Amanda May Show.* Kay didn't believe in bad luck, but it didn't seem an auspicious beginning.

"Don't think about it," Del told her again and again on the brief flight. They hadn't seen much of each other during the past week; Del had been out of town on behalf of other clients, and she had been totally absorbed at work. "You can't do anything about it now, so just concentrate on the job ahead. We'll figure out what to do about Mott later, after we get back."

"Easy for you to say," Kay muttered, and because she was so upset, said something she hadn't intended. "It's not Mott that bothers me so much, it's the news about Pennington Robotics. They made a breakthrough on the same system we're working on at Stockwell, and if they take the patent, well...I can kiss that government grant goodbye!''

Del heard the frantic note in her voice. "Don't think about it now," he insisted. "You can't do anything from Chicago, so just do what you have to do here. This could be as big a breakthrough in its own way as Pennington has had there. Er...by the way, what exactly did they break through on?''

But it was too complicated to explain in the plane, and Kay was too upset to think coherently about it. Anyway, Del was right. She should concentrate on the present. She'd had several more sessions with Del's people; she had even gone on a whirlwind shopping trip with the color consultant to select what she was going to wear today. Now, restyled, modified, coached and color coordinated, she hardly recognized herself; her only comfort in all this was that if she made a good impression, it would have been worth it.

"You're not nervous, are you?" Del said a short while later, as they were waiting in the Green Room before Kay was called. He was wearing a dark blue suit today, with a red tie and white shirt. He looked handsome enough to take her breath away—if she'd had any to spare, Kay thought, and clasped her cold hands together so he wouldn't see them shake.

"No, I'm not nervous," she lied. Now that she had committed herself to this, she wanted to do a good job. So much depended on her educating the public about robotics—and about what Stockwell Engineering was trying to do—that she felt a hard knot in her stomach. She was sure that if they didn't call her name soon, she'd faint.

Del took her clammy hands in his. His fingers were warm, his touch reassuring. He made her look at him. "You're going to be just fine. Better than fine," he said, mesmerizing her with those blue eyes. "You're going to go out there and do what you have to do and do it superbly, just like you do everything else. Right?"

"Right," she whispered. And then, to break her tension, she said, "Why don't you come out there with me?"

He smiled. "Nope. This is your show."

"Oh, God, I just wish it were over...."

A production assistant came to the door just then and beckoned, and Del gave her a quick kiss on the cheek. "Knock 'em dead," he said.

Surprised at the gesture but unable to think what it meant with the assistant frantically gesturing to her, all she managed to do was smile a quick goodbye, then she was picking her way over cables lying on the floor and skirting people standing around with big headphones on. The glare of lights was blinding as she stepped onto the set. Someone rushed up to pin a microphone on her and ask for a quick sound check. Thank goodness they were running a commercial, Kay thought. She needed a few seconds, at least, to get her bearings.

Amanda May, a physical clone of Georgette, with blond hair, blue eyes and long, crimson fingernails—but with a sharper, more predatory look in her eyes—had met briefly with Kay in the makeup room before rushing out to the set. She had promised a more in-depth show than the one Kay had done in Springfield and had even given her a few sample questions to think about. Clinging to the hope that maybe this time she would actually get to talk about robotics, Kay took her place and spoke into the microphone for the sound level. A technician hovering signaled to someone invisible in the darkness beyond the edge of the set, and then Amanda May appeared again from the sidelines, where she'd been taking a sip of orange juice. The woman's perfume was overpowering as she carefully took her seat, but Kay was encouraged by her brisk smile.

"Ready?" Amanda May asked.

"As ready as I'm ever going to be," Kay had time to reply. The red light over the big camera blinked on as the director finished the countdown, and Amanda May smoothly turned to introduce her next guest. They were on.

True to her word, Amanda May did allow Kay to give her brief speech on robotics. Both she and the studio audience seemed receptive as Kay explained what a robot was and what it did and how it operated, and Kay was even given a chance to explain some of the work Stockwell Engineering was doing now and what her plans were for the future. But just when she was beginning to relax and starting to think this wasn't so bad after all, things changed. Amanda May, who had been skillfully prodding her along with pertinent questions, suddenly altered her approach. Instead of asking Kay about future developments in robotics, she took a completely different tack.

"I'm sure you'll agree that engineering is mainly a man's field, Ms. Stockwell," Amanda May said. "And since that's so, perhaps you could tell us why you want to compete with men."

At first Kay didn't see the pitfall. Buoyed by what had gone before, she said, "Just because something has been considered men's work doesn't necessarily make it so," she said pleasantly. "In fact, if we turn that around a little, I'm sure you'll find millions of women who would be more than willing to share, or have men completely take over, a so-called women's field of expertise called housework."

There was an appreciative laugh from the audience but only a cool smile from Amanda. "I can't argue that. But one can hardly compare housework with something as complicated and demanding as engineering, now, can one? Could you tell me whether your choice of profession has had any effect on your marital status? For example, you aren't married, are you? Is that a function of your work?"

Kay could feel herself getting tense. "No, that's a function of the fact that I haven't found a man as interesting to me as my work."

There was another laugh from the audience but not even a cool smile from Amanda this time. "But you were engaged, weren't you, for a time, to now Senator Adam Cordell?" she pressed.

Kay stiffened. She didn't want to talk about Adam. "Yes, I was," she said briefly.

Now Amanda did smile, a predatory little smile that raised the hairs on the back of Kay's neck. "So you did find a man...er...who could compete with your profession. But he broke the engagement, did he not? Was that because he didn't approve of your work?"

"I don't think the reason is any of your business," Kay said between her teeth. "But even if it were, one has nothing to do with the other."

"Oh, doesn't it? But you do admit that you were having an affair with the senator."

"I'm not admitting anything," Kay said, her green eyes flashing. Her temper was very close to the surface, and she held it in check with an effort. She'd done okay so far; she couldn't blow it now, no matter how tempting it was to put this smug woman in her place. Coolly, she said, "What I can't understand is why you're so interested, Amanda. Or why it should matter. As they say in your business, those are yesterday's headlines—if they even were *that* important. I think we have better things to discuss than old gossip, don't you?"

Amanda May's eyes flashed, too. "Indeed," she said. "But unfortunately our time is up." She turned smoothly to the camera. "That was Kay Stockwell, of Stockwell Engineering, ladies and gentlemen, who was here today to discuss the future of robotics. A future that does not, obviously, include rising young Senator Adam Cordell, who will be our guest next week. Until then, this is Amanda May Crosby, saying...keep talking."

Kay managed to sit there until the camera's red light blinked out and the director shouted that they were clear. Then she shot to her feet. "How dare you!" she said angrily to her hostess, who was unpinning her microphone from her white wool suit. "You had no right to ask about Adam! You never mentioned a word!"

Amanda shrugged. Someone had brought her another glass of orange juice, and she took a delicate sip before answering. "Hey, honey, it's all in the game," she said. "It would have been worth it if I could have shocked you into saying something juicy."

"Juicy!"

Imperiously, Amanda handed the glass back to a hovering assistant. "The name of the game is ratings, my dear," she said, standing and smoothing her skirt. "And sex gets ratings. So does a little scandal and gossip. Adam is going to be here next week, and I just thought—"

"Well, you thought wrong! In fact, if—"

But she didn't get a chance to finish, for just then Del appeared out of the people milling around and took her arm. "Thanks, Amanda," he said quickly. "It was a good show."

Amanda gave him a look that told the shocked Kay they were old friends. "You're welcome, doll," she said. "Anytime I can help." Then she turned back to Kay. "You ought to learn to lighten up, honey. Roll with the punches. It's the only way to stay ahead in this business."

Kay looked at her coldly. "I'm not *in* your business, Miss Crosby," she said. Then she jerked her arm out of Del's grasp, turned on her heel and left the set.

Del came with her as she found her coat, left the building and looked around to flag a taxi. She ignored him the whole time, and finally he took her arm again and forced her to face him.

"You're angry," he said, stating the obvious.

"Damned right, I'm angry!" she exploded. "You knew what she was going to do the entire time! How could you?"

He shrugged. "It was a good show. People will remember you."

Her eyes flashed with fury. "I don't *want* to be remembered because I was engaged to Adam!" she cried. "I thought I was there to talk about robotics!"

"You were," he said reasonably. "You did. But you needed something to... to spice up the show, make people connect."

She gave him a look that would have shriveled a lesser man.

"Well, now they will, thanks to you," she said, her eyes smoldering. "I can't believe I was so stupid and naive! I thought you... Well, it's obvious I was wrong. Everything would have been fine if I'd followed my first inclinations and refused to listen to you, but no! I had to put myself in your hands, so you could *change* me and *mold* me and tell me what colors to wear and how to fix my hair and . . . and how to speak! Well, I'm speaking now, Del Rafferty, and you're going to listen to what I have to say. I'll make it so clear that not even you can get it wrong! You're fired, all right? You're *f . . . i . . . r . . . e . . . d.* How do you like *that* diction?''

A cab came just then and she waved it down, climbing in and slamming the door before Del could join her. The cabbie's eyes met hers in the rearview mirror. ''Where to, lady?''

''The airport,'' she said, ignoring Del, who was standing nonplussed on the sidewalk. ''And hurry.''

With a wary glance at her angry face, the cabbie put the car in gear, and they were off. In the back seat, holding on to her composure by a thread, Kay was so furious she didn't dare look around. At this point, she didn't know whether she'd curse or burst into tears of rage.

CHAPTER TEN

DEL COULDN'T BELIEVE IT, but Kay seemed to have taken the only cab in the entire downtown area of Chicago. Feeling foolish because she'd left him standing on the street corner, he finally managed to flag another taxi, but by then he'd missed the plane back. Not that he wanted to fly home with Kay, he thought blackly; after that little exhibition of temper and pique, the last thing he wanted to do was sit next to her in a tiny plane. He managed to find one going back at a later time but was still seething when he got home, not at all in the mood to discuss this second debacle or to explain or defend himself to his daughter. He should have known Jennifer would meet him at the door with an eager, "Well, how'd it go?"

He was too tired and angry to argue about it. "I don't want to discuss it," he said, brushing by her so he could toss his briefcase onto the hall table. He went into the living room, where he threw himself into his easy chair, which tonight felt like a bed of nails. He got up immediately. With Jennifer following, he went into the kitchen to see what Mrs. Nivens had left for supper. Not that he was hungry, he thought direly, but it was something to do.

But no good smells emanated from either the range or the oven, and when he looked, even the microwave was empty. Enraged out of all proportion, he slammed the microwave oven door and swore. "What happened?" he demanded. "Didn't Mrs. Nivens come in today?"

"Yes, she was here, but I told her I'd fix dinner," Jennifer answered. "Dad, what—"

That shocked him momentarily out of his preoccupation with his own troubles. "You? *You* volunteered to cook?"

Jennifer brushed aside the startling news because she was more interested in finding out what had gone wrong. Obviously something had, and she said impatiently, "Yes, but can we forget that for a minute? Tell me how things went today!"

He still didn't want to discuss it. "Not well," he said brusquely. "But I don't want to talk about it, all right? Now, what's for dinner?"

She narrowed her eyes. "I don't know," she said defiantly. "I'm not sure I want to fix anything now."

He held on to his temper with an effort. "Then we'll go out and get something."

Her voice rose. "Not until you tell me what happened today. Come on, Dad, I've got a right to know! Kay is my friend, too!" She looked at him in sudden awful comprehension. "You didn't let that Amanda May be nasty to her, did you?"

"She wasn't nasty," he said quickly, but even to himself, he sounded defensive, and he frowned. More strongly, he added, "But even if she had been, Kay can certainly take care of herself."

"Oh, I *knew* it!" Jennifer cried, obviously deciding right then and there that he was to be denied the benefit of the doubt. "I knew something would go wrong. Dad, how *could* you!"

He was trying very hard to hang on to his composure. "The only thing I did, Jennifer," he said through his teeth, "was my job. Now—"

"That's always your excuse!" she cried. "Do you know that? That's always your excuse! The only thing you ever care about is how something *looks*, not how people feel!"

Appalled that she could say such a thing, he said, "That's not true! I—"

"Oh, yes, it is!" she shouted. "You've always been that way, even when I was a little girl! You're *still* that way! It's only what *you* want! *You're* the only one who counts!"

Did she really believe that? "Jennifer, that isn't true!"

"Oh, yeah? Then why did I suddenly have to come and live with you this year? Tell me that!" she demanded in a confusing about-face. "I always wanted to—oh, yeah, when you and Mom got divorced, I wanted to come and live with you, but did you want me then? No! Then, when I *wanted* to go to Europe with Mom and Leif, you decided you wanted me to stay with you! Why is it always what *you* want? Why doesn't anyone ever ask me?"

Feeling that he was rapidly losing track of the conversation, if that's what it could be called, he said, "What do you mean you wanted to come and live with me after the divorce? You never told me that!"

"Why should I have to?" she said shrilly. "Why didn't you want me?"

"I *did!* I begged your mother for joint custody. I even—"

"But you didn't ask me!"

"You were only seven years old!"

"So what? You think kids don't have a right to an opinion? Well, apparently not, since you didn't ask me this year when you decided that you finally wanted me to come and live with you! You never ask! You just order!''

"Jennifer, you don't understand."

"You bet I don't!" she cried, and before he could say more, she turned and ran out of the kitchen, thundering up the stairs and slamming the door to her room. Feeling like a leaf swept up by a whirlwind and deposited willy-nilly, upside down on the ground again, Del stared blankly at the door through which she'd just vanished. Briefly, he debated about shouting for her to come down or going up to her room and demanding to be let in.

No, no, neither would do, he thought, and slumped against the counter, not knowing how to handle it. He didn't want to use his parental authority to force her to confront him; he wouldn't accomplish anything that way. Maybe he should just let it go. The more he thought about it, the better the idea seemed. *Handle it tomorrow,* he told himself, and thought longingly of a cigarette, the kind he'd given up years ago.

Muttering another curse, he rubbed a hand over his eyes. This definitely hadn't been one of his better days.

BY MORNING, things didn't look much better. Realizing that life went on and that he still had to go into the office no matter what a disaster he seemed to be making of his personal life, Del got up at his usual time, showered and shaved and was downstairs having coffee when Jennifer appeared. She took one look at him and turned away without saying anything, attending to her breakfast in injured silence.

He tried to talk to her. "Jennifer, I—"

"I really don't want to talk about it," she said stiffly, and carried her orange juice and cereal out so she could eat alone in the dining room. By himself in the kitchen, Del sighed and poured the rest of his coffee down the sink. Then he took his briefcase and went to work.

But the office wasn't much better than home, for even though he immediately plunged into a myriad of details regarding other accounts, he couldn't get Kay out of his mind. In addition, the things Jennifer had said to him the night before came back to haunt him, and he wondered if she really believed what she'd said. Did she honestly think he hadn't wanted her? And did she really believe that his only concern was how something *looked,* not how people felt?

Frowning, he had to admit that, on the surface, it certainly seemed to be true. Then he could feel himself getting defensive again. He had to address the problem of Jennifer feeling neglected with her directly, which he planned to do tonight. But as far as his work was concerned, finding the right image for people was his *job,* he decided, and he did it very well. How could either Kay or his daughter condemn him for doing what he did best?

But then, insidiously, he began to wonder if he was trying to justify it himself. After all, just because he had a knack for manipulation didn't make it right, he thought, and then felt even more impatient at the situation than he had before. Why all the questions? he demanded of his obviously overwrought conscience. And why now? Until this latest furor, he had believed that he had come to grips with all this years ago. Why was he having second thoughts at this point in his career?

The treacherous questions continued to demand answers he didn't have at the moment, so he deliberately put it all out of his mind and tried to get back to what he'd come here for: work. He was supposed to be analyzing one of the ads his advertising department had worked up for his approval, but as he stared down at the glossy, polished page, he found himself wondering how the public—and it *was* the public, he told himself; he wasn't alone in this—had gotten to the point where even negative publicity was considered good press. How had it happened that even saying something bad about someone was better than saying nothing at all, and who had decided that scandal and gossip weren't things to be ashamed of, but things to be eagerly and avidly sought?

It wasn't his fault, he tried to tell himself; he hadn't made up the rules, so he shouldn't be blamed for taking advantage of them. After all, that was the way of the world. He had learned that at an early age, hadn't he? Earlier than even he wanted to think about now, and he quickly thrust away a bitter memory of graffiti-covered tenements and barred, broken windows and scraps of trash blowing down cold, mean streets.

Closing his eyes, he tried to get a grip on himself. What was the matter with him today? he wondered. But then Kay's face flashed into his mind again, and when he thought that she was trying to do something good, even noble, in her work, he felt even more ashamed and guilty. What did that have to do with her affair and broken engagement to a senator, even one who was making a name for himself in Washington now?

Restlessly, he got up and went to one of the windows in his office. But he didn't really see what he was looking out at, for he was feeling a growing disquiet at the thought that he might have some responsibility in this awful turnaround. When had he stopped questioning? When had he come to accept the philosophy that just because something *worked,* it was right?

He still wasn't ready to answer that question or the host of other disturbing doubts that had come to mind since Kay had left him flat-footed outside the television studio yesterday afternoon. But the more he thought about it, the more chagrined he felt about Kay herself. He should have known better than to treat her like that, he thought; he *did* know better. But he had been so intent on showing her how good he was that he hadn't thought about much else. Jennifer had been right; his only concern had been how the show would *look,* what ratings it would get, how his client would come off. He hadn't really considered how Kay would feel.

Feeling increasingly ashamed of himself, he debated how he could make it up to her. The obvious thing to do was apologize, but there were other things he could do, too. On that thought, he called in the people he'd assigned to assist him with the Stockwell account. All of them had seen the tape of the *Amanda May Show,* and he knew from their expressions they believed, as he had done before Jennifer forced him to review a few things, that the show was a success. Wondering how he could have missed the real point, he opened the meeting by saying, "The reason I've called you in here is because I want to change the focus of the ads and promos for the Stockwell campaign."

He had anticipated the protest that would arise, and he wasn't mistaken. Everyone started to talk at once, the consensus being that since they'd already done all the preliminary work and had storyboards and mock-ups ready to go, and since the taping yesterday had gone so well, there was no reason for the change.

For once, he overrode their protests by sheer weight of authority. "You don't have to understand," he said, not wanting to explain because he wasn't sure he understood himself. "Just do it."

There was a silence. Then, hesitantly, someone spoke up. "Whatever you say, boss. But... er... what direction do you want us to take now? After all, things were... um... working pretty well, we thought."

"Yes, that's true. It's just time for a change in focus, that's all," he said, knowing he sounded a little unfocused himself. Well, he couldn't help it. Plowing on, he added, "Let's just say the client doesn't like the... strident approach we've been taking."

Someone groaned. "You're not going to give us the kinder, gentler jazz, are you? That's been done to death, and it was boring as hell to start with, anyway!"

Del reddened. He wasn't used to backtracking on himself like this; usually he just decided which direction a campaign was going to take, and they took it. "No, I'm not going that far. But... let's concentrate on the contribution Stockwell is making to a better society, all right? I want a theme that says something like, 'Stockwell Engineering—focusing on *your* future.' Or, 'Stockwell Engineering, working toward a better future.' That sort of thing."

"You're kidding, right?"

He fixed the speaker with a hard glare. "Does it sound like I'm kidding? Now, drop everything and work on this."

Another chatter of protest arose. Out of the babble, he heard someone say "... other things more important..." and he glared in that direction, too.

"Nothing is more important than this," he said flatly, and looked around the group. "Got it?"

He didn't have to say anything more. It was rare that he played the heavy-handed boss; usually he gave them as much creative space as they needed, figuring that's what he was paying them for. But occasionally he did override them on their wilder flights of fancy, and they could all recognize the tone he used when he wanted no argument. Muttering, they filed out, shaking their heads. When Del looked up, Stella was standing in the doorway, looking at him. Catching her knowing eye, he warned, "Don't say it."

Stella grinned. "I wasn't going to say anything, boss. I've got work to do myself."

"Then you'd better get to it," he growled, and sat down at his desk.

As soon as his secretary went back to hers, he reached for the phone. Now that he'd made his stand and looked like an idiot to his staff, he thought he might as well call Kay and make a fool of himself with her, too. But he had a change of heart when he was dialing her number, and slowly, he put down the receiver. Maybe he should go in person, instead, he thought. After all, it would be harder to kick him out of the office if they were face-to-face. If he called, all she had to do was hang up on him.

Stella was typing something when he came out and announced that he had to be away from the office for a while.

"Whatever you say, boss," she said agreeably.

Was that a giggle he heard as he started toward the door? He turned quickly to see if she was laughing at him, but she was bending over the keyboard again, typing furiously away.

"Stella . . ." he started to say.

She looked up innocently. "Yes, boss?"

She didn't fool him for a minute. She was too quick by far, he thought, and glared at her a moment until he realized it wasn't worth the trouble.

"I'll be back later," he said, and didn't realize he'd forgotten his coat until he was out in the parking lot.

Thinking he'd be damned if he'd go back to his office and face his smirking secretary again, he got into the car and headed toward Stockwell Engineering. It didn't occur to him until he was halfway there that Kay had fired him, and for the space of a block, he thought about turning around and going back to his office. Then he decided to hell with it. If she'd really meant it, he'd know soon enough, he thought, and drove grimly on.

KAY HADN'T BEEN HAVING a good morning herself. She'd been so furious when she finally got home from Chicago that she'd spent half the night mentally composing the scathing letter she was going to send to the Better Business Bureau about Rafferty Associates. As the night wore on, she shredded her imaginary missive and began to feel remorse. What had ever possessed her to leave him standing on the curb like that, while she melodramatically flung herself into a taxi and commanded, "The airport!" Every time she thought about it, she cringed.

By this morning, she'd reached the point where she'd almost convinced herself to call Del and apologize to him. She felt even guiltier when Brice came in and congratulated her on the taping.

"I don't think it went well at all," she said brusquely. "In fact, I think I really blew it."

His smile disappeared. "What do you mean?"

She told him what had happened. Everything had gone so well in the beginning, she said, until Amanda May had mentioned Adam.

"I thought you handled it very well. You didn't lose your temper."

She glared at him. "No, I didn't lose my temper," she said peevishly. "I'm not *that* lacking in control. But it really was none of her business."

"What did Del have to say about it?" Brice asked.

She didn't want to talk about Del Rafferty. "I don't know. I didn't give him a chance to talk about anything."

"But you had to fly back—"

"We took different flights," she said flatly. Then she decided she might as well tell him the whole humiliating tale. Defiantly, she looked him in the eye. "But before that happened, I fired him."

Brice didn't say anything; he just sat back looking...well, she couldn't describe the look he was wearing. Something between poleaxed and paralyzed, she thought, and frowned. Quickly, she glanced down at the desk.

"I'm sorry," she muttered. "I know how much you were counting on him to—"

"No, no, it's all my fault," Brice said. "I tried to force you to do something you obviously didn't want to do, and I was wrong. I'm sorry, Kay. I really did think it would be a good idea."

"It *was* a good idea," she said. "It's just—" She paused and then made herself say, "I think that if I hadn't had that awful experience with Martin Winslow, I wouldn't be so sensitive. But..." She faltered again. She couldn't bear the disappointment in his eyes; it made her feel even worse. But the worst part of all was that she couldn't explain it fully to him. How could she say that her own disillusionment stemmed from the fact that, despite her misgivings, she *had* begun to trust Del? She had really started to believe, not necessarily in all he was doing, but that he was right about some aspects of this image business, at least. She couldn't forget one discussion they'd had, for instance, where he had asked her to explain why she wore business suits to important meetings with potential backers and not sweatshirts and jeans.

"Appearance and good grooming aren't *image*," she'd argued, and, even as she'd said it, she'd known it was a weak stand. What else were they, if not that?

Wisely, he hadn't really pressed the point. All he'd said was "Image isn't substance, I agree. But in this visual world of ours, it's what makes the most impact—at first. When the public is bombarded by visuals from the moment they wake up until the time they finally go to sleep, it's difficult to get anyone's attention in all the babble. To do it, you have to extend the bounds a little. Then, once you have the floor, you can say what you want."

There had been a flaw in that argument, she knew it. But she'd been so mesmerized by that blue gaze of his that she couldn't find it. Was that why she had agreed, against her better judgment, to do the *Amanda May Show?* Why *had* she allowed him to talk her into it? Was her growing attraction to him obscuring everything else? Maybe on some unconscious level she'd realized it, and that was why she had fired him.

Then she realized she didn't know *what* she thought anymore; she was even more confused this morning than she had been before, and it didn't help that Brice was sitting across from her looking as though he'd lost his best friend. Guiltily, she said, "Maybe Rafferty Associates wasn't the right firm, Brice. Maybe we could try again with someone else."

He shook his head. "There isn't time for another firm to step in," he said. "Besides, Del's the best. I don't know what someone else could do for you that he hasn't already thought of, or done. No, it just wasn't a good idea, Kay. I'm sorry I even brought it up."

When he stood and started out, she felt even worse. "Brice..."

He turned to look at her, but she realized she couldn't keep saying she was sorry again and again, so she just shook her head. "Never mind. But Brice... we'll think of something."

He was determined to be upbeat and positive, even though he looked so defeated. Trying to be encouraging, he said, "Sure we will. And you do have the Senate subcommittee appearance coming up, so maybe we'll gain some ground there."

She had to ask it. "Any news about George Mott?"

He shook his head. "Nothing more. Our legal department is still working on it."

"Well, keep me apprised."

"I always do," he said, and went out.

Once he had gone, Kay slumped in her chair. This was awful, she thought. And it was all her fault. The conversation with Brice had been painful but she realized she'd let her injured pride get in the way when she should have been thinking with her head. She never should have allowed Amanda May's questions about Adam get to her. What difference did it make now? Who cared? It was yesterday's news, if that. Both she and Adam had gone on to other things.

Or she'd thought they had, until the show. She hadn't realized until yesterday just how much the ending of that relationship still rankled. To have it all brought up again on national television was too much, and she had blamed Del for having to go over it all again. She had trusted Del; she had started to believe in him. And it had seemed to her, then, that he was doing the same thing to her that Adam had done—wanting her to change, to alter herself to fit a certain image, to present a different picture because the real one somehow wasn't quite...acceptable. *That's* what had hurt, and *that* was why she had run away from him. Now she knew she should have stayed and faced him, had it out, told him just what she was thinking and why. She hadn't done it with Adam, and that's where she had made another mistake. She never should have left without telling him exactly how she felt.

She glanced at the phone. She could call Del and explain, she thought, and then rejected the idea as soon as it occurred to her. No, it was better this way. She was getting too involved with him, and she should just end it right here. From the beginning she had realized how easy it would be to move from a professional to a personal relationship with him, and she had already made one mistake after another where he was concerned. She'd been playing with fire, and she'd gotten burned. So it was best just to leave it like this, she told herself, and decided it was time to get to work. She had a million things to do today, all of them involving some much-hated, but necessary, paperwork. Wondering how it was that she had become an administrator when her heart was really in the laboratory working with Mort, she sighed and pulled a stack of papers toward her.

KAY LOOKED UP from the half-finished stack and rubbed her eyes. In two hours she had managed to make some progress, but the effort at concentration was exhausting. She'd be reading reports and suddenly realized she was thinking of Del—how he looked when he laughed and how intense his gaze could be, or how a dimple appeared in his lean cheek when he smiled...a dozen other things. Annoyed with herself for not being able to put him out of her mind, she pushed the papers away and stood up to stretch.

She walked to the window and looked down. The protesters were still there but much quieter these days, almost bored looking, in fact, as they trudged back and forth before the front gates, carrying their signs. They had become such a familiar sight that she hardly noticed them anymore, and she realized how dangerous that could be. Things might be quiet, but nothing had really been resolved; if it had been, they would have gone back to their homes, their jobs, their lives. Wearily, Kay was rubbing her eyes again when Rachel buzzed through with the news that Del was in the outer office asking to see her.

Kay's first thought was to send him away. She'd spent all last night and the better part of the day telling herself she was better off without him, and the idea of confronting him and explaining it all nearly sent her into a panic.

Then she told herself not to be ridiculous. She was a grown woman, the head of a prominent engineering company. Del was—had been—an employee whose services she no longer required. As long as she remembered that and refused to be distracted by the look in his eyes, she'd be okay.

Before she could change her mind, she reached for the intercom. "Send him in," she said, and took a seat behind the desk. She intended to play it formally.

When Del entered the office, she nearly forgot her resolve. He was carrying a briefcase and was dressed in a dark blue business suit with white shirt and blue striped tie. He looked polished and professional, assured of himself...and very handsome. *Damn him,* Kay thought, and said coolly, "This is a surprise. Please, sit down."

He obeyed, commenting that he wouldn't be here very long. "I just came to apologize," he said with his disarming smile. "And to ask you to reconsider letting my agency go."

"And why should I do that?" she asked frostily.

He sobered. "Because despite what you think, I can turn this thing around for you. I know you believe I pulled a fast one yesterday—"

"With that barracuda Amanda May, you mean?" Kay said sweetly. "Yes, it would be fair to say I think that. I suppose you've got an explanation for that, too."

He reddened slightly but held his ground. Reaching for the briefcase he'd put on the floor, he opened it and pulled out a paper or two, one of which he handed across. "I thought you might like to see this."

She looked at him suspiciously. "What is it?"

"Analysis of your on-air performance. Data on audience reaction. Projections for what it will mean for Stockwell Engineering's . . . er . . . image."

She glanced down at the paper. She was so keenly aware of him sitting across from her that the neatly typed lines looked like squiggles, and after a moment she put it aside. Hedging a little, she said, "Is this supposed to change my mind?"

He gave her an intent look. "I'd hoped it might."

"In other words, you feel it's all right for me to humiliate myself as long as I achieve—" she flicked a disdainful finger toward the paper he'd given her "—high ratings."

She had the satisfaction of seeing him flush but not the pleasure of goading him into an argument. "I disagree with your assessment of what happened, naturally, but you—a scientist—can't deny these figures, Kay," he said, and handed her another paper.

"What's this?" she asked, even more wary.

"Results of the latest survey we did regarding your company. If you'll compare the figures before my agency got involved with those calculated just yesterday, you'll see that in just a few weeks, Stockwell's image with the public has gone up considerably."

She took a quick look, then put down the paper. Tired of fencing, she demanded suddenly, "Why are you doing this, Del? I thought we—"

Something crossed his face—some emotion she couldn't quite identify. "I'm doing this because I...I believe in you, Kay," he said simply. "I believe in what you're doing. I think other people should believe in it, too. Now, maybe we haven't gone about it the right way—according to you, anyway. And if that's so, I'd like another chance so that we could direct the campaign the way you'd like it to go. What do you say? Can we meet halfway?"

She didn't know what to say. She knew there was more to this than he'd told her. She felt instinctively that he was here not only because he believed in the work she was doing, but because of... her. *She* was the drawing card, and as her heart began to race, she looked at her hands, clasped tightly atop the desk, and knew that she was going to accept his offer for the same reason. For her, also, he was the drawing card.

"All right," she said, speaking evenly, although inwardly she wanted to get up from the desk and dance around the room with delight that it wasn't over between them...yet. "We'll give it another chance. But first..."

He was good, but he couldn't hide the eager, relieved light in his eyes. "What?" he said.

She started to smile; the smile became a wicked grin, then she almost laughed. When the idea had occurred to her just now, she wondered why she hadn't thought of it before. She'd been wanting a chance to show him what she was *really* about, to have him see why she believed in the things she did, to demonstrate why substance meant so much more to her than image. And what better way to do that than to take him back to her own roots?

"First," she said, "I want to invite you and Jennifer for a weekend. Jennifer said she'd like to visit my grandfather's farm, and I . . . I think this would be the perfect time."

Del couldn't have been more surprised if she'd said she wanted to sing "The Star-Spangled Banner" on television. "Visit the farm?" he said. "But—"

"You wanted to meet halfway, remember?" she said. "Well, maybe it's time for you to get away from all your high-tech stuff and get back to basics. A farm is about as real as you can get, and right now, I think we both need a little dose of reality."

"But I've never been on a farm before," he said.

"Good," she said. "Then it's about time, don't you think?"

It was obvious that Del didn't know what to think. But this time, she had boxed him in as neatly as he'd done to her with the *Amanda May Show* in Chicago. "Well, I..." he started to say, and then saw the look in her eyes. Straightening his tie, he said, "Jennifer isn't speaking to me at the moment, but if I can open the lines of communication long enough to ask her, I'm sure she'd be delighted to come. So would I. What time?"

They agreed to meet at Kay's Saturday morning. But just before Del left, clearly wondering what he'd gotten into, he turned to her one last time.

"What happens on Monday?" he asked.

Kay forced herself to hold that intent blue gaze. Her voice suddenly a little husky, she said, "Why don't we just wait and see? Maybe by then we'll both be feeling a little differently about things, and we can decide then."

"Kay..." he started to say, and then paused. Finally, he just went on simply, "I'm glad you reconsidered."

She wasn't going to let him know how delighted she was that he had accepted. "As they say on the farm," she told him severely, "don't count your chickens before they're hatched."

CHAPTER ELEVEN

WHEN KAY AWOKE on Saturday morning, she was pleased to see that the day looked clear and calm—almost balmy for Springfield this time of year. In fact, it looked to be one of those rarities, a time of lingering Indian summer—always a joy in this state of flat landscapes, where it wasn't uncommon for temperatures to plunge overnight no matter what the season. Hoping that the fine weather would hold this weekend, at least, she let Duffy out, took a quick shower and was ready when Del and Jennifer arrived.

Father and daughter were on speaking terms again. It had taken a long discussion with apologies on both sides, Del confided to Kay, and the lure of a visit to the farm hadn't hurt. Everyone was looking forward to the trip. But when he suggested they drive down in his car, a sleek new-model sedan, Kay was doubtful.

"I don't know," she said. "I thought Duffy would go, too, and you don't want dog hairs all over your back seat, do you?"

"If Jennifer doesn't mind, I don't," he said, winking at his daughter. "Besides, we can always vacuum later."

"Well, all right," Kay agreed, wincing despite herself when Duffy jumped up on the back seat. In addition to dog hairs, she could picture footprints all over that plush upholstery, but since Del didn't seem to care, she decided to put it out of her mind, too. Besides, Jennifer was clearly delighted that the dog was going along; when the teenager climbed into the back and Duffy cuddled right up next to her, Kay thought that a few paw prints were worth the smile on Jennifer's face.

"I'm ready," Jennifer announced. "What's keeping you two?"

Del grinned at Kay. "Obviously, we're holding up the parade. Are you ready?"

"I just have to lock up," Kay said, and a few minutes later they were on their way. An hour's drive east took them to the road into the farm, and as they drove in, Del stared in amazement at what seemed to be miles of plowed land on either side of the road. Although it was fallow season now and the fields were cleared of all but the rich black soil for which the state was famous, it was still a grand sight.

"How big is your grandfather's farm, anyway?" Del asked.

"About three hundred acres," Kay answered, pleased that he was impressed. She was proud of her grandfather, proud of her roots here, and without realizing it, she had wanted Del to like it, too. But she added, "Granddad doesn't farm it all like he used to. These days, he only has about two hundred acres in production."

"What does he grow?"

"Mainly wheat and barley, but in the past few years, he's begun to experiment with fruit trees—apples and peaches." She smiled fondly. "He says tending to an orchard will be easier on his old bones than bouncing around in the combine or the tractor."

Del looked again at the vast acreage spreading out on either side of the road. Speechless, he just shook his head.

"Look!" Jennifer exclaimed excitedly from the back seat just then. "There's a house!"

The farmhouse stood at the end of the two-mile drive like a lonely sentinel manning an outpost. As they approached, the new orchard could be seen fanning out behind, with much larger shade trees—the native oak and hickory and hard maple, bare of leaves now—surrounding the big farmhouse. The place stood two stories and looked, Del commented, like something out of a storybook. Kay laughed.

"Granddad does take care of the place, doesn't he?" she said, her eyes sparkling as she tried to see it through Del's eyes. Even to her, the house looked imposing and well cared for. Built of clapboard, it was painted white with a high, sloped roof of gray shingles. A row of dormer windows on the second floor glittered in the sunlight, and a big porch spanned the entire front length of the house. To Jennifer's delight, there was even an old-fashioned porch swing on one end, upon which, Kay told her, she'd spent hours as a girl cuddled up with a book.

Out back were the other buildings: a big barn, with storage for hay and stabling for the farm horses Emmett used to have; a chicken house; a tool shed and garage; Emmett's workshop; and a cleared, fenced area for the garden he planted every spring. Everything looked immaculate and carefully tended, and as Del stopped the car, he shook his head again.

"How does he do it all?" he murmured in wonder.

"You'll see when you meet him," Kay said with a laugh, and got out of the car. "Granddad! We're here!" she cried, and ran up the front steps.

Emmett Stockwell looked just like the picture Kay had of him on her bookcase at home. Tall and only slightly stooped from age, he looked years younger than eighty-six, with snapping blue eyes and a shock of silver hair that was still thick and luxurious. In honor of visitors today, he was wearing khaki jeans, a checked flannel shirt and boots, and his handshake was as strong and firm as his voice when Kay introduced him to Del and his daughter.

"Pleased to meet you," he said, with the slight southern drawl that sometimes characterized the "downstater," as Chicagoans referred to anyone who lived on Illinois land south of U.S. Route 80.

"And you, sir," Del said, genuinely respectful. "It's very generous of you to invite us as weekend guests."

"No trouble, no trouble at all," Emmett replied with a fond glance at Kay. "Though I have to say, it's not often my granddaughter brings people out. You two must be mighty special, I'd say."

Kay blushed. "Oh, Granddad, the things you say!" she protested, aware of Del's smile. "Now, are you going to invite us all in or not?"

Emmett smiled at Jennifer, who was hanging back shyly. To Del and Kay, he said, "Well, now, I think I'll let you two get settled while I take Miss Jennifer on a tour. What say, Jennifer—would you like that?"

Jennifer glanced at her father, who nodded. "Yes, I'd like it very much, Mr. Stockwell," she said politely. Then, "Can Duffy come, too?"

"Sure, bring him along, good-for-nothin' hound that he is." But he grinned when he said it, and he ruffled the dog's ears as Duffy fell in beside them on the way to the barn.

"Well," Kay said, watching them, suddenly very much aware that she'd neatly been left alone with Del. "I think Jennifer will get along just fine."

Del's glance followed the couple. "Your grandfather is quite a man," he said. "I like him."

Kay smiled. "He likes you, too."

"How do you know? We just met."

Her eyes sparkling, she shrugged. "A granddaughter can tell."

Del paused, then he asked softly, "And how does the granddaughter feel?"

Kay wasn't sure. Del looked so handsome in this setting, with his black hair glistening in the sun and his eyes a bright, deep blue. She knew something was building between them, and while part of her savored the anticipation, another part still wasn't sure she was ready, even now. So she said lightly, "The granddaughter likes him, too. Now, I think we should bring the bags in and get everybody settled. Afternoon chores will begin soon, and we don't want to be late."

Del seemed intent on giving her all the space she needed. "Chores?" he said in mock dismay. "You mean you invited us out here to work?"

Pleased that he was playing along, she laughed. "Everybody works on a farm," she said teasingly. "Didn't you know that?"

"How would I know?" he countered. "I've been a city boy from the word go."

"You'll have to tell me about it while we're slopping the hogs," she joked, and then laughed again at his expression. Enjoying herself thoroughly, she pretended to take pity on him and said, "Don't worry, Granddad got rid of all the hogs last spring. Now we only have to bring in the cattle and round up the sheep and catch one of the chickens for supper. You do like fried chicken, don't you?"

Del looked a little sick. "I think I've just turned into a vegetarian."

Kay laughed. "Come on, I'll show you where you're staying."

Carrying his and Jennifer's suitcases, Del paused when Kay led him into the farmhouse, staring at the pegged wooden floors, waxed to a shine, at the big, round rag rugs, at the homey furniture, with antimacassars on the backs and arms of the overstuffed chairs and sofa, at the fieldstone fireplace that looked big enough to roast an ox, at the years-old hurricane lamps on the mantel, the only source of light when the power went out during the heavy snowstorms that battered the farmland during the winter.

"It looks just like a . . . a movie set," he said.

Kay smiled knowingly. "Except that this is real, Del," she said, and led the way upstairs.

The guest room was at the top of the landing, a room as immaculate as the rest of the house, with a double bed covered by a handmade quilt in a pattern called "Flying Geese." When Del remarked on the intricate color blocking, Kay smiled again and ran her fingers gently over the quilt top.

"My grandmother made this," she said. "See how tiny and even the stitches are? I couldn't do it in a million years. I'd never have the patience."

"It's beautiful, all right," Del agreed, and put his suitcase on the floor instead of the bed so he wouldn't disturb the quilt.

"Jennifer and I will bunk together," Kay said. "We'll use my old room because it has twin beds."

"Whatever you think best," Del said. "Your grandfather has been so welcoming, but I don't want to put him out."

Kay glanced out the window. Below, just coming out of the barn, she could see her grandfather and Jennifer, and when she saw what was in Jennifer's arms, she smiled and gestured to Del. "I think everything's going to be fine, don't you?" she said, pointing.

Del joined her at the window. Even from this distance, he could see the cat Jennifer was carrying, and he shook his head. "I'm not sure this is a good idea," he said. "You already put the bee in her bonnet about getting a dog. Now I can just hear all the pleading about a cat, too."

Smiling wickedly, Kay said, "That's no problem. Granddad always has a half a dozen barn cats around. I'm sure if you asked, he'd be glad to give you one."

"That's *not* what I meant."

"I know," Kay said, turning to look up at him. She had intended to say something else, but the expression that suddenly leaped into his eyes as he gazed down at her stifled her smile, and without warning, she felt off balance again.

She had been trying this whole time not to feel so acutely aware of him, not to smell the spicy scent of his after-shave or notice how his eyes changed color depending on what he was thinking, but the single look was her undoing. Suddenly she felt flushed and hot, having to fight the desire for him that swept over her. Knowing that she couldn't give in to that feeling, no matter how demanding—at least not here, not right now—she made herself look away. Hardly aware of what she was saying, she said distractedly, "Barn cats aside, I always loved my time at the farm. I hope Jennifer likes it, too."

Del seemed to be having as much trouble controlling his breathing as she was. He, too, looked away from her, out the window. Jennifer and Emmett were just heading in the direction of the big workshop, and he muttered, "I know it will be good for her—for both of us." Then he looked down at Kay again. His voice husky, he added, "I hope it will be good for you and me, too."

She had to do something to lighten the moment, to give herself a little emotional space. She was feeling too overwhelmed by Del, and the double bed with the Flying Geese quilt was only inches away. "We'll see," she said quickly, and forced a laugh. "After Granddad puts you to work this afternoon, maybe the only thing you'll want is to go home."

His eyes held hers. "I doubt it."

She didn't know what to say to that, so she hastily picked up Jennifer's suitcase. "I'll just take this along to the other room and leave you to get settled," she said, and escaped down the hall.

A little while later, her precarious equilibrium restored—or so she told herself—Kay had changed into jeans and a long-sleeved checked blouse and invited Del down to the barn. Emmett kept only one cow these days—for sentimental reasons, he said, since he couldn't possibly use all the milk—but he had promised to teach Jennifer how to milk, and Kay wanted Del to be there for the lesson. Grandfather and granddaughter smiling at each other, they all gathered around Pansy, a big, placid black-and-white holstein Emmett had already brought in and tied in a stall. He was carrying a low stool and a stainless steel pail, which he proceeded to place in the proper position. Then, lithely squatting on the stool, he looked up at Jennifer.

"Now," he said, "most people think that all you got to do to milk a cow is squeeze a little on the teat, but that's not so. It's like making bread—you have to *knead* as you go, workin' two at the same time, always—" he grinned "—aiming for the inside of the bucket."

He demonstrated, expertly sending twin streams of foaming milk clattering against the side of the pail. "See? Easy as pie," he said, and then, because two of the barn cats had gathered around, he aimed two jets of milk directly at them. When both cats opened their mouths and drank greedily, Kay smiled at the identical expressions of wonder on both Del's and Jennifer's faces.

"Pretty good, Granddad," she teased. "Did you practice that little act just for us?"

In answer, he pretended to aim a spout at her, but she just laughed. She knew he'd never waste good milk that way, and when he turned to Jennifer and she backed up a step, wide-eyed, he smiled and said, "Here. You try."

"Oh, no, I couldn't!"

"Sure you can," he said, and plunked her down on the stool, taking her hands and showing her how it was done. When two streams of milk hit the pail, she looked up excitedly at her father. "Dad! I did it!"

"You sure did, Button," he said, and laughed with the other adults as Jennifer bent to the task with renewed vigor. She got more milk outside the pail than in, but it didn't matter—especially to the cats, who crowded around.

"Now we'll separate it," Emmett said when the cow's udder was empty.

"You mean make butter?" Jennifer asked, wide-eyed again.

Emmett laughed and patted her shoulder. "Not unless you want to spend half the night churning."

"You don't want to do that, take my word for it," Kay said with a laugh. "It's easier to buy it in the store, believe me. But you won't believe the cream!"

She was right. When Emmett put the milk to separate and the cream rose to the top, both Raffertys were amazed. "Cream never looks like this in the store!" Jennifer exclaimed.

"It doesn't taste like this, either," Kay said, using a spoon to scoop it out of the separator. Made this way, it was the consistency of mayonnaise. Spread on bread the old-fashioned way, with a little sugar sprinkled on top, it was one of the best childhood treats she could remember.

Jennifer seemed to agree—and Del, who seemed just as impressed as his daughter. "This *is* good," he said after gingerly taking a taste. He took some more, grinning while Kay laughed at his expression.

"I told you," she said, and then glanced slyly at her grandfather. Indicating the big, crusty fresh loaf from which she'd been cutting thick slices, she said, "This is homemade bread. You didn't make it, did you?"

To Del's amusement, Emmett actually reddened under his weathered tan. "No, it's from that widow, Martha Green. She's been comin' around, pesterin' again."

With twinkling eyes, Del said, "I wouldn't mind being pestered like this. I've never tasted better bread."

"Well, she's a good cook, I'll give you that," Emmett muttered.

Kay laughed. "But Granddad is set in his ways," she said, her own eyes sparkling as she looked from Del to her grandfather and back again. "And he doesn't want some darn fool woman interferin', right, Granddad?"

Since her voice was a perfect imitation of Emmett's, everybody laughed, including Emmett. Then Jennifer giggled and pointed. While they were occupied, Duffy had gotten into the top of the separator, and when the dog looked up, his whiskers were covered with white. He looked so comical—and so guilty—that everybody laughed again, and then it was time to start supper.

LATER THAT NIGHT, after her grandfather had retired and Jennifer had gone up to bed, exhausted, replete and happy, with Duffy by her side, Kay found Del out on the front porch, leaning against the rail, staring out at the darkened, empty fields surrounding them. It was so quiet that they could hear a meow from one of the cats down in the barn, and at first Kay didn't know whether to disturb him or not. As she stood uncertainly in the doorway, Del became aware of her presence and turned toward her with a smile.

"Hi," he said. "I was just trying to decide if I wanted to go for a run to try and work off all those calories from the cream and whatnot, or if I should just stay here and enjoy a cigarette."

Surprised, she came out onto the porch. "I didn't know you smoked!"

"I don't," he said. "I gave it up five years ago. But sometimes..."

She smiled in return. "I know what you mean. It's been even longer since I stopped, but there are times to this day when I think longingly of one. I know it would taste awful, and I'd be sorry, but still..."

They were both silent for a few minutes, enjoying the night. Then Del said thoughtfully, "It's funny, isn't it?"

"What's that?"

He turned to stare out again. His voice low, he said, "Things I haven't questioned in years suddenly seem... questionable... out here." Then he laughed, sounding embarrassed. "It sounds silly, doesn't it?"

"No," she said quietly, joining him at the rail. "In fact, I think it would be odd if you *weren't* affected by things out here." She, too, looked out. Taking a deep breath of the crisp, clean night air, she added, "I've always been glad I've got the farm to come back to. It gives me a . . . a base, something to rely on. Things are so *real* out here. It gives me perspective when I'm confused or sad or disappointed—or angry."

"Now that I've been here myself, I understand why," Del said solemnly. "In fact—" he hesitated, then went on "—I can understand a lot more now that I've seen you here."

It was what she'd been waiting to hear him say. But she didn't want to rush him, so all she said was, "Oh? What things?"

"Why you are the way you are," he said quietly. "Why I'm the way I am. You grew up with what was real, Kay, but in the finest, cleanest sense there is. But what I grew up with was real, too." Something changed in his voice— a harshness crept in and he glanced away, muttering. "All too real."

She was almost afraid to ask. But she sensed that they had come to another fork in the road of their relationship, and she needed to know everything about him. Gently, she put a hand on his arm. "Tell me about it," she said.

For a moment, she thought he wouldn't. She could feel him tense under her touch, and she wondered if she'd made a mistake or misjudged things. But after a second or two, he let out a heavy sigh.

"There's not much to tell," he said in a tone that indicated otherwise. "I grew up in a tenement in Chicago, with graffiti on the walls and bars over the windows— what windows there were, after the gangs went through. I learned to run like hell when I thought I could get away from someone who was chasing me . . . and to turn and fight when I knew I couldn't escape. I'm not proud of it, but in my teens I carried a switchblade in my pocket and wore a chain for a belt, and never a day went by that I didn't dream of getting out of there and leaving it all behind."

Kay was silent, shocked. She had never imagined this, and she didn't know what to say. Then he turned to look at her, and in the light that spilled out onto the porch from the living room windows, his eyes were shadowed. She couldn't see his expression, but she could hear the pain in his voice.

"I've had enough 'substance' to last me a lifetime, Kay. That's why I got into the business I did." Then he seemed to realize just what he'd said, how much he had confessed, for he laughed shortly. "But I didn't mean to burden you with all this...this angst," he said, embarrassed again. "I'm sure the last thing you want to hear is my life story."

"You're wrong, Del," she said quietly. "I understand how painful things can be. I...I didn't have a childhood like yours, but I was lonely just the same. My mother died when I was so young, you see, and my father...well, my father didn't get over it for a long, long time—if he ever did. I don't know what I would have done without Granddad. I spent so much time out here with him that it was almost as though *he* were my father."

"He's a remarkable man, all right," Del agreed, and glanced around. "And I can see why you loved it here."

Kay hadn't intended to mention it, but it seemed a night for confessions. On impulse, she said, "I'd like to show you something, Del. Something I've never shown anyone else. Not even...well, not anyone."

"What's that?"

She held up her hand, indicating that he should wait there. Then she went inside and grabbed two coats from the collection hanging on the coatrack in the hallway—a long mackinaw her grandfather used during storms, and a parka with a sheepskin lining that she left for the times she was here. Handing Del the mackinaw, she put the parka over her shoulders and gestured conspiratorially.

"It's in the barn," she whispered.

"What?" he whispered back, intrigued.

But she put a finger to her lips, grabbed his hand and led the way. When they reached the big double doors, she pulled one open so they could slip through. It was so dark, Del couldn't see anything, but he thought he heard a strange noise and was startled—until he realized it was the cow, contentedly chewing on something. Her cud, he remembered, thinking that he was going to have to abandon some of his city ways. He turned to Kay. She had taken a flashlight from its place by the door, and she was shining it on the ladder that led to the loft above.

"Do you think you can climb up there?" she whispered.

Del grinned. "You ask this of a kid who used to leap ten-foot chain link fences in a single bound? Do you want me to lead the way?"

Kay went first, scrambling up the ladder without hesitation. Del followed, almost as expertly, and as he emerged into the deeper darkness of the loft, he was surprised that it was noticeably warmer up here. Remembering that heat rises, he clambered up the last rung and took her arm. "Now are you going to tell me?"

Kay flashed the beam of the flashlight onto the piles of straw covering the loft floor. "This way," she said, and started toward what Del perceived to be the faint outline of a door at the other end. They had almost reached it when she said, "I hope the light works. I rigged it a long time ago, but it's been *years* since I've been up here. In fact, I haven't even thought of this place in longer than I can remember. I only did tonight because we were talking about our childhoods. Since this is where I used to spend so much of mine, I thought I'd let you see it."

"It" turned out to be what looked like a workshop. At least, Del thought it was—that or a museum of sorts for all kinds of toys and inventions. The light did work, and when Kay pulled the string to switch on the bulb that was hanging by a cord from the ceiling, he looked around in amazement.

"What in the world . . . ?"

Kay grinned. "This is where I grew up—surrounded by all my toys," she said, obviously delighted at his expression. "What do you think?"

He shook his head. "Well, I know that girls no longer play with dolls as a matter of course, but this . . ." Tentatively, he reached out and touched a model of some kind of complicated waterwheel with a fan built in. It stood about eighteen inches high and was constructed down to the last detail.

"What's this?" he asked.

"Oh, that's a model of an electricity-producing waterwheel I built when I was . . . oh, about ten, I think. The idea was that Granddad would be able to generate all his own electricity and irrigate at the same time."

Del examined it more closely. "It looks like it could work."

"Oh, it would," she said, and reddened slightly. "Except for the fact that the farm doesn't have the kind of stream or falls it needs to turn the wheel." She laughed. "A slight miscalculation on my part. But otherwise a great idea, don't you think?"

He did, indeed. Moving on to another model on the long table that took up most of the room, he stopped before a complicated arrangement of pulleys and levers and various other parts that seemed designed to work in unison. "And this?" he asked, marveling at the workmanship.

She smiled in remembrance. "That was one of my science projects," she said. "I'd studied the layouts of some of the ship locks around the world and wanted to try my own design." She frowned, trying to think. "It won some kind of award.... I don't remember what now."

Del just shook his head. Moving on down the table, he had her explain one design after another, each more intriguing to him than the one before, until he came to the last. "And this?"

With an expression of chagrin on her face, she reached out and picked it up. "My first attempt at a robot hand," she said, gazing at the pincerlike object that looked like a high-tech version of a complicated wrench. "When I think of the eggs I broke trying to calibrate it to those fine tolerances..." She laughed suddenly, almost like a girl. "Granddad could never understand how all those hens could lay so few eggs while I was here. I never told him, of course. He's a loving man, but to a farmer, it's a sin to waste food, even in the name of science."

Del was still bemused at what she had shown him. On the one hand, he was impressed by the level of intelligence and creativity it had taken to build such things, but on the other, it was all too easy for him to picture the lonely young girl who had spent all those hours alone up here. "It's hard to believe you did all this at such a young age," he said finally.

She was determined not to feel sorry for herself—or allow him to. "It's amazing what you can do when you're motivated," she said, and then grinned. "Especially if your grandfather pretends not to know what's going on up here. I used to sneak out at night and work on things, and he never said a word. I thought I was being so clever, skulking around under cover of darkness, but it wasn't until I was almost a teenager that I realized you can see the light up here from the house." She nearly giggled at the memory. "What a clown I was! I even hauled up one of my grandmother's comforters so that I'd always have a comfortable place to nap when I got sleepy. It's around here somewhere...."

She glanced around, then her eyes widened. "Now, what...?" she said to herself.

"What is it?"

She pointed. There, in the corner, as fluffy and fresh as if it had been put there the day before, was a comforter. It seemed to have been recently laundered, and when Kay went over and pressed down on it, she smiled tremulously.

"I'll bet Granddad did this," she said. "I'd be willing to bet it was just put up here."

"But why?" Del said, and then understood because he would have done the same thing for Jennifer. "He probably does this every time you come, Kay, sort of as a welcome home present."

Kay was having a hard time controlling her sudden emotion. "But I never knew, until now. Why didn't he say anything?"

But Del understood that, too. "He didn't have to. It was enough to know it was here, ready for you, in case you found it."

Kay was silent a moment. Then, her voice shaky, she said, "Men! I've lived around them all my life, and sometimes I don't think I'll ever understand them."

Del smiled. "Would it surprise you to know we feel the same way about women?"

"Then we're even," she said softly, and came to a sudden decision. Straightening, she said, "Del, there's something else I wanted to tell you about. I realize now that I overreacted about that business with the *Amanda May Show,* and I want to apologize. I never liked to talk about my relationship with Adam Cordell, and when that woman kept pressing me...well, I blamed you unfairly because she tried to pry into my private affairs."

"You were right to be angry," he said somberly. "It was a mistake, and if anyone's sorry, it's me."

"Well, it's over now, and I survived," she said. "And in fact, now that I've had time to think about it, I realize you did me a favor."

"A favor? How do you mean?"

"That show was the first time I've been forced to talk publicly about Adam. I thought I wouldn't be able to do it, but now I realize it's not so hard. I just don't care anymore. It's all in the past."

Del looked relieved. "Do you mean that?"

"Absolutely," she said, realizing it was true. Then, because she felt she owed him something in return for his confession, she added, "It was a bad time in my life—I don't deny that. Adam really hurt me. Oh, it wasn't just that he wanted to break our engagement—I think I could have handled that, because, after all, people change. But it was the way he changed, the things he said and did, the way he wanted me to change. That hurt the most." She looked away, absently picking up the robot hand, then putting it down again. "I'm ashamed to say it now, but I allowed his political consultant to dictate everything to me because Adam wanted it. I'll never forget the... the *awful* shade of blue he insisted I wear for the camera. A nonintrusive shade, I think he called it. And to think I actually did it!'' She shuddered.

"You gave in to your feelings," Del said quietly. "That does funny things to people."

"Yes, I suppose it does," she agreed, but she didn't sound convinced.

"For instance," he said, putting his hands on her arms and turning her to face him. "They're doing some very funny things to me right now."

And just like that, things changed. Maybe she had known they would, bringing him up here; maybe she had been playing with fire again, or tempting fate. But whatever it was didn't seem to matter now, for it seemed the most natural thing in the world to step into his arms in that dark, dusty childhood workroom of hers and look up at him in wonder as feelings, dormant for so long, began to rise to the surface.

Then she realized that this had never happened to her before. She had thought she was in love with Adam, but she knew now that what she had felt for him couldn't compare to her feelings for this man, especially when he drew her slowly toward him until their bodies were touching.

"I know it sounds trite," he whispered, staring down into her wide eyes. "But I think you're the most beautiful woman I've ever seen, Kay. And I've wanted you from the moment we met...."

She didn't know what to say, even if she could have spoken. A lump had formed in her throat, and she was having trouble breathing. The night chill had disappeared, and abruptly the loft seemed hot, heavy and humid; perspiration suddenly prickled her forehead as she looked up at him mutely, with intense longing.

One of his hands went to the back of her head, burying itself in her hair; the other slipped under her parka to her waist. She could feel his arm shaking as he pulled her to him, but by then she was trembling so badly herself she hardly noticed. Inch by inch, his head came down until their lips touched.

She had known passion before, but just like the first time Del had kissed her, she was instantly swept away by emotion and nothing else mattered. A tornado could have ripped through and she wouldn't have noticed; a lightning bolt could have split the tree outside the barn and she wouldn't have heard. The instant Del's lips touched hers, she thought of nothing but him. She had longed for this moment, she realized; she had fantasized about it, dreamed that it would happen. But nothing in her imagination had prepared her for the exquisite reality of being in his arms with his mouth hungrily seeking hers—not tentatively, as he had the first time, when both of them had been aware they could be interrupted at any moment, but with a man's full passion, demanding a woman's response. She gave it to him with all the force of her being. Wrapping her arms around his neck, she didn't even notice the parka slipping off; she never wanted to let him go. Slowly, still wrapped in each other's arms, they sank onto the comforter, and the thought flashed through her mind that she had never appreciated her grandfather more. That was the last thought she had of Emmett, for Del's hand was on her breast, and even through the fabric of her shirt, she felt his burning touch. His mouth clinging to hers, his hands moved to the buttons of her blouse and unbuttoned them one by agonizing one, taking his time so that she yearned to finish the task for him. She wanted to feel his skin against hers, and when he finally pulled the blouse off her shoulders and

reached for the wispy lace bra she wore, she couldn't wait
any longer. She ripped open the snaps of his shirt, practically tearing the garment from his body.

He laughed softly, tilting her head up to his. Her eyes
were brilliant with desire as she looked back at him, and
the laugh died in his throat and became a moan. He
pulled her to him again.

"You're so beautiful," he murmured, stroking her
back. His mouth moved to her throat, and he kissed the
wildly beating pulse there while she arched up against
him. He cupped one firm breast in his hand, bending his
head to tease the nipple with his tongue.

She was never sure how they got the rest of their
clothing off. By the time they came together, skin against
skin, flesh to flesh, the sensation was so blissful that she
just wanted to lie there savoring it. But her body seemed
to have a mind of its own, and she couldn't control the
undulating movements of her hips against his.

"Be careful," he murmured, his lips against her ear.
"Any more of that, and I won't be responsible...."

And she whispered back, "I won't hold it against
you."

He laughed softly and moved over her, and she discovered then that he was a wonderful lover. She was prepared for him to be experienced, expert in the art of
making love—after all, he was a handsome, sophisticated man. But she wasn't prepared for the fury of desire he aroused in her, nor she in him. He was a gentle
lover at first, considerate and passionate at the same
time, but as his own passion rose and took over, one
magic moment led to another and then another, until finally the touch of hands and legs and arms and tongues
wasn't enough. She wanted to feel him inside her, to draw
him deeper and deeper within, until the moan she heard

was torn from his throat, too, and not just wrenched from her.

"You're lovely, Kay," he murmured once, gazing down into her eyes. His fingers brushed her tangled hair back from her flushed face. "So beautiful. I never thought...I never dreamed it could be like this."

And she looked up at him, thinking how extraordinary it all was. "You feel it, too?" she whispered.

He closed his eyes as she drew his head down to hers again. Opening her mouth, she took his tongue inside. He groaned and rolled on top of her, both hands beneath her, cupping her to him, holding her with the same frantic desperation she was beginning to feel. Sweat broke out on both their bodies as they writhed against each other, and when she guided him inside and raised her hips to meet him, he moaned and buried his face in her hair.

She could feel herself being swept away with every thrust. He was driving into her, deeper and deeper with each answering rise of her body. She ran her hands up and down his strong back, pulling him farther into her, arching her back to present her aching breasts. He bent his head, sucking first on one swollen nipple, then the other, kneading her soft flesh with his hand. Their bodies were slippery together, and she felt the hard muscles of his legs and arms, his flat belly tight against hers. Then she couldn't hold back any longer, and the rhythm of her hips increased until he pulled back his head and groaned. Through the stinging sweat running down her face, she saw the muscles of his neck cord with effort, and she pulled him down again, crying, "Del...!"

His cry matched hers, and the pleasure seemed to mount and mount until she thought she would faint from it, and still it went on. She heard another sound and didn't realize it came from her as he thrust into her for the

ast time. Her body wasn't her own; it had become ethe-
real, a being that could fly.

Then Del laughed in exuberant release, and she came
reluctantly back to earth.

"Lord," he gasped, and collapsed beside her.

AS MUCH AS THEY BOTH wanted to, they couldn't spend
the night in the loft; they were too aware of the two people they'd left behind in the house—or at least, Kay was.
When at last she roused herself and sat up to search for
her clothes, Del opened one eye and muttered hoarsely,
"What are you doing?"

"Getting dressed," she said, finding his shirt and
tossing it to him. "Come on, we can't stay out here all
night."

He moaned. "Why not?"

She snapped the catch on her bra and reached for her
shirt. "Do you want to explain to your daughter where
her roommate was tonight?"

Sighing, he said, "No." Then he pulled her to him
again and kissed her soundly. "But just because we don't
have a loft back in town doesn't mean—"

She laughed and tossed him his jeans. "Last one down
the ladder is a rotten egg," she said.

"No fair," he protested, standing on one leg while he
hopped around trying to get the other into his jeans. The
leg was turned inside out and he had to start all over
again, and by that time she was fully dressed and looking at him with sparkling eyes. "Don't forget to turn out
the light," she warned, and danced out of the way as he
grabbed for her.

Laughing like a couple of children and putting their
hands over their mouths to stifle the sound, they left the

barn and crept back to the house. Del left her at her door with a kiss.

"You were...wonderful," he said, gazing down into her eyes.

She knew that if she didn't play it light, she wouldn't be able to leave him. Her lips still felt bruised from the passion of his kisses; her body ached to hold and be held by him again. Telling herself jubilantly that there would be other times, she twinkled up at him. "You weren't so bad yourself," she said, and skipped inside before Duffy could sound the alarm.

CHAPTER TWELVE

THEY DIDN'T GET BACK to Springfield until late Sunday night. When Jennifer had discovered that the farming community was giving a square dance on Sunday, she begged to go. She'd never been to one, and even though she didn't know how to dance, she wanted to see what it was like. Del was so surprised that she was interested that he talked it over with Kay, and in the end, they all went— Emmett dressed up in his best western shirt with the silver collar points, starched jeans and "stompin'" boots, his guests not quite so authentic in their loafers and flats. Kay had found dresses for herself and Jennifer so they wouldn't look out of place, but as soon as they arrived, it was obvious they were still "city slickers."

The dance was held at the Farmers' Grange, and even before they drove in, they could hear the lively music pouring from the open door. People streamed in and out, men with their western-style shirts and jeans, women wearing checked dresses with puffed sleeves and so many starched petticoats that their skirts stood out like open umbrellas. All the women had on black slippers, most wore bows in their hair and not a few stopped to greet Kay. After all, this was a close-knit community, and she had lived among them summer after summer for half of her life.

Emmett, too, was popular, and was soon deep in conversation with other weathered-looking men as they discussed what farmers dwell on the world over: prices, weather, predictions for winter and spring, crops. On the other side of the big room, the ladies hovered around the buffet, and as Jennifer headed in that direction and the band started tuning up again to begin the first square, Del looked at Kay.

"You go ahead," he said. "I think I'll just watch."

"No way," she answered with a grin. "They've got a beginner's square, so you don't have an excuse in the world."

"How about the fact that I don't have any idea how to square dance?"

"You've got two feet, don't you?" she said wickedly. "Then let's go!"

Grabbing his arm, she half dragged him over to one of the several groups that were forming. Just as they took their places, the band swung into high gear, the caller stepped up to the microphone, and they were off.

Whirled around, pushed this way and that, stepping in and stepping back, Del felt as though he'd walked into a kaleidoscope of music and movement and laughter and noise. Half the time he couldn't hear what the caller was saying, and the other half he didn't have the faintest idea what the man meant. What was "trade the wave" or "spring-chain the gear" or "load the boat"? About the only thing he did know was promenade, but that was simple enough; he just followed everybody else. Finally, sweat running down his face, he was just starting to get the hang of it, he felt, when the last do-si-do was called and suddenly everything stopped. Streams of people headed toward the punch bowl, and he was left standing there, panting from exertion and wondering if he was going to have a heart attack.

"Hey, Dad," Jennifer said, coming up. "You did pretty well for a beginner."

"Thanks," he gasped, taking out his handkerchief to wipe his dripping face. "But I didn't see *you* out here. What's the matter? Can't keep up with your old man?"

Jennifer grinned. "It's more fun watching. See you."

And before he could stop her, she dashed away again. Three of the ladies were just bringing out cakes, and when he saw that Jennifer was first in line, he shook his head. But he couldn't worry about it now; he had to get his breath first. Wiping his face again, he looked around and saw Kay grinning at him.

"Well, how'd you like it?" she asked.

"I'm not sure," he said, breathing heavily. He looked at all the white-haired men and women who seemed to take this horrendous exercise right in stride. "How do they do it?" he marveled. "I'm years younger than most of these people, and I feel like I'm going to pass out."

Kay laughed. "They work hard all day. They're fit."

"Fit! I've seen marathoners who weren't in such good shape!"

"Would you like some punch before the next dance?"

He looked at her in horror. "There's more?"

She laughed again, genuinely amused. "The night is young, Del," she said. "And you were the one who wanted to put on your dancing shoes."

Wiping his forehead again, he muttered, "That was Jennifer. And I haven't noticed *her* out on the floor. Besides, when I said dance, what I had in mind was a waltz or two. Or, maybe, if we were really feeling frisky, I thought we might break out in a fox-trot. I didn't think I'd be involved with a group who'd put the Green Berets to shame."

She tried to hide her smile. "Maybe you'd like some air."

"Only if it comes in an oxygen tank."

Laughing again, she put her arm in his. "Come on. We'll sit the next one out."

He allowed her to lead him to one of the benches pushed up against the wall. "You think I'm a wimp, don't you?" he said plaintively, only half kidding as he collapsed onto the bench.

She hid another smile. "No, I think you're a city boy," she said. And then, because of their new intimacy, felt comfortable enough to tease him a little. "I don't imagine there were many square dances where you came from."

He glanced at her from under his brows. "No, but there were occasions when we were called upon to move...fast," he said, and closed his eyes. "But if they could see me now—"

"You see? You're just not used to that anymore."

He looked at her again. "How come you are? Do you keep this up as a hobby?"

She laughed and shook her head. "No, it's too energetic for me. But I have been coming to these things since I was small, so I can fake it for a while."

Remembering how gracefully she had danced, how beautiful she had looked, with her laughing eyes and flushed face, Del said, "You fake it very well. But then, you should, since you're the most beautiful woman here."

She flushed at the compliment. "Why, thank you, sir," she said lightly. "But flattery will get you nowhere. You've got to do another square, or Granddad will never forgive us."

"Your grandfather has his own problems," Del said, and pointed.

Kay looked in that direction in time to see a very large woman dressed in a red-and-white checked dress puffed up with layers of petticoats heading determinedly toward Emmett, who was deep in another conversation with a group of men. The woman was so big and her petticoats stood out so stiffly that she looked like a ship in full sail, and Kay chuckled when she billowed up to Emmett and took his arm. The expression on his face was priceless, and Del laughed.

"I take it," he said, "that that's the widow Green."

Kay nodded. "Granddad's had it now," she said in delight. "She'll stick to him like glue. There's no place to hide."

Del looked at her. "If he's like me, he won't want to," he said, and before Kay could reply, he grabbed her hand and jumped up. The lively music was just starting again, and he hauled her out onto the floor for a spirited, if inexpert, rendition of the very complicated "Texas Star." The entire time they were dipping and weaving and changing partners and promenading around, Kay felt proud. Watching Del as he partnered other women in the square before turning back to her again, she wondered how she could ever have thought she was in love with Adam.

She caught his eye just then, and with a wide grin, he gestured with his chin toward another circle. Looking over her shoulder, Kay saw what Del had been gesturing at: the widow Green, her eyes closed, a fatuous expression on her wide, homely face as she clung to the man of her dreams—Kay's own grandfather, Emmett. When she saw that, Kay smiled. Just then, the square changed, and

Kay was whirled right into Del's arms. Looking up into his handsome face, she knew just how the widow felt.

BECAUSE JENNIFER had school the next morning, and they had a long drive back to Springfield, they left before the dance was over. Emmett had so many friends and neighbors in the community that he wouldn't have any trouble catching a ride back to the farm—although, as he muttered to Kay while he gave her a hug goodbye, he'd be "durned" if he'd sit in the back seat with Martha Green.

"Oh, Granddad," Kay teased. "She just thinks you're a handsome fella, as do I."

"Handsome is as handsome does," he said obliquely, and then whispered that she had a pretty good-looking fellow, too.

"He is nice, isn't he?" she said, and gave him another hug. "Thanks for having us, Grandad. I'll talk to you soon."

"You can bring him back anytime," Emmett replied. "Jennifer, too. Seems to me she could use a little time on the farm. It was always good for you."

"True," Kay agreed, holding his hand fondly before she got into the car. "Thanks again...!"

After Del had thanked Emmett for his hospitality and Jennifer had impulsively given him a hug, they were off. In the back seat with Duffy, Jennifer fell asleep on the way back to Springfield, but Kay and Del didn't talk much, either. Content to be in each other's company, they rode in companionable silence, and Kay herself was almost asleep when Del finally pulled up in front of her house. As he cut the engine, he turned to give his sleeping daughter a quick glance, then he reached for Kay and gave her a deep, heartfelt kiss.

"I had a wonderful time," he said huskily, staring into her eyes.

"So did I," she whispered, mindful of Jennifer in the back seat.

"We'll have to do it again."

"Granddad says you're welcome anytime."

He held her glance. "That wasn't exactly what I meant."

But she knew what he meant, and she could feel something stirring inside just at the idea. "Maybe I can have you over for dinner one night," she suggested.

He smiled. "I'd like that. I can send Jennifer to a movie."

Kay couldn't help herself. Innocently, she said, "Oh, she's welcome, too."

He glowered. "There's such a thing as a little *too* much togetherness, you know."

"Dad's right," came a sleepy voice from the back seat. "I know you two want to be alone, so just let me know when, and I'll go... hang out. If you want to get rid of Duffy, too, I'll take him along."

Embarrassed that Jennifer had not only apparently overheard their conversation but had already put two and two together, Kay immediately protested, "It's not that we want to get *rid* of you!"

"Yes, it is," Del said matter-of-factly. "Okay, Button. Thanks for the offer. We'll let you know."

"Del!" Kay objected.

He shrugged. "Can't keep much from teenagers these days—right, Button?"

"Right, Dad," Jennifer said, a grin in her voice. "G'night, Kay. Thanks for a wonderful weekend. I really enjoyed it, and your grandfather's the best."

Kay gave up. "I enjoyed it, too," she said. "We'll do it again."

"I hope so."

Del helped Kay with her bag. But as they stood for a moment on the front porch, Duffy off on some errand of his own around the yard, Del took her into his arms once more and kissed her soundly. "I *did* have a good time," he murmured. "In all respects. Can I call you tomorrow?"

And every other day, Kay thought, and smiled. "Absolutely," she said, and couldn't help adding, "After all, we've still got a campaign to run, remember?"

His eyes twinkled as he looked down at her. "As a matter of fact, it had slipped my mind. But don't worry. I'll go home and take a long, cold shower and get back on track."

She laughed, and he kissed her again lightly on the lips. Then, waving, he went back to the car and got in. Kay watched until the taillights disappeared, then, with a heartfelt sigh, she called Duffy and went inside.

JENNIFER HAD CLIMBED into the front seat with her father before he drove off. After buckling her seat belt, she said, "Dad?"

Del was clearly preoccupied. "Um?"

"Dad, Kay said she'd take me shopping."

"That's good."

"No, I mean *shopping*. You know, like Mom used to. So I can get a whole new wardrobe."

"Oh?"

She heard the wary note in his voice and smiled. "Don't worry, I won't spend a fortune. It's just that I'm . . . I'm tired of jeans and sweats. Do you mind?"

She definitely had his attention.

"Mind? Of course not. It's just..."

She could practically feel him hesitate, but she knew that he had to ask, and he did.

"I think it's a great idea," he said, proceeding cautiously. "But I'm curious about the sudden turnaround. Why the big change, when you've been wearing the same thing ever since you got here?"

"I don't know," she said. "It's just...well, Kay always looks so nice, don't you think? Even in jeans, she's a knockout, while I just feel like a sack of—"

"You look fine to me," he said quickly, and then glanced across the seat at her. "I don't want you to look like Kay, honey—as attractive as she is. I like you just as you are. I want you to look like yourself."

"But I hate the way I look!" she said, shuddering. "I've gained so much weight that I look like a blimp! I mean it, Dad, I'm going to change my image. I'm going to get serious about losing weight, and I...I want to change my name."

Del was silent for a few seconds. "You...what?" he finally asked.

"I want to change my name," she repeated, obviously relishing the thought. "Jennifer is so *yuppie*. I hate it. I want something else—something simpler, more direct. Like...Kay."

He couldn't hide his dismay. "You want to change your name to Kay?"

She giggled. "No, silly, of course not. I just meant that I want a name *like* that."

Feeling as though he were rapidly losing control of the conversation, Del cleared his throat. Wondering how Maxine would deal with this—wondering what Maxine would say about it—he asked carefully. "Do you have something in mind?"

"As a matter of fact, I do," she said with satisfaction. "Now, I knew you would freak out at this, so I thought the easiest thing would be to start using my middle name. After all, if you called me Jennifer Patricia, you must have liked it. So, what do you think?"

"I think Patricia is a lovely name," he said fervently.

"Not Patricia—Pat. From now on, you can call me Pat, okay?"

Relieved that he'd gotten off so easily, he said, "Okay. I'll try to remember."

"And Dad . . ."

What now? he wondered. "Yes?"

"I think it's great that you and Kay are going to-gether."

He shifted awkwardly in the seat. *How much does she know?* he wondered uncomfortably, and said, "We're not actually *going* together."

She grinned. "You could have fooled me. If you're not, why were you sneaking off to the barn in the middle of the night last night?"

He felt his face turning red. Do kids see everything? he wondered, and protested, "We weren't sneaking! Kay wanted to show me a workshop in the loft she'd had as a child, and—"

"Oh, sure. You think I believe that?"

"You can ask her yourself."

He sounded so aggrieved that she giggled again. "Hey, I don't care. I think it's great. Kay's wonderful, Dad. No wonder you're in love with her. It's about time, don't you think?"

He wasn't going to touch that one with a ten-foot pole. "I think this conversation has taken enough convoluted turns to last me a lifetime," he said. "Now, if you don't mind—"

"No problem, Dad," she said solemnly, but he could hear the laughter in her voice and was glad they were finally home.

But she wasn't finished with him yet, for as they were collecting their things from the car, she turned to him and said earnestly, "And don't worry. The next time you want to see her alone, I'll make myself scarce. You'll see."

"Thanks, Pat," he said weakly, and led the way inside.

AT THE END OF THE WEEK—the first opportunity after a busy workweek that he and Kay had time to get together—he related the story to Kay, and she burst into laughter. Her eyes sparkling, she said, "I guess we weren't so clever, after all, were we?"

They were sitting in her living room in front of the fire having coffee after dinner. Jennifer—or Pat, as he was trying to remember to call her—wasn't there. She had gone to the movies with Trudy, and then she was going to spend the night with her friend.

"So you'll have plenty of time to be with Kay," she had said with that innocent look that was starting to drive him crazy. He'd thanked her dryly and, after dropping the girls off at the local burger stop before the show, hurried to make his date.

Now, he was sitting on the floor with Kay, his arm around her, her head on his shoulder, feeling more content than he had in a long time. He loved being with Kay, loved hearing her laugh, loved seeing her expressive face light up, or watching how her eyes sparkled, or how her mouth moved as she talked. It had been so long since he'd felt like this that he almost believed he were young again. It was a wonderful experience, and as Kay turned to say something to him, he had such a strange expression on his face that she said instead, "Del, what's wrong?"

He looked at this woman whom he was sure he was coming to love, and shook his head. "Nothing," he murmured, and drew her close to him. "Nothing at all that you can't fix...."

With the fire crackling and the dog sleeping contentedly near the hearth, he took Kay into his arms and kissed her. There was nothing youthful in his kiss; his passion was a man's passion, and Kay reacted instantly. They both knew that the evening had been leading up to their being together again, and anticipation—the drinks before dinner, the dinner itself, then dessert and finally the espresso he had fixed—had only made the waiting more exquisite. This time they were alone, without having to worry about anyone but themselves, and that knowledge, unspoken between them, added to the electricity of the moment.

Her eyes shining in the firelight, Kay broke away from the kiss to look up into his face. "Let's go upstairs," she whispered.

He smiled into her lovely face. "What?" he murmured. "And leave our romantic fire and the hard floor and couch pillows that never stay in place?"

Softly, she laughed. "Ah, where did youth go?" she said. "There was a time when we wouldn't have given it a thought."

Del grinned as he stood up. As a precaution, he banked the fire and put the screen in place. Then, reaching down, he pulled Kay to her feet. "I'll show you youth," he said, and followed her upstairs.

Kay's bedroom reflected her personality: organized and functional, neat and feminine without being frilly.

When Del noticed the puffy comforter on top of the bed, he grinned.

"You seem to have a thing about comforters," he said. Then he took her in his arms again and kissed her until she was breathless.

"I do," she said, gasping as they pulled away to take a breath. "You want to see why?"

Still in his embrace, she reached behind her and whipped the comforter, along with the blankets, down to the foot of the bed. Turning back to him, she said, "You see how easy it is?"

"Always on top of things, I see."

"Not always," she replied with a wicked smile that made him reach for her again.

This time, it was he who broke away, gasping for breath. Looking down at her, he touched her face with his hand, his expression both ecstatic and marveling. "You don't know what you do to me, Kay," he murmured. "I don't think I've ever felt like this...."

She looked up at him, wide-eyed and wondering herself. "I haven't, either. Oh, Del—"

"Shh," he murmured, placing his hand at the back of her neck. "Don't talk...enjoy."

And they did. With the house to themselves, they had no sense of urgency this time. They took time with each other as they hadn't before: undressing each other, then touching and caressing and exploring with delight, until finally their bodies betrayed them again, and anticipation could be denied no longer. Falling into bed between the fresh sheets, they lay side by side, just gazing at each other in the soft light that came into the bedroom from the lamp they'd left on in the hall. Slowly, Del moved to kiss her, and she drew him to her. With one thigh over his hip, she guided him inside, and they began to move as one, ever so slowly at first, but then, as that wonderful warmth spread, faster and faster, until they were swept along with no will of their own. As before, the climax shook them both, and they strained upward with exquisite shared pleasure. At the peak, Kay dug her nails into his back, and he cried out her name.

Exhausted, they fell back, breathing hard.

"That was . . . wonderful," Del gasped, holding on to her tightly.

Kay was so happy she grinned. "You enjoyed it, then."

A slow smile spread across his face. "I don't know. Maybe we'd better try it again."

"Fine," she said faintly. "When I can move again."

His eyes were already closing. "All right, just let me know. . . ."

Kay smiled again. Enough energy had returned so that she could reach down and pull the comforter over them. "Another reason why I like these things," she said, snuggling under the softness, next to Del's warm body. "It's—"

But just then, some kind of cannonball hit the end of the bed and bounced. Rudely jolted out of his pleasant reverie, Del sat bolt upright. "What the hell!"

"Duffy!" Kay cried, but she was caught under the comforter while the dog jumped around on the bed. It was obvious that Duffy thought it was some kind of game, for every time Del tried to snatch the dog's collar, Duffy barked and bounded over to the other side of the bed. It was like being on a raft in a sea of bouncing tennis balls. With Del swearing and the dog barking, Kay started to laugh so hard she couldn't stop, and the sight of a naked Del jumping to the floor and finally wrestling the exuberant dog off the bed made her laugh even harder.

"Oh, Del! If you could see yourself!" she choked out, sitting up with the covers in a tangled mess. Glowering, Del looked up from his crouched position by the side of the bed. When he looked down at the dog he had pinned under him, Duffy barked excitedly again and began to furiously wag his tail. It was still a game to him, and the dog looked so comical that Del started to laugh, too. He loosened his hold, and when Duffy jumped up and began to lick his chin, he put his face in his hands and shook his head.

"Not exactly the kind of romantic ending I had planned for the evening," he groaned.

Still laughing herself, Kay threw back the covers and got up. Grabbing her robe, she quickly belted it around her and went around to collar Duffy.

"You really know how to put on a grand finale, boy," she scolded. How was she going to teach him there were some times when his presence at the foot of her bed was definitely not welcome? It was a problem that had never arisen before.

"I'll put him out," she said.

Del hauled himself ignominiously up from the floor. "No, it's all right. I've got to get home, anyway."

She looked at him in dismay. "But I thought you said that Jennifer was spending the night with a friend!"

He pulled on shorts and slacks and looked around for his socks. "Yes, but that doesn't mean I can," he said reluctantly. "She already suspects too much. Can you imagine the flack I'd take if she got home in the morning before I did?"

She hadn't thought of that. Crestfallen, she said, "I guess you're right."

He came around to where she was standing. Tilting her head up so that she had to look at him, he said, "But that doesn't mean we can't have the rest of the weekend, does it? I'll tell you what. How about we plan a picnic at the lake? You'd like that, wouldn't you?"

"At this time of year?" she said, scandalized. "If we go out there now, we'll freeze to death!"

He grinned wickedly. "Not if we cuddle."

She grinned suddenly back. "The three of us?" she said. "Or, rather, four, if we include Duffy. He *loves* the lake. We could all go."

Del's grin faded. "Do we all have to?"

"No," she said, laughing and rising on tiptoes to give him a quick kiss. "And I'd love to do something—even have a picnic in the cold weather. But after I take Jennifer on her shopping trip tomorrow, I've got to spend the rest of the weekend working."

"Working? On the weekend?"

"Is there an echo in here?" she teased. "And don't tell me you've never heard of the concept—you, whom Jennifer calls a workaholic of the first order."

"Speaking of Jennifer," he said, momentarily diverted as he finished dressing, "what do you think of this business of changing her name?"

"She hasn't changed her name. She just wants to be called Pat. Isn't Patricia her middle name?"

"Well, yes, but—"

Kay laughed. "When I was her age, I wanted to change my name, too. But I hated my middle name—Lynn—so I had to stick with plain old Kay. Don't worry, Del, she'll get over it. And even if she doesn't a lot of people go by their middle names. Or shorten their first," she added pointedly. "Otherwise, we'd all be calling you Delan, wouldn't we?"

He shuddered. "God forbid. All right, I take your point. Have you seen my other shoe?"

Fifteen minutes later, wearing both shoes and after several lingering kisses at the front door, Del regretfully departed. "But I'll be back," he assured her as he went down the walk.

Dreamily, Kay leaned against the door. "I certainly hope so," she said.

He stopped at the end of the walk. "You sure you don't want to go on that picnic? When will I see you again?"

"I'll call you next week," she promised, and couldn't help adding, "after Jennifer...Pat...and I have had our shopping trip and you've had a chance to get used to the transformation in your daughter."

"Transformation?" he repeated, alerted. He looked doubtful. "You're not going to turn her into something I'll regret, are you? The way kids dress these days—"

"Trust me," she said wickedly, reminding him of the time he'd said that to her. Then she grinned and shut the door.

CHAPTER THIRTEEN

KAY DIDN'T SEE MUCH of Del the following two weeks. They spoke often by phone, but they were both so busy at work that there just wasn't time to do more. Del made several quick trips out of town to see clients, while Kay was swamped at the office, and as he told her once during a hurried five-minute call, he had so many things to do in this preelection season that he sometimes wasn't sure whether he was coming or going.

Kay sympathized, but things weren't going well at Stockwell, either. With her appearance before the Senate subcommittee coming up in the new year, she found herself working longer and longer hours in preparation. She was at the office so much, in fact, that she finally hired Jennifer to "pet-sit" Duffy for a few hours after school every day—a job that Jennifer was delighted to accept even without the pay Kay insisted she take. Each day Jennifer would take the bus to the corner near Kay's house and then spend some time with the dog, feeding him before she went home. Since Duffy had taken a shine to Jennifer, and Jennifer was clearly in love with him, it was working out, but Kay still felt guilty. She didn't want the dog to think she had abandoned him.

But, as Del reminded her one night when they met briefly for coffee before rushing off to other obligations, certain things had to take priority.

"And, selfishly, I have to say, Jennifer's new responsibilities with Duffy and everything else you've done for her have made her a changed person," Del told her in the café. He gave her a grateful look. "I can't believe the difference in her, and it's all due to you."

Kay laughed. "I think you're giving me too much credit, Del. All I did was take her shopping a couple of times—"

"And give her confidence and make her feel important," he said, then added a little forlornly, "I couldn't do that, no matter how I tried."

Kay put her hand over his. "She's just going through a difficult adjustment, Del," she said quietly. "Give her time."

"Time, I've got," he said wryly. "Space, I'm not so sure of."

"What do you mean?"

He looked askance. "You mean you haven't heard the latest? Now we're into health foods. And vitamins and minerals and God knows what else. The kitchen is so cluttered that Mrs. Nivens told me the other night she can't get in to clean or to cook."

She smiled. "It sounds harmless enough."

"Oh, I haven't finished. In addition to the stuff in the kitchen, now we've got some kind of science project festering in the main bathroom—which I'm no longer allowed to enter, by the way, for fear I'll upset the delicate balance of whatever it is she's working on."

"Well, you did want her to improve her studies," she reminded him solemnly, but with a twinkle in her eye.

"Yes, yes, I did, and I suppose if she doesn't blow us both up in the process, this project of hers, whatever it is, will help pull up her grades. But in the meantime, I have to fight my way into the other bathroom, which always has...things hanging up all over the place.''

''Things?'' she said curiously.

He gestured. ''You know, panty hose and underthings.'' Dolefully, he shook his head. ''If I didn't know better, I'd think her mother had moved back in. I haven't had nylons hanging from the shower door since I was married!''

She was doing her best not to laugh. ''You wanted her to take an interest in her appearance,'' she pointed out.

''An interest, yes. I didn't think she'd become *obsessed!*''

''She's not obsessed, Del,'' Kay said, laughing despite herself at his expression. Picturing the new Jennifer, pounds lighter because of her diet, her hair trimmed to just below her shoulders, wearing the latest in teen garb and looking much happier these days, she squeezed Del's hand. ''She's just spreading her wings a little. It's about time, don't you think?''

''I don't know,'' he said. ''I'm not sure. One day she's a little girl, and the next...'' He sighed. ''I guess all fathers feel this way.''

''I'm sure they do,'' she said. ''It's part of the process, I think.''

''Well, when is this process complete?''

''You'll have to ask Jennifer,'' she said. ''And you two are getting along much better these days, aren't you?''

''Oh, yes, I can't deny that. And I suspect it's all due to you, too.'' He looked at her keenly. ''You had a talk with her, didn't you?''

Smiling into her cup, she said, ''We discussed a few things, yes.''

His glance held hers. ''Well, whatever you said, I'm grateful,'' he said quietly, entwining his fingers with hers.

And then, "What would we Raffertys do without you, Kay?"

Warmed by the compliment, she countered, "I think the question is, what would we Stockwells do without you and Jennifer? I can't speak for Duffy, but you've certainly helped me to turn the company's image around. In addition to other...er... benefits," she added, blushing with memories of their intimacy.

His fingers tightening on hers, he grinned. "I've enjoyed those, too, believe me. But where the company is concerned, you're responsible for the upswing, Kay. I merely showed you how to manage it. The rest was up to you."

It was her turn to sigh. "I hope the worst is behind us now."

"You haven't heard any more from George Mott?"

"Not since his threat to sue, no. I'm hoping the letter my lawyers sent scared some sense into him."

"So am I. But if there's trouble, you know where to find me."

She smiled, then glanced at her watch with horror. "And you know where to find me," she said. "I'm sorry, Del, but I've got to go. I'm supposed to meet Mort in five minutes."

"I've got to get a move on, too," he said reluctantly. He gave her a kiss as they went out to where their cars were parked. "Maybe when I get back from California, we can take a couple of days off—just the two of us," he said. "Would you like that?"

"More than anything in the world," she answered, staring up into his eyes. When he looked at her like that, she wanted to ravish him right here in the parking lot. "When will you get back?"

"I'll be gone until at least Thursday."

"And Jennifer? She could stay with me, if you don't want her alone in the house."

"Thanks, but Mrs. Nivens is going to stay over. Something about Jennifer having to be there morning and night to do whatever it is to her science project. I certainly hope she isn't growing some kind of fungus in there. I have nightmares about it escaping and creeping up the stairs to get us in our sleep."

Kay laughed. "You do not."

"I swear."

"Then maybe *you* had better come and stay with me for a while."

She had meant it as a joke—or had she? Suddenly breathless as his eyes met hers, she felt her heart skip a beat when he said softly, "I'd like nothing better."

Aware that they had suddenly stepped onto different ground, Kay pulled back. "Then maybe we should talk about that when you get back," she said lightly.

He gave her another brief kiss. "That, and other things," he said, opening her car door for her. "In the meantime, let's hope that everything stays quiet so that we can take those few days off."

"Amen to that," she said fervently.

But as it turned out, Del's plane had hardly taken off when all hell broke loose at Stockwell Engineering. It seemed that George Mott hadn't been intimidated by Kay's lawyers, after all; he'd merely been waiting for the right opportunity before he struck. As Kay knew only too well because of Del's involvement with his clients, next year was an election year, and Mott was a friend of Sanford Granger, the man who was running for mayor. To dislodge Farley Troxell, the aging incumbent, Granger needed an issue, and because of his friendship with George Mott, the issue turned out to be Stockwell Engineering. Before Kay knew it, Mott had filed a multimillion-dollar damage suit against the company and had encouraged Granger to call for an investigation not only into Stockwell's hiring and firing practices, but also into the defense contracts Stockwell was rumored to be negotiating.

As before, the media loved it. In a slow news season, Stockwell became the much-needed source of controversy, and Kay was abruptly plunged right back into the maelstrom. Demonstrators and protesters returned to the gates in greater numbers, carrying their placards and chanting their slogans; their sheer number made it difficult for Stockwell's employees to get to work. Even though there was no repeat of the rock-throwing incident, tensions were running high again within days, and after conferring with the company attorneys and two of her top executives from other departments, she called a meeting with Brice and Mort Lachlan, who had been working night and day on the QSA. They met in her office two days before Del was due home, and Brice's first question was about him.

"Have you talked to Del about this, Kay?"

She knew how busy Del was in California, and she hadn't wanted to bother him. "Not yet," she said, avoiding his eyes because she knew what his reaction was going to be. "He's out of town."

"Yes, I know. But his staff should be fully apprised—"

She had anticipated his objection, and she said, "I don't want to deal with his staff. I only want to deal with him."

"But if he's not here—"

"He'll be back by Friday," she said, ending the discussion. "In the meantime, we need to decide what to do now." She turned to Mort. "What's the status on the QSA?"

Mort slumped in the chair. "Not good. I still haven't worked through that glitch we talked about."

She knew how hard he'd been working, because many nights she'd worked right beside him. So she didn't argue about it or demand results he couldn't give. All she asked was, "Any projections?"

He looked even more downcast. "Not at this time. I hope we'll be ready by the time you go to Washington, but with all this other business..."

He gestured toward the front gates. Even from behind closed windows, they could all hear the chanting of the crowd. Hoping that the increasingly cold weather would drive the demonstrators inside soon, or at least cool their zeal, Kay nodded. "I understand. I know you're doing what you can, Mort. If you need any more people—"

"That's not what we need," he said, meeting her eyes.

She and Brice both knew what he meant. The truth was that they needed more money. With the renewed media attention, a mayoral candidate calling for an investigation and protesters milling around the front gates, several of the venture capitalists Kay had persuaded to invest were backing out. As she had discovered so painfully, investors didn't mind publicity about their projects and good works—just as long as the publicity was favorable and the works continued to look good. Nothing dried up capital so quickly as censure and protest, and Kay knew that if she didn't do something soon, Stockwell would never recover from the damage.

"I'm going to give a press conference," she announced abruptly. "I'm going to tell those—"

"Er...Kay," Brice said quickly. "Do you think that's a good idea?"

She gave him a hard look. "You have any other suggestions?"

"Yes, I think we should wait until Del gets back."

"And what's he going to do?"

"I don't know. But he's the expert. After all your hard work to turn things around, do you really want to jeopardize the situation now?"

She didn't like the way he put it, but she bit back her quick retort. Besides, she had already considered the question and answered it in her own mind. After all, this was *her* company, not Brice's, not Del's, and she couldn't just stand by or wait for someone else to handle things. Not even Del, she thought. "The situation already is jeopardized, Brice. I've got to say something, defend what we're doing here and make it clear that George Mott doesn't have a leg to stand on. If I wait, it just gives people more ammunition, and I think we both agree that's the last thing we need."

Mort was following the exchange with wide eyes, but Brice looked increasingly anxious. "Let our lawyers do it, Kay. They'll take Mott on in court."

"Do you know how long that will take?" she demanded. "By the time the lawyers get into court, Stockwell Engineering could be out of business, and then the point will be moot!"

"I still think you should wait, or at least call Del and ask what he thinks."

But the more he pressed her to get Del's permission, the more resistant she became. She more than anyone knew what was good for her company. Del might be a whiz with images, but Stockwell Engineering was real to her, and she was going to defend it.

"Opinion noted," she said, ending the discussion. "Thank you, gentlemen."

Along with Mort, Brice reluctantly got to his feet. "What are you going to say, Kay?"

"I haven't decided yet," she said, although she had. She glanced at the silent engineer. "Just keep on it, Mort. Try not to let all this distract you. I'll take care of it—somehow."

When they had gone, she slumped in her chair. Faintly, she could hear the chanting from outside. She closed her eyes and put her head in her hands. Right now, she would have eagerly given up the president's chair in exchange for not having to make this decision. She had been so sure of herself when she was talking to Brice and all her other executives, but now that she was alone, all the possibilities of failure loomed threateningly before her, and suddenly her decision didn't seem so clear-cut.

Maybe she should wait until Del got back, she thought. Or at the least, maybe she should call him.

And ask him what? she asked herself derisively. *Whether I have his permission to act on the situation here?*

She had hired Del to overhaul the company's image; she had done everything he'd suggested. But then she had abandoned one of her own hard rules and gotten involved with him, and now she had to wonder how much of their personal relationship was overlapping into what should have been a professional association. She couldn't abide the thought that she had become so dependent on him that she couldn't make a move without him calling the shots or giving her a script. Once she had allowed Adam to dictate to her, and she had vowed never to give anyone that much power over her again.

But Del isn't Adam, a little voice whispered at the back of her mind, making her frown. She knew that, but still...

She glanced at the phone. Would it hurt just to call him? she asked herself. Hesitantly, her hand reached for the receiver, then dropped again. She couldn't call, she thought; she didn't know where he was staying tonight. His schedule was so erratic....

But his staff will know, the little voice said, and she knew it was right. All she had to do was call Del's secretary and ask for his itinerary. Stella would know, she thought; Stella knew everything.

She looked at the phone again, not sure why she was so reluctant to pick it up. Was it because she didn't trust herself where Del was concerned? What would happen if Del advised against calling a press conference to set the media straight? What would she do? Take his advice or go ahead and do what she felt was right?

Right now, she was getting nowhere. There were more questions than answers whirling around her head, so she decided to put the whole business out of her mind for a while and get some work done. She had a stack of reports and memos to go through, and if she was going to speak to the press, she'd better have all her facts at hand. Feeling tense and out of sorts, she got down to work.

It was almost five when she looked up again. Rachel poked her head through the door and announced that if Kay didn't need her for anything else, she was going home.

Wearily, Kay rubbed her eyes. "Fine, go ahead. I'll see you tomorrow," she said, and then glanced at the window. It had grown dark while she was working, and she asked if the protesters had gone home.

Rachel shook her head. "Some of them, I think. But there are still some out there." Then, in a rare display of emotion, she exploded, "It's so unfair! Don't they understand what you're trying to do here?"

Smiling at such staunch support, Kay said, "They won't until we tell them, and we can't do that until the Senate hearing."

"Well, I've heard of being between a rock and a hard place before, but this is ridiculous!"

Kay agreed. As her secretary closed the door again, she stood and stretched. Was she tired because she'd been working so hard or because of all the strain of the past week? Probably a little of both, she thought wearily, going to the window and staring down at the little knot of demonstrators who had set up camp outside the gates. She seemed to be doing this a lot these days. She was just wondering why they didn't go home when the phone buzzed. Glancing over her shoulder, she saw that it was her private line and immediately felt a stirring of apprehension. Was that Del? If it was, what was she going to say?

Before she could think about it, she picked up the receiver. "Hello?" she said cautiously.

It was Del, and he was mad. Without preamble, he demanded, "What's this I hear about you giving a press conference?"

"Hello to you, too," she said, immediately feeling defensive. She made an effort to be calm. Nothing would be accomplished by getting into a fight. "I take it you heard from Brice."

"Yes, he just called me—right out of a meeting, I might add!"

This wasn't going well. She didn't care for his tone of voice, and her own was considerably cooler when she said, "Well, Del, I'm terribly sorry for the inconvenience. Brice shouldn't have called. I told him not to."

"You what? Never mind. Why didn't you call me? If I'd known there were problems out there, I would have—"

"What? Come yourself? Interrupted your important meetings to fly back and rescue me?"

That stopped him, but only momentarily. "Well, no," he said reluctantly. "I would have put someone from my staff on it."

"I don't want anyone from your staff."

"But you didn't call me!"

"Only because I thought I could handle it, Del. Honestly, don't you think you're overreacting?"

"Overreacting! We've done all the groundwork to change Stockwell's image, and you're going to blow it by calling some spur-of-the-moment meeting with the press, and you think I'm overreacting?"

Her voice dropped ten degrees. "What makes you think I'm going to—as you so succinctly put it—blow it?"

Even through his own ire, he could hear the frost in her tone, and he made a belated attempt to make amends. "I'm sorry, I didn't mean it like that. What I meant was, we need time to prepare you."

"Prepare me!" she said indignantly. "You make me sound like a Thanksgiving turkey or something!"

He sounded exasperated. "That's not what I meant, and you know it. You've been around me long enough to know how carefully we research things, Kay. Giving a press conference isn't like having a coffee klatch with the neighborhood housewives. It's serious business!"

"Well, thank you, Del Rafferty. If you hadn't told me, I never would have realized it. Here I was, thinking that I was going to win over a hostile press by handing out fresh coffee and home-baked rolls!"

"Now, Kay—"

"Don't you 'Now, Kay' me! You're being insulting as well as rude, and you have no right to be either one!"

There was a silence. Then he said, obviously forcing himself to calm down, "I'm sorry. It's just that when Brice told me about the situation there and what you planned to do, well, I guess I did overreact."

It was too late for his conciliatory tone. Ungraciously, she said, "Yes, I guess you did."

He obviously wasn't going to take all the blame. "But you're at fault, too," he said, inciting her temper again. "You should have let me know. You know what they say—I'm as close as the phone."

"I know what they say, Del," she said, her teeth clenched. "But the fact is, I don't have to call you over every little thing!"

"This isn't a little thing! For crying out loud, Kay, why can't you understand that?"

"I do understand it. That's why I'm going to speak to the press myself tomorrow."

"Tomorrow! I can't possibly get there by then!"

"No one asked you to."

"This is insane! You can't do this!"

She'd heard enough. He was talking to her as though she were a recalcitrant child, and she didn't like it. Adam had treated her in a similar fashion toward the last, and she wasn't going to stand for it again.

"Yes, I can, Del," she said coolly. "And if you're in doubt, watch the evening news. Oh, I forgot. This will only be local, won't it? Well, don't worry. Since you're so insistent that I call someone, I'll phone your office and tell your people to record it and analyze it and do whatever else they do with these things. You can see it when you get back."

"Don't do it, Kay," he warned.

But she had already made up her mind. And if she hadn't, this conversation had done it for her. "Goodbye, Del. And thank you so much for calling. It's been a real pleasure."

"If you go ahead with this, I'm off the account," he said as she was starting to hang up. "I mean it, Kay. If you won't work with me, we'll call it quits."

Slowly, she put the phone back to her ear. She couldn't believe he'd said such a thing. "Are you trying to blackmail me?"

"No blackmail, just common sense," he said, his voice hard. "If you won't listen to my advice—"

"You mean, if I don't do everything you say!"

"I *am* the expert here, Kay. I don't tell you how to construct your robots, do I?"

"No, and I don't tell you how to run your business, do I?" she flashed back angrily.

"Well, my business is advising you how to present yours, so I'm asking you one more time, Kay. Don't give the press conference until I can get there and we can discuss it. Will you do that much, at least?"

But he had gone too far. "No," she said coldly. "Oh, I was right! I never should have listened to Brice in the first place or allowed you to talk me into this stupid image business! It hasn't worked out, it's never going to work out, and I'm sorry I even tried!"

He was silent a moment. Then, very quietly, he said, "Are we just talking about business, or does this go a little deeper, Kay?"

She'd often gotten in trouble because of her temper; she thought she had taught herself long ago to think before she spoke in fury. But she forgot all those hard, painfully learned lessons now; all she could think of was that it was Adam all over again. Everything had been fine as long as she did whatever he said, but the instant she deviated from the program or expressed a different opinion or demanded her own identity, the reaction was the same: hostility. She was furious with herself for being in the same position again.

"Yes, it does go deeper than that," she said tightly. She felt threatened and betrayed and hurt all at the same time, and she was too furious to figure out why. "Yes, it does!" she repeated again stridently. "I see now that as long as things were going your way, everything was fine. But the instant I protested or changed my mind or decided to do something my way, you felt you had the right to threaten me. Well, you might be able to do that with your other clients, Del, but you're not going to do it with me—not professionally *nor* personally." Then she said a truly hateful thing, which she instantly regretted. "I fired you once and I'm doing it again, but this time, it's for keeps. Send your bill to accounting. I'll see that it's paid immediately. And don't bother to call again—for any reason. Understand?"

"Absolutely," he said, sounding just as enraged. "And there will be no bill, by the way. Since you're obviously dissatisfied with the services of Rafferty Associates, we wouldn't dream of charging you for a thing. Goodbye, Kay, and good luck with your press conference."

He didn't need to add, *You're going to need it;* the implication was there, and that made her even more irate. With an angry exclamation, she banged the phone down and then stood there, breathing hard, trying to get herself under control. She fully expected it to ring again, for Del to be on the other end, saying he was sorry. Well, he wasn't any sorrier than she was right now, she thought wrathfully. But what she was sorriest about was that she'd gotten involved with him in the first place. How could she have been so blind?

But that night, not even the sight of Duffy running eagerly to greet her could cheer her up, and when she saw the cheery note Jennifer had left for her, propped against the Crock-Pot in the kitchen, she felt like crying. In all the furor, she'd forgotten Jennifer, and for once she had no idea what she was going to say.

THE PRESS CONFERENCE the next day was a disaster from beginning to end. The select group of reporters she had invited began rushing around snapping pictures the moment they entered the gates. The security guards she'd hired tried to corral them, but they pushed back. A shoving match immediately ensued, and before things could get out of hand, she went out—against Brice's advice—and spoke to the unruly crowd herself. She was so tense by that time that it seemed a miracle when her plea for order worked, and as the group shamefacedly filed into the conference room she had set aside, she tried to compose herself. Then she stepped to the front of the room to give her prepared speech.

She never got a chance to say a word of it. Before she could open her mouth, one of the reporters, a man she knew by the name of Tony Mercer, called out.

"George Mott has recently filed suit claiming he was fired because he tried to protest new defense contracts Stockwell was pursuing," the reporter said aggressively. "How do you respond to that?"

How she wanted to respond was to say that George Mott was a vindictive little man who wasn't above lying to get his name in the paper. What she did say, holding firmly on to her temper, was, "George Mott has his facts wrong."

Instantly, there was a babble. A self-satisfied Tony emerged, his tape recorder at the ready again. "Then you're denying that Stockwell Engineering is going after contracts from the Department of Defense?" he said. And before she had time to answer, went on, "Do you also deny that you're scheduled to appear before a Senate subcommittee in the new year to ask for government contracts?"

She was really getting to dislike this man. Coolly, she looked at him and said, "Which question would you like me to answer first, Mr. Mercer?"

Before he could respond, someone else spoke up. "I'd like you to address the problem of Stockwell's contributing to unemployment by turning to robotics, Ms. Stockwell. What do you have to say to that?"

She turned to look at the woman, whose name was Marian something-or-other. When she saw the avaricious gleam in the reporter's eyes, she felt herself stiffening. The unemployment rate was a favorite campaign theme. Because of the growing problem in this part of the state, Granger was generating a lot of followers because of his stand on the issue. What he intended to do about it wasn't really clear, but it sounded good when he said he believed every able-bodied Illinoisan deserved a good job at a decent wage. Kay didn't disagree with that, but that was hardly the point here.

"I say it's rubbish," Kay said evenly. "Stockwell is not trying to put people out of work. In fact, quite the contrary. We—"

"Then you're saying that all these fancy robots you and everybody else are building aren't going to take over the workplace?" someone else aggressively demanded.

"Not in the way you mean," Kay said, reminding herself to hold on to her temper. "What they *will* do, however, is make valuable contributions to society. And in fact, they already have. Who, for instance, went in to clean up the nuclear accident at Chernobyl?''

"An accident the world shouldn't have had to deal with in the first place!''

"I agree. But that's not the argument," she said, dismissing him. Turning to the other reporter again, she said, "Robots are being utilized in many dangerous operations, both on land and undersea. For example, I'm sure none of you object to deep sea exploration. Surely it makes more sense to have scientists monitoring incoming data safely on the surface while robots do the dangerous explorations and send the data back?''

"That sounds all fine and good, Ms. Stockwell," Tony sneered. "But you still haven't answered my earlier question. Why did you fire George Mott?''

She wasn't going to fall into that trap. Her lawyers had warned her not to comment on the case because it was a legal matter now; they had impressed upon her the fact that an incautious remark could jeopardize Stockwell's position. "I don't think that's any of your concern, Mr. Mercer," she said, ignoring the angry buzz that followed her words.

"Yeah? Well, Mott is making it our concern. You *are* aware that he's filed a multimillion-dollar suit against Stockwell, aren't you? What are you going to do when you get to court?''

"I let my attorneys handle that, Mr. Mercer," she said. "I've got other things to do."

"Like building robots for the Defense Department?'' someone demanded.

"Like making sure an honest man is cheated out of an honest day's work by a pile of nuts and bolts?'' came from the other side of the room.

Kay knew it was hopeless. She could feel her temper seething just below the surface and knew that if she said much more, she'd end up saying something she was sure to regret. With a curt "That's all for now," she started out, only to be halted by Mercer again.

"Just one more question," Tony said snidely. "What gives you the right to fire loyal people who worked for your father for years? What gives you the right to start something that'll put other people out of work? Who died and made you God?"

Slowly, Kay turned back to face him. She had almost reached the door, but even though Brice was frantically signaling her just to keep walking, she couldn't ignore what had just been said.

"What gives you the right, Mr. Mercer?" She turned the question back to him, her eyes flashing. She walked toward him and leaned forward so that they were looking eye-to-eye. "What gives you the *right* to ask your questions and demand answers to things that can't possibly be any of your business? Questions, I may add, that totally misinterpret what I'm doing here."

She could see he wanted to rear back from the blaze in her eyes but couldn't because he'd lose pride. "Yes, but I'm the press," he said.

"The *press*," she repeated, contemptuously. "Does that mean *your* rights supersede mine? Let me ask you something, Mr. Mercer. Why are *you* free to harass me and to print your lies and your innuendos and conjectures in the paper without having to prove *your* sources? And just what gives you the right to dictate to me, to try and intimidate me, to take *sides,* when you're not even in remotest possession of the facts? You explain *your* rights, Mr. Mercer, and then perhaps I'll defend mine!"

And with Brice groaning and holding his head, Kay turned on her heel and walked out. Behind her, the silent and stunned group looked at each other for a few seconds, then, as though they were lemmings with but one mind and thought, they wheeled around and raced for the gates.

THE HEADLINES in the business section of the paper the next morning made even Kay cringe. Kay Stockwell Blasts Freedom Of The Press was one of the least lurid, and as she forced herself to read the accompanying articles, each one painting her in a worse light, she pulled the loyal Duffy close. What Del's reaction would be to this, she didn't want to think—if he dwelt on it at all, she thought, recalling their awful quarrel. He'd been right and she'd been wrong, and now that the damage was done, it was too late to tell him. She'd made it clear she didn't want to see or talk to or hear from him again, and since she was too proud to call herself, she knew he never would after what she'd told him.

"I think I've done it this time, Duffy," she said mournfully.

And as though he understood, Duffy reached up and gave her cheek a sympathetic lick.

CHAPTER FOURTEEN

DEL FLEW HOME from Los Angeles the day after Kay's disastrous press conference. He was still upset about his quarrel with her, but as he entered the house, he sensed something was wrong there. Ominous silence greeted him when he unlocked the front door, and he put his suitcase down warily.

"Jennifer?" he called. Not a sound. *"Jennifer!"*

Still nothing. *Well, that's just great,* he thought, slamming the front door behind him. She was supposed to be home from school at this hour, so if she wasn't she was probably punishing him—blaming him for the debacle at Stockwell Engineering. They'd had a brief conversation about it when he called to tell her when he'd be home— very brief, it turned out, for when Jennifer found out that he was through with Kay's account, she'd slammed the phone down in his ear. Thinking that was another thing he was going to talk to her about, he decided he needed a cup of coffee.

In the kitchen, he was just taking a cup down from the shelf when he paused. Something was wrong, he thought, and glanced around. Then he realized what it was, and he turned slowly back again. Where were all the bottles and jars and bags of things Jennifer had been bringing home from the health food store since their trip to the farm? The counters were swept clean, and a quick check of the cupboards revealed only the usual things found in any kitchen. What was going on? he wondered, and then saw the telltale evidence. Smashed down in the kitchen wastebasket in the corner were the remains of some fast-food meal, complete with a crumpled cellophane bag that had once held some kind of cookies. Like everything else, that bag was empty now, and when he saw the morning edition of the paper stashed beside it in the basket, a portion of the article about Kay's press conference showing, he knew what had happened.

"Oh, no!" he groaned. Leaving the kitchen, he turned and headed toward the stairs. Jennifer's bedroom door was closed. If she was up there, after all, the reason she hadn't heard him was because she was probably lying on her bed with her stereo headphones clamped to her ears, as she had done the first two months she'd lived here. Seeing all the progress they'd painfully made slipping away before his eyes, he was just starting to go up to confront her when he noticed a strange smell. He stopped, sniffing, trying to identify the odor. It smelled like...sulfur. And then, galvanized, he thought, *Is something on fire?*

Panic surged, and he almost shouted for Jennifer to run, escape, when he caught hold of himself. If the house was on fire, he'd smell smoke, not that rotten egg odor, he realized, and once he decided that, he began to get angry. What in the hell had been going on while he'd been gone? Where was Mrs. Nivens, who was supposed to be keeping an eye on things?

"Jennifer!" he shouted, trying not to lose his temper along with everything else. That would only make things worse, he knew, but when he wondered why he couldn't leave the house for a few days without some disaster occurring, he could feel rage building. "*Jennifer!* You come down here at once!"

When there was still no answer, he debated a moment, not sure whether he wanted to go up and break down her bedroom door or try to locate the source of that horrible odor. In the end, the stench won, and he was just heading toward the bathroom where Jennifer had been keeping her science project when the front door opened. As soon as he saw his daughter, he didn't bother with a fatherly greeting.

"What in the hell is that smell?" he demanded.

His tone set her off. Throwing the books she was carrying down on the hall table, she faced him defiantly. "It's the remains of my science project."

"What? What do you mean 'the remains'? Why does it smell so bad?"

"Because it does, all right? Because I made a mistake and added something I shouldn't have and ended up having to trash the whole thing! *Which* I wouldn't have done if I hadn't been so upset about Kay! Oh, Dad, how *could* you? How could you have abandoned her when she needed you the most?"

"I didn't abandon her," he said harshly. "But even if I had, it has nothing to do with you, and *that* has nothing at all to do with whatever happened to your science project! What do you mean, you added something you shouldn't have? Suppose you'd blown up the whole house?"

She gave him a withering look that told him he obviously hadn't the faintest idea what he was talking about, then she turned and started up the stairs. "Wait a minute!" he said. "Just where do you think you're going?"

"To my room!"

"Not until you tell me what's been going on around here! What's happened to all the health food? And what's all the stuff in the kitchen wastebasket?" He no-

ticed then that she was wearing an old, shabby pair of
jeans topped by a sweatshirt that had definitely seen better days. She hadn't worn either of those things since the
shopping trips with Kay; that gave him part of the answer, and he demanded to know what was going on.

"Oh, what do you care?" she cried, trying to brush by
him. He reached out and grasped her none too gently by
the arm.

"Just a minute. You're not going anywhere until we
talk about this. I *do* care. What's the matter with you?"

Blue eyes glittering with unshed tears, she looked at
him as though she hated him. "Why did you quit Kay's
account?"

"I…" He'd been about to say he hadn't quit, but that
wasn't quite true. "It's not that simple," he said angrily.
"It was a mutual decision, which, I remind you, has
nothing to do with you!"

"It has everything to do with me!" she cried. "I like
Kay, too! You shouldn't have quit, Dad! Now she's gone,
and it's all your fault!"

"Gone?" Del said, immediately alerted. Unconsciously his grip tightened on Jennifer's arm. "Who told
you that?"

"Kay's secretary did," Jennifer answered, her face
crumpling, "when I called to find out what had happened."

"Where did she go?"

"I don't know!" Jennifer wailed. "All her secretary
would say was that she wasn't there!"

"She must have told you more than that."

"No!"

Del thought quickly. He knew Kay; she was many

things, but she wasn't unfair. "She wouldn't just...
leave...without telling you, Jennifer," he said finally.
"You must know more than you're telling me."

"No, I don't!" Jennifer cried. "She called when I
wasn't home and told Mrs. Nivens that she was going
away and that she was going to take Duffy so I didn't
have to come over and take care of him! So now she's
gone, and it's all your fault because you quit the account when she needed you the most!"

Torn between wanting to explain to her and trying to
find out where in the hell Kay might have gone, he said
distractedly, "I told you, it was a mutual decision."

"But why?"

"It's a long story...."

It was the wrong thing to say. Her face convulsing with
new tears, she jerked her arm away. "No, it isn't!" she
shouted. "It's always the same thing with you! She didn't
do what you wanted, so you didn't want her anymore!"

"That's not true!"

"It is! It is! You only like people when they do what
you say! When they don't, you just throw them away!"

He was appalled. "You don't believe that!"

"Yes, I do! I do!" she shrieked, her cheeks suffused.
"And now that I've messed up my science project and
gone off my diet and disappointed you, you'll throw me
away, too! Well, fine! I never wanted to stay here, and I
can't wait to go live with Mom again!"

He felt a chill of fear. She couldn't mean it, he thought
desperately, and said, "Now, just a minute. You're not
going to leave and go to live with your mother in the
middle of the school year!"

"I will! I will! I'll call her and tell her that I can't stay
here! She'll come and get me then—she will!"

He knew that wasn't true. "Jennifer—"

"Don't try to talk me out of it, Dad! I'll go, I swear I will—just as soon as Mom comes to get me!"

He was rapidly losing what little grip he had on his composure. "Jennifer, this is ridiculous!" he said sharply. "You're getting hysterical, so just calm down!"

"No, I won't! I won't! I hate you, Dad! I hate you!"

He was so shocked that he couldn't think of a response. He could only watch as she thundered up the stairs and stormed into her room without looking back. The slamming of her bedroom door acted like an exclamation point to all the angry words that had passed between them, and as a vibrating silence descended, Del sank onto the bottom step of the staircase and put his head in his hands. When he thought that Kay was gone... Gone? What did that mean? She couldn't have just *gone,* he thought. He didn't know what to do.

Now what? he asked himself. He intended to talk to Jennifer, eventually, but even if he could find out where Kay was, what could he say?

"You've really made a mess of things, buddy," he muttered to himself, and wondered where in the world to go from here.

KAY CRIED ALL THE WAY to the farm. After reading the articles in the paper and reliving the awful press conference over and over in her mind until she thought she'd scream, she realized she couldn't face anyone at Stockwell until she sorted a few things out. She had never called in sick, but she did that day, asking Rachel to tell Brice that she wouldn't be in for a few days. She couldn't talk to him yet, either, so she took the coward's way out and was ashamed of herself.

But it seemed she had a lot to feel ashamed about these days, and, because she didn't know what else to do, she threw some things together, locked up the house and fled to the place she always went when she had a problem: to the farm and to her grandfather, who always understood. With Duffy on the seat beside her, soulfully looking up with liquid brown eyes as though he didn't understand but loved her anyway, she went . . . home.

As always, Emmett welcomed her with open arms. He knew something was wrong, but he didn't say anything, and the instant she felt her grandfather's comforting embrace, Kay knew she'd made the right decision. The farm had always given her perspective, and more than anything else, she needed that now. She had never felt so lost and alone—not even when she had come home without Adam.

"Oh, Granddad!" she said mournfully. "Everything that could have gone wrong has, and it's all my fault!"

"Shh," he murmured, holding her close. "Don't you worry now. Ain't nothing so bad it can't be fixed."

"I'm not so sure of that," she said, sniffing against his chest.

"Do you want to talk about it now?" he asked.

She shook her head. She knew if she tried, she wouldn't make sense. It was all so jumbled in her mind: Stockwell, her great plans for the robotics division, Jennifer . . . Del. Every time she thought about it, she wanted to cry all over again.

"Not now, Granddad," she said, looking up at him with tear-filled eyes. "Do you mind?"

"Not a bit," he said without judgment. "You always did need some time to work things out. I figure you'll come to me when you're ready. Until then, you're welcome as long as you want."

Wiping her eyes, she gave him a quick hug. "Thanks, Granddad . . . ."

Smiling, he touched her hair, the color of deep copper in the sun. "No need for thanks," he said huskily. "It's what families are for."

It was two days before Kay could bring herself to talk about that press conference, and even then she was loath to tell her grandfather what she had done. The more she thought about it, the more humiliating it seemed. Emotions had no place in business. Hadn't her father drilled that into her before he died? It had been her credo for a long time. When had she forgotten something that important?

When she'd gotten involved with Del, that's when, she realized. Everything had been fine until she had abandoned her own rules and allowed her attraction to him to ruin everything.

Follow your instincts, trust your reactions, and rule with your head and not your heart. Her father had told her that over and over again, and she thought she had it memorized. But then Del Rafferty had walked into her office, and it seemed she'd forgotten everything in the blaze of his deep blue eyes. Oh, what a fool she'd been! Now she stood to lose it all.

"I don't know what happened, Granddad," she said finally one night after supper. She had spent the entire day making pies and cookies and muffins from the pumpkins she'd harvested from Emmett's pumpkin patch behind the barn, and tomorrow she planned to can applesauce, which she knew he liked.

But as busy as she'd kept herself since she got here—giving the house a good cleaning, airing all the blankets and quilts, even taking up the rugs and polishing the floors until they shone—she hadn't been able to keep herself active enough to forget the reason she'd come. As always, Emmett had given her all the time she needed to work things out; he hadn't said anything himself, but she felt she owed him an explanation, so she joined him in the front room, where he was having his after-supper coffee. Handing him a piece of pie, she sat down by the fire and tried to gather her thoughts. Enjoying his dessert, Emmett waited patiently.

"You always could make good pumpkin pie," he said in satisfaction, taking another bite. "A pity we didn't have any cream for it, now, isn't it?"

Mention of the cream only reminded her more painfully of Del and her last visit to the farm. Turning to look into the blazing fire Emmett had built, she said in a low voice, "Granddad, I really made some big mistakes where the company is concerned."

Emmett put down the empty plate. "You ready to tell me about it?"

So she did, reluctantly, but with painful honesty, omitting nothing, not even the foolish pride that had compelled her to ignore Del's advice and call the press conference herself. Emmett listened silently to the whole tale, not changing expression even as Kay forced herself to relate every last humiliating detail.

"And so that's the story, Granddad," she finally finished. "I know I shouldn't have lost my temper, but what George Mott is doing just isn't right!"

Emmett smiled slightly. "You're just like your father," he said, shaking his head. "In his day, he would have said and done the same thing."

Despite her preoccupation with her' troubles, she looked at him in amazement. To her, Jim Stockwell had always been cautious and conservative; she couldn't remember him ever losing his temper, and she absolutely could not picture him in the situation she was in now.

"You're just saying that to make me feel better," she said. "I don't think Dad ever raised his voice in his entire life!"

"Don't you believe it," Emmett replied. "Your dad had a temper in his day, indeed he did. It used to get him in more trouble than you've seen yet."

"I don't believe it!"

"It's God's truth. So you see," Emmett said, "you come by it honestly."

Kay was so taken aback, she didn't know what to say. At last, she said with a shake of her head, "I just can't picture Dad that way. He was always so careful, so cautious...." She looked up. "Something must have changed him.... What?"

Emmett looked into the fire, his gaze far away. "I'm not certain, really," he said. "Maybe it was your mother dyin' so young. He wasn't ever the same after that. Her death took him by surprise, I think, and he...got scared."

"Scared?"

"It's the only way I can explain it. He was never one to take the safe path afore then. He was always the rebel...." Seeing her incredulous expression, Emmett smiled. "Oh, yes, I know it's hard to believe, but what do you think made him pick up and leave the farm to get that engineerin' degree of his? It wasn't my idea, I'll tell you. I needed him here, but no, he must go, and so I gave him my blessing. And it was right," he went on thoughtfully. "No father should expect his son to follow in footsteps that aren't right for him."

"But Dad loved the farm!" she protested.

Emmett smiled again. "Your father loved comin' *back* to the farm. It would have killed him stayin' here and takin' care of it. He just wasn't meant for it. I could see that when he was just a lad.''

"How?" she asked curiously. Emmett had never talked about her father—his son—in quite this way, and she wanted to know everything there was to know.

Her grandfather grinned at her. "How? Well, let's say that that workroom above the barn was his long afore it was yours. Oh, yes, I used to see that light on at all hours with him, too," Emmett said, smiling at her expression. "And he used to sleep up there sometimes, just like you used to." He shook his head. "You both thought you had the old man fooled, didn't you?"

Remembering how clever she thought she'd been all those years, and how she and Del had found that fresh comforter up in the loft, Kay felt her face turn red. Embarrassed, she said, "I guess we were the ones who were fooling ourselves."

"Not much goes on around here that I don't know, honey. I'm not as smart as you and your Dad—no, no, it's true—bookwise, that is. But I pride myself on what I do, and it's a poor farmer I'd be if I didn't keep my eye on things—isn't that right?"

"Oh, Granddad, I think you're smarter than anyone I know—and that includes Dad," she said fervently. "But if you knew all this time, why didn't you ever say anything?"

"And ruin your secret place? Everyone needs one of them, and I knew something good would come out of all those hours, first that your dad, and then you, spent up in that loft. And look what happened. Your dad started his company, and now you're carryin' on with it. So I was right, wasn't I?"

She'd been smiling, but now her face fell. "I'm not so sure about that, Granddad," she said, reminded again.

"Dad started the company, all right, but I haven't done such a good job carrying on with it, I don't think. Look at what a mess I'm in right now."

Emmett was sitting in his favorite rocking chair; he rocked a few times back and forth before he said, "Well, that's true—I'd be a fool to deny it. From what you say, you've got yourself a peck of trouble at the moment. But you'll do the right thing to fix it, honey. I've no doubt about it."

"But what's the right thing?"

She gave him a bleak look from her position on the floor. Beside her, as though he sensed her disquiet, Duffy stirred and thumped his tail on the rug, giving her encouragement. But if she had expected an easy answer from the man who always seemed to know everything, it wasn't forthcoming.

Rocking again, he said complacently, "You'll figure it out—I know it."

"You make it sound so simple."

"Not simple," he corrected. "But then, nothing is, until you face it."

She looked at him quickly. "Are you saying that I ran away?"

He looked calmly back. "It's not up to me to say, honey. It's up to you."

She glanced at the floor. Duffy's tail thumped again, and she absently stroked his silky head. After a moment, she sighed. "You're right, Granddad. I did run away. I'm not proud of it, but I...I guess I needed some time to think things out, to decide what to do."

"And have you?"

She didn't look directly at him. "Yes—about the company, at least. Brice has been telling me since this thing began that I should go public with what we're really working on there—you know, our big system for the physically impaired. But I haven't wanted to do it because we weren't ready to give details. It's been so expensive that I didn't want anyone to get the jump on us just when we're almost there, but I think now my silence was a mistake. Maybe if people knew what we were trying to do, things would turn in our favor, and everything would get back to normal."

"And George Mott?" he asked.

"I'll let my lawyers take care of him. According to them, he's trying to get mileage on a nonissue, and once we go to court, he'll realize how futile it is."

"And Del?"

She kept her eyes on Duffy. "I . . . don't want to talk about Del," she said.

"I see," Emmett said noncommittally, seeing too much, as always. "Well, that's too bad. I liked your nice young man."

"He's not *my* young man!" she protested. "In fact, he's not a *young* man at all!"

"Anyone below sixty is young to me," Emmett said incisively, and rocked back and forth for a few minutes. Then, straight-faced, he said, "Can we at least agree that he was nice?"

"No," she said sullenly, but even she realized the absurdity of her stand and had to smile. "Well, maybe sometimes," she said grudgingly. "But that's not important now."

"Well, it's a shame," he said. "I liked his daughter, too."

She still felt badly about Jennifer. "So did I—so do I," she amended. "But it just didn't work out."

"That's too bad."

"Will you stop saying that? With everything else I have to deal with right now, a relationship is the last thing I need!"

"All right, all right. Don't get all het up, as your grandma used to say. It was just a comment."

She glared at him. "You never *just* make comments."

He looked indignantly back. "Are you saying I'm an interfering old man?"

Despite her troubles, a slight smile curved her mouth. "Well, I wouldn't say *old*," she told him.

"I'll show you old," he harrumphed. "When I get up at four tomorrow morning to bring in the last of that squash, I'll make sure you're out there collectin' with me."

"You can try," she said, a light suddenly gleaming in her eyes. She'd just had an idea, and she couldn't wait to get out to her workshop to try it. "But I'll be busy the next couple of days. And it won't be making pumpkin pie!"

He didn't ask her what she had in mind; he'd seen that look in her eyes before. Instead, he grumbled good-naturedly, "Well, thank the Lord for that. The way you've been going at that stove in the kitchen, I'll have pumpkin this and pumpkin that comin' out of my ears until next spring. As it is, the next time you see me, I'll probably have turned as orange as can be."

"Oh, Granddad," she said, getting up and giving him an impulsive hug and kiss. "I do love you. You're so good to me."

Embarrassed as always by her shows of affection but deeply pleased inside, he gave her arm an awkward pat. "No better than you are to me," he said gruffly. "But Kay..."

"What, Granddad?"

"Think about that young man of yours, won't you? He seemed like a nice fellow to me."

BUT KAY DIDN'T ALLOW herself to think about Del during the next couple of days; she had to bring all her concentration to bear on the problem that faced her at Stockwell. To save the day, she needed a breakthrough on the QSA, and with the idea she'd had taking shape and form in her mind, she threw herself into her work. While Duffy kept Emmett company, she spent every waking moment either at the kitchen table with her lap-top computer and printer, or up in her workshop performing endless experiments—the lack of sophistication was sure to make Mort laugh, until she explained what she'd worked out. She became so obsessed and absorbed working on the changes in the QSA program that she would have forgotten to eat if her grandfather hadn't reminded her.

But at the end of those two days, she had an answer. It wasn't the total answer, but it was enough to move them forward. She knew it—she could feel it in her bones—and she was so elated that she wanted to shout, to dance, to tell the whole world that she'd finally made the breakthrough she and Mort had been searching for all these months.

I did it! she thought, looking down at the complicated calculations she'd worked out. She was up in the loft, and pages and pages of printouts were strewn from one end of the workbench to the other. She was so thrilled that she wanted to call Mort right that second and tell him everything. He'd be as excited as she was, she thought, and jumped up before she realized what time it was. Midnight had long come and gone. To her surprise, she realized it was almost dawn.

She'd wait until he got to the office, she thought deliciously, and nearly gave herself a hug of delight. Now Brice could say what he wanted to the meddlesome press; he could shout it out to anyone who wanted to listen, and she wouldn't care! He could even tell George Mott right to his face that if this worked out the way she expected it to—and she had no doubt that it would, not now—Stockwell was well on its way to taking a patent that was going to revolutionize robotics. At the thought, she threw back her head and laughed aloud. Wouldn't he be surprised! Wouldn't they all be surprised! She could hardly wait to tell Del!

That last thought stopped her in her tracks. She'd been reaching for the coffee she'd brought up to the loft—a cup that had gone cold hours ago—but her hand froze. She hadn't allowed any thoughts of Del to interrupt her work until this minute.

But now she had her breakthrough, and without warning, Del's face flashed into her mind and wouldn't leave. *Oh, Del,* she thought. *What am I going to do about you?*

It was the farm, she realized. They'd had such a wonderful time here that she could never forget it, even if she wanted to. And she didn't want to forget that magical weekend. Even now she could remember everything they had done or said or laughed about or discussed when they had first discovered each other here at the farm.

Now that she'd started thinking about him, she couldn't seem to stop. In her mind's eye, she could see Del's expression as he watched Jennifer learning to milk, and she remembered how they had all laughed at Duffy that afternoon—a dog instead of a cat caught for once with the cream on his face. And she recalled the night they went square dancing, as well, and how handsome

Del had looked and how blissful she'd felt being twirled around the floor in his strong arms. Oh, she remembered so many things she had tried to forget, she thought, and made the mistake of glancing toward the comforterbed in the corner of her loft. Stabbed with sudden pain, she closed her eyes as every detail of their lovemaking rushed back at her. As exhausted as she was from the intense work of the past two days, she could still remember the feel of Del's mouth on hers and how well they fit together; she knew how strong and lean his body had been and how wonderful it had been with him. She felt hot with the memory of how incredible their time here had been.

And at home as well, she recalled, thinking of the night they had gone upstairs after dinner. He'd been so tender and gentle then, so passionate—such a thrilling lover. She could still smell the scent of his skin and feel the crispness of his chest hair under her fingers, and she could still see his eyes....

It was the memory of his eyes, so intent on her face, so blue they almost looked black at times, that made her realize she couldn't just let it all go. Something had happened to her since then, something she'd thought would never, ever, happen again. It wasn't only that, against all resolve, she seemed to have fallen in love with him; it was that knowing him had made her see that sometimes things were just not what they appeared to be. He wasn't, that was for certain. But neither was she. She had presented an efficient, organized, formidable front to the world, when behind it, she was just as uncertain as everyone else seemed to be. Catchphrases and buzzwords and sound bites and spins—it was all part of the way the world was now, but it didn't have to be the sum total of things. Del had allowed her a glimpse behind his mask, and she had laid herself bare for him. How could she pretend it had never happened? Style could never replace substance; form and content were two different things. But what she had learned was that sometimes one was as necessary as the other.

Suddenly consumed with the need to talk to Del and to tell him what she had come to understand about him, and about herself, she quickly gathered up all her papers and calculations and switched off the light. She felt her way down the ladder, gave the cud-chewing Pansy a last pat, then left the barn and ran back to the farmhouse. She was packed and ready to go by the time Emmett came down; she already had coffee made, and during a quick breakfast, she told him what she had finally figured out.

"Good for you," he said, pleased. "I knew that, given enough time, you'd come to it yourself."

"How did you get to be so wise?" she asked fondly, and gave him a kiss and a fierce hug goodbye before she left.

She thought about what she was going to say to Del all the way back to town. But as eager as she was to see him, she stopped at the office first to hand over the precious papers she'd brought and explain things to Mort. He listened skeptically at first, then with increasing excitement, and by the time she finished telling him what she had worked out, he was practically quivering, eager to try out the experiment. Leaving a message for Brice, who hadn't arrived yet, she sped off again. She didn't want to call Del at his office or see him there with everyone else, so she headed directly to his house. She knew exactly what she was going to say, but she never got the chance. When she arrived, Jennifer answered the door. Dressed in jeans and the baggy old sweatshirt that Kay thought she'd given to charity, she was eating a double egg sandwich for breakfast. Her father wasn't here, Jennifer said. She didn't know where he was, and she didn't care. Then she promptly burst into tears.

CHAPTER FIFTEEN

SEEING JENNIFER IN TEARS, Kay quickly stepped inside and shut the door. "Honey, what's wrong?" she asked, alarmed. A sudden thought occurred to her, and she put her arm around the weeping girl's shoulders. She knew how protective Jennifer was of her, and she said, "You and your dad didn't have a fight about what happened out at Stockwell, did you?"

Jennifer's response was to cry even harder. It was too awkward to continue standing in the entry, so Kay guided her into the living room, where she gently forced her to sit on the couch. Jennifer was still clutching the egg sandwich, which was starting to ooze yolk, and when the girl looked around distractedly and then seemed about to put it on the coffee table, Kay hurried into the kitchen, grabbed a paper towel and brought it back to wrap up the remains. Setting the sandwich aside, she took Jennifer's hands.

"Tell me," she said.

"Oh, Kay, it was aw...aw...awful!" Jennifer sobbed, hardly able to get the words out. "He wouldn't talk to me and he was so...so...so *unfair!* I wanted to find out what had happened, but you were gone, too, and so I..." She broke down again, crying as though her heart would break.

Feeling even worse, Kay said quickly, "I'm sorry, Jennifer, but I called before I left, and you weren't home. I left a message with Mrs. Nivens—"

"Yes, but you didn't say where you went! And Dad wouldn't talk to me, and now he's gone, and—"

"Gone?" Kay echoed, wondering if something awful had happened to Del. "What do you mean—gone?"

"I don't know and I don't care!"

"But—"

"It doesn't matter!" Jennifer said shrilly. "Because I won't be here when he gets back—if he ever does! I'm going, too!"

"What? What do you mean?" Kay asked, alarmed. "Where are you going?"

"Why should I tell you? You don't care, either!"

Shocked, Kay exclaimed, "Jennifer, that's not true! Of course I care!"

"No, no, you don't! If you did, you wouldn't have gone away like that! Or, at least, you would have told me where you were going!"

"But I..." Kay started to say, and then stopped. Jennifer was right, she thought guiltily; she should have said something more, or at least tried to explain. But she hadn't, and now she realized how much she had hurt Jennifer and how deeply she had betrayed her trust. Ashamed, she began to be angry with both Del and herself for dragging Jennifer into their fight. Personal problems were one thing, but she and Del were supposed to be adults. It wasn't fair to put Jennifer on hold while they sulked or tried to decide if they wanted to work things out, and she despised herself.

Reaching for Jennifer's hands again, she tried to make the girl look at her. "You're right," she said quietly. "I'm sorry, Jennifer. What I did was…inexcusable. I was just thinking of myself and what a mess I'd made of things.''

Jennifer was sobbing again. ''You *never* make a mess of things! Only I do that!''

Kay smiled slightly, bitterly. ''I'm afraid that isn't true, either. Your father was right—I shouldn't have given the press conference without thinking it through a little more. But I was so determined to do things my way that I mishandled the whole thing. I'll have to figure out how to repair the damage myself, I'm afraid, but in the meantime, it doesn't have anything to do with how I feel about you.'' She tightened her grip on the girl's hands. ''I'm so sorry I treated you this way, Jennifer,'' she said sincerely. ''I hope you'll be able to forgive me. Adults make mistakes, too, you know, and here's one who's made some doozies lately.''

Despite herself, Jennifer smiled. ''That's funny, coming from you,'' she said, hiccuping through her tears.

''Maybe to you,'' Kay said, relieved to see even a small smile. ''But unfortunately for me, it's all too true.'' She hesitated. ''You said your father was gone. You really don't know where he went?''

Jennifer's smile vanished. ''No, I told you—and I don't care! I'm leaving myself, and then he'll be sorry!''

Kay had been too preoccupied to notice before, but now she saw a duffel bag sitting by the door. Sensing how volatile Jennifer was right now, she knew that she had to play it as casually as she could. ''I see,'' she said. ''Well, I can't blame you for wanting to teach us both a lesson, but I hope you'll be more considerate than we were to you. Can you give me a hint about where you're going?''

Jennifer gave her a suspicious look. It was obvious that she hadn't expected Kay to be so calm, and she said defiantly, "I'm going to be with my mother!"

"I see," Kay said, wondering how Del was going to react. "Well, I can understand why you'd want to, but . . . does she know you're coming?"

Jennifer looked even more dubious. "No, but I'll explain when I get there."

"Oh. And what about your dad?" Kay said. "I guess you haven't told him you're leaving, have you?"

"No, but I told you, he doesn't care!"

Kay might not be sure of many things right now where Del was concerned, but this was one she did know about. "Oh, honey, it isn't so," she said. "Your father loves you. He loves you very much."

"No, he doesn't!" Jennifer said shrilly.

"He does," Kay insisted. "Why do you think he wanted you here with him, why he's wanted you here for years? He cares very deeply for you, Jennifer. He's so proud of you."

"No, he's not! He's not! He only likes people when they do what he wants them to, and I haven't done that since I came. I've messed things up again and again, and he's not proud of me at all!"

"How can you say that? He—"

"I can say it because it's true! Everything was fine when I went on my diet and started losing weight and dressing like he wanted me to and doing better in school! But the instant I stopped doing those things, he acted like I wasn't worth bothering about at all!"

"But why did you stop doing those things?" she asked, ignoring the melodramatics. "I thought you were pleased that you'd lost weight. And you enjoyed our shopping trips and getting new clothes. And you were proud of doing so well in school.''

Confused, Jennifer glanced away. "Yeah, I was," she muttered. Then she looked back defiantly again. "But I can get mad, too, you know! And when I saw how Dad just...just *quit* you because you didn't do what he wanted, well, I thought...I thought that he could do the same to me, you know? I didn't *mean* to ruin my science project, and I didn't *want* to go off my diet, but then, when you left and took Duffy, too—well, everything got out of control! And when he came home and got so mad at me for messing up, well, I..." The tears came again, choking her so that she could barely speak. "It's so hard sometimes!" she wept. "I try to do good, but I know I'm going to make mistakes, and then...and then... Oh, it's not fair!" she bawled. "Dad shouldn't expect me to be *perfect* all the time!"

"Dad doesn't expect you to be perfect, now or any other time," a new voice said just then, from behind them. "In fact, Dad's made so many mistakes himself that he doesn't have a right to expect anything of you at all.''

Both Kay and Jennifer whirled around at the sound of that voice. When they saw Del standing in the doorway, they just stared. It was obvious that he'd been listening to part of the conversation, at least, but they had both been so preoccupied that they hadn't even heard him come in. Shocked, they exclaimed at the same time.

"Dad! What are you doing here?"

"Del! Where have you been?"

He glanced at Kay. "I might ask you the same thing," he said, and then looked at his daughter. He had already seen Jennifer's duffel bag by the door, and he smiled crookedly, tiredly. "If you're going someplace, I can tell you one thing, Button...."

Jennifer seemed transfixed. Tears drying on her cheeks, she whispered, "What?"

"No matter where you go, your problems always go with you."

DEL HAD BEEN TO CHICAGO and back. But this trip he hadn't spent in the luxurious hotels and restaurants near the Loop, or North Michigan Avenue's posh Gold Coast. Responding to a need he felt but hardly understood, he had gone back to his roots, to the darker, poorer section of the city, where he had been born. There, far from the glamour and glitz of the city's finest parks, beaches, museums and opera houses, he'd walked amid rows of tenement houses and mean streets, where windows were barred and trash littered the sidewalks, trying to come to grips with his life.

For years now, he had put everything about his past out of his mind—or tried to. Having come so far from where he had started, he hadn't wanted to remember any of it—the gangs, the violence, the friends he'd had who had been shot or knifed or sent to prison, or who had ended up drunk or stoned... or worse. All through his youth, his sleep had been interrupted with noise and confusion and the sounds of screams and curses and fighting that rent the night, and from the age of eight, when his best friend, a boy named Willie, had died of a drug overdose, he had vowed to get out. While other boys were out roaming the streets proving how tough they were by skipping class, he had been working hard and hitting the books. To support them, his mother had worked as a maid at two hotels downtown, while he'd tried to help out by unloading groceries at night at a market for cash.

He never knew who his father was; his mother wouldn't talk about him. And when he was fifteen, his sister, who was older than him by a year, left for Hollywood to become a star. Six months later she was dead, and his mother had never been the same. The doctor said his mother died of emphysema, but he knew that her heart and her spirit had been broken when his sister had gone the way of Willie, his best friend.

And he had never been the same again, either, Del thought that day in Chicago, walking down one street after another. He didn't know where he was and didn't much care. It didn't matter what the street signs said; to him, they all read the same: these were the streets where dreams came to an end.

But he'd gotten out, he thought, as he walked along, his shoulders hunched against the cold, his collar turned up to shield his face against the rising wind. Trash disturbed by his passing swirled up and then scuttled down the curb again, blowing aimlessly, like so many of the people here. He'd been so preoccupied that he hadn't noticed it was getting dark, and he knew he should be leaving soon. Even for someone who had grown up here and knew how to handle himself, it wasn't smart to be wandering around at night, alone.

So he turned back toward where he'd left the rental car, not even sure it would still be there. Addicts were always looking for car parts to sell. At this point in Del's life, the car was low priority; he could always replace it, but the real question was whether he could repair the damage he had done to his daughter and the woman who had stolen his heart.

Again and again, the things both Kay and Jennifer had said to him churned through his mind. *You only like people when they do what you say!* Jennifer had shouted at him, while Kay had accused him of caring only about how something looked, not how a person felt. With both, the battle had been between image and reality, but as he glanced around at the faceless, featureless brick buildings marred by gang graffiti and bars on the windows, at the bare dirt where there could have been grass, at the garbage in streets that should have been swept clean, he felt his stomach tighten and wondered how he could be blamed for wanting to put a gloss on things.

But that's all part of the past, Kay had told him once, when they were talking about childhood things. Even then, he hadn't been completely honest with her; ashamed, he'd never been able to bring himself to tell her the complete truth about his growing up, how mean it had been, how shabby and poverty-stricken.

And it's what you do with the past that counts, she'd gone on to tell him. *Look at you. No one would ever guess where you had been.*

Del shook his head. He'd purposely hidden his past from everyone. But knowing Kay had made him see things differently, and having Jennifer come to live with him had reinforced his new perspective. And as he walked back to his car, he suddenly realized a truth that had been eluding him until now. Being here had made him see things more clearly than he had in a long time, and as he reached the car, he glanced around again. He'd gotten into the image business because he wanted not to change things, he realized now, but to cover them up, to pretend they were better than he knew them to be. The only problem was that, as Kay had said to him, he couldn't cover up forever. And, as she had tried to point out to him again, by her work and by example, the only thing he—or anyone—could do was try to change the part of the world he lived in or was responsible for. She was doing it with her robotics research, trying to help those less fortunate, while he... All he'd been doing was putting a gloss on things.

It was a sobering thought, and suddenly, without warning, he was ashamed of himself and filled with the urgent need to go back and tell them both—Kay and Jennifer—how wrong he had been. But first... first, he had something important to do, something he should have done long before now. Just thinking about it made him smile, and feeling better than he had in years, as though a weight had been lifted off him, he unlocked the car and got in. After he made one stop, he'd be on his way home.

KAY WAS THE FIRST to get herself together. Del's unexpected appearance had startled her; she had been so occupied with Jennifer that she'd almost forgotten the reason she'd come to the house in the first place. Seeing Del reminded her, and she stood up uncertainly. She hadn't been able to gauge his reaction yet; she didn't know if he was angry that she had come or even if he wanted to see her at all. But she had to say what she'd come to say, and she cleared her throat.

No matter where you go, your problems always go with you, Del had said, and Kay knew he was right. Tentatively, she said, "These past few days, I've discovered for myself that you can't run away from trouble."

Del didn't move from his place in the doorway. He seemed as wary as she felt. "Where did you go?"

She smiled slightly. "To the farm, where else?"

"So that's where you went!" Jennifer exclaimed. "I should have known!" She turned to her father. "And where did you go?"

Until Jennifer asked the question, Del seemed unable to take his eyes off Kay. Now he looked at his daughter. Somberly, he said, "I went to Chicago. I had some thinking to do, Button."

Jennifer looked apprehensive. "About what?"

"About you. About me. About—" he glanced in Kay's direction "—about Kay."

"And?" Jennifer squeaked.

Del came into the living room. "And," he said, his voice low as he spoke to Jennifer, "I realized that I had some big apologizing to do—to both of you," he added with a quick glance at Kay. He sat down beside Jennifer. "Going back to Chicago made me see things a little more clearly, honey, and I realize now that I wanted you with me so much that I refused to see how unhappy you are here. So if you want to be with your mother, I'll—"

He never got a chance to finish the sentence. Stricken, Jennifer launched herself at him, burying her face in his chest, bursting into renewed tears. "Don't send me away, Dad! I didn't mean what I said earlier! Can't I stay here?"

If the situation hadn't been so serious, Kay would have laughed at Del's expression. He looked so confused and bewildered as he glanced up at her, begging for help, that she sat down beside Jennifer, too.

"I think what your dad is trying to say, honey, is that he knows how difficult it's been for you, so if—"

"I don't want to go!" Jennifer bawled. "Oh, Dad, please don't make me!"

Del's baffled eyes met Kay's over his daughter's head. "I'd never *make* you go, darling," he said. "I thought you *wanted* to. You've been telling me since you got here how much you miss your mother and how exciting it would be to go to Europe. I just—"

Jennifer's face was still buried against his chest. Her voice muffled, she said. "I just said that because I was being mean. I never wanted to go with Mom. I don't like that Leif at all! But I didn't think you wanted me here."

"Not want you!" With difficulty, Del made Jennifer sit up so that she had to look at him. "How can you say that, Button? I love you! I've always wanted you with me!" Then, because he finally believed she was old enough, and because the urgency of the moment seemed to require it, he told her something he'd never said before. "Long ago, when your mom and I divorced, I tried to work out something with her so that you could stay with me. But she thought you'd be better off with her, and . . . and the judge agreed. But I never did, darling—please believe me. I used to *beg* your mother to let you come and stay with me, but she never would . . . until this summer. Now, I . . . I know you accused me of not considering your feelings, and you're right—I should have asked you. But I was so thrilled at the thought that we'd finally be together that I guess I didn't think beyond that. I didn't want to, because I knew at the end of the year, Maxine would probably insist that you go. And I didn't want you to. I wanted you here with me forever."

Jennifer's eyes had started to glow halfway through Del's heartfelt speech. By the end, her entire face was shining. "Oh, Dad, you mean it?" she whispered.

"With all my heart," he said, holding her tightly and looking over her head again into Kay's eyes. Then he held Jennifer away for a moment. "So it's all settled between you and me?"

"Oh, yes, Dad," Jennifer said fervently. "I'm so glad I get to stay! Now that I have friends, Trudy and Susan and Eddie—Did I tell you he asked me for a date?"

Del glanced at Kay again. She smiled; they were both thinking the same thing: how resilient young people were. "What did you say, Button?" he asked.

"Well, I said I'd have to ask you," Jennifer answered. "That's because I haven't decided yet. Because as cute as Eddie is, I think I like Perry Alden better."

Del looked confused again. "But I thought you said he was too smart—"

"No, I said he always had his nose in a book—there's a difference. Besides, there's nothing wrong with being smart," Jennifer said cleverly. "Look at Kay."

But Del wasn't sure he wanted to look at Kay. Now that the moment had come, he didn't know what he wanted to say. He took no satisfaction from being right because he knew that he'd acted like an insensitive jerk. But even if he admitted that, would Kay be able to forgive him?

"Go ahead—apologize," Jennifer said in a loud whisper. "Kay and I know you come on a little strong sometimes, but maybe if you promise to be a little more *real* from now on, she'll forgive you, anyway."

Knowing he wanted a great deal more than a pardon for his behavior from Kay, Del looked her way. She met his eyes, but before he could decide what she was thinking, Jennifer sighed.

"Oh, brother," she said. "Is this what I have to look forward to if I fall in love with somebody?" She saw their faces and grinned. "Come on, you know it's true. It's written all over your faces...and has been for weeks. You're not only crazy about each other, but you'd be good for each other, too. So come on, what do you say?"

Del took himself in hand. "I'm sorry, Kay."

Kay spoke at the same time. "I'm sorry, Del," she said.

Jennifer sighed again, this time with pure pleasure. "*Now* we're cooking," she murmured.

Del decided it was time to take charge. He hadn't done all his soul-searching in Chicago without coming to realize how he felt about this woman, and he reached for Kay's hand and held it tightly, as though he were afraid she would leap up and run away. "I hadn't planned it quite this way, but . . ." he started to say, and then took a deep breath. "I know I've done just about everything wrong that I could have done wrong, but will you give me another chance, Kay? I'll prove to you that I can change—that I *have* changed—if you'll only let me try."

"Well, I—"

His fingers tightened on hers. "Jennifer's right about one thing," he said, holding her eyes. "I am crazy about you. I have been from the first. Maybe that's why I did so many stupid things—I don't know. But when I went to Chicago, I realized what you've been trying to tell me all along, and if I'm confused about so much else, one thing I know for sure is real, and that's that I love you."

It was Kay's turn. She was so happy that she wanted to cry. But she had a few things she had to say to him, too. Brushing at the tears in her eyes, she managed to say, "I've been a little obstinate myself, I admit. And I've done some pretty awful things to you. I wouldn't listen to your advice, and I held that stupid press conference when you didn't want me to, and . . ."

Hope and relief and joy had leaped into Del's eyes. Through the grin that was threatening to break out and swamp his face, he said, gruffly, "Well, we'll have to talk about that, all right." Then he abandoned his pose. "But if we can start over again—"

"Start over!" Jennifer exclaimed. "But I thought it was already decided!"

Kay smiled—a little shakily. "I think we'll just take it one step at a time, okay?" she said to Jennifer, and then looked at Del. "What do you think?"

Jennifer was sitting between them, but it didn't matter. When Del reached for Kay and pulled her close for a blissful kiss, Jennifer sat back with another sigh.

"Well, thank heaven for that," she said with satisfaction. "I thought you two would *never* get together! We'll be a real family yet, you'll see!"

Del gave Kay's hand a squeeze as he looked down at his daughter. "Maybe sooner than you think, Button," he said, and reluctantly released Kay so he could get to his feet. "Excuse me, I'll be right back."

"Where are you going?" Kay asked, alarmed. Now that she had him, she didn't want to let him go.

Del just grinned. "You'll see," he said, and disappeared out the front door.

Left alone, Jennifer and Kay looked at each other. "What do you think...?" Jennifer asked.

Kay just gave a bewildered shrug. Then she heard a bark and groaned. Oh, Lord, she'd forgotten about Duffy, waiting in the car. Del must have seen him on the way in and had gone out to get him. Thinking that she was getting to love this man more and more, she was just rising to her feet when Duffy trotted into the living room, looking proud as punch, as though to say, "See what I found?"

Jennifer gasped. Right behind Duffy was the most beautiful little dog she'd ever seen. Part cocker, part heaven knew what, the caramel-colored little puppy had long, silky ears, a nub of a tail and two great brown eyes that looked around wide-eyed at the world. With Duffy standing guard, the puppy plopped down right by Del's foot.

As though unable to believe her eyes, Jennifer looked at her father. "Dad . . . ?"

"You've been wanting a dog ever since you met Duffy," he said huskily. "And when I found this one at the pound, something told me she'd like to come home to be yours."

Jennifer looked from her father to the little dog, who was still sitting shyly by Del's foot. "Mine?" she whispered. "Really mine?"

Del's eyes met Kay's and saw the love shining there. "Name her and she stays," he said, reaching a hand out. Kay took it, and he pulled her to him. Together, they stood with their arms around each other while Jennifer got down and gathered the puppy to her, tears spilling over onto her cheeks.

"Daisy," she said, wiping her face. "That's what I'm going to call her. Doesn't she look like a Daisy to you?"

Apparently she did to Duffy, who gave a quick bark of approval. They all laughed, and then Jennifer stood with the puppy in her arms. Solemnly, but with a suddenly adult look in her eyes, she said, "I think Duffy and I should take Daisy for a walk, get her used to the neighborhood. Will you two be all right while I'm gone?"

Del's arms tightened around Kay's waist. "I think we'll manage," he said, winking at his daughter.

Jennifer smiled at Kay, the smile of a girl who was fast becoming a young woman. "I thought so," she murmured, and then on impulse gave Kay a quick kiss. "I'm so glad things worked out," she whispered.

Kay gave her a heartfelt hug. "So am I," she whispered back.

"And so am I," Del said, when Jennifer had taken the dogs out. And he proceeded to prove it by kissing her until she gasped.

EPILOGUE

TWO MONTHS AFTER their engagement party, Kay and Del flew to Washington for her appearance before the Senate subcommittee to ask for the robotics research grant. As they waited in the big corridor outside the imposing room where the committee was to meet, Del took her hand.

"You look beautiful," he said, and then gave her a wicked grin. "Even if you aren't wearing blue."

She was too tense to smile. "Maybe I should have," she muttered. "I think I'm going to need all the help I can get."

"Nervous?" he asked.

"No, why do you say that?" she said, and stopped twisting the square-cut emerald ring he had given her to celebrate their engagement. "Well, maybe a little," she confessed. "This means so much to me—to everyone at Stockwell."

"You'll do fine—you always do. Look what you did to George Mott. He was so soundly defeated in court that I think he's even left the state."

As absurd as it was, she still felt badly about that. "I hope he finds what he's looking for. We had our differences, but he did know his field. Anyone can make a mistake," she added. "Look what happened between you and me."

He didn't like being reminded of how close they had come to losing each other. "Yes, but we were smart enough to remedy that."

"Swallow our pride and grovel, you mean."

"Well, that never hurts as a last resort," he said, smiling.

She glanced toward the closed ornate doors of the committee room. "What's taking them so long?"

"They have to get their pomp and circumstance in order before they call you in. Don't worry, it'll be soon enough."

She was worried. "What if I don't remember everything?" she asked. Then, panicked, she said, "What if I forget my speech?"

"You won't forget. You're thoroughly prepared. And you know what you're talking about."

"Yes, but you didn't help me with it!"

He looked amused. Holding his hands up in pretended surrender, he said, "Didn't I promise never to interfere again?"

"Yes, you did. But what good's having my own image consultant if he doesn't give me his professional opinion once in a while?"

"You want my professional opinion?"

"I'd rather you went in there and gave this speech for me."

"Sorry, can't do that. You're on your own, kiddo. But don't worry, Jennifer and I are rooting for you. And Brice. And Mort—and everybody at Stockwell, who all think you're a genius, anyway."

He was referring to the breakthrough she'd made with the QSA. Once she'd made the discovery out on the farm, work had been proceeding at a feverish pace, and she had come today equipped with a model and a video, both of which she intended to use as part of her speech in a few minutes. The progress they'd made would surely guarantee a grant, she thought, and rubbed her clammy hands together. What if it wasn't enough?

"Here," Del said, with that uncanny knack he had at times of reading her thoughts. "Jennifer thought you might need a little moral support, and since she couldn't be here herself, we decided this might be the next best thing."

"What's this?" she asked, looking down at the locket Del had pressed into her hand.

He smiled. "Open it...."

When Kay obeyed, she felt tears come to her eyes. The locket opened to reveal two tiny pictures, one of Del on one side, the one opposite of Jennifer with Daisy and Duffy. As she was so often these days, Jennifer was smiling—and had reason to be. Fifteen pounds lighter now due to a sensible diet, her grades were high again, and she had a new boyfriend—Perry Alden—who was rapidly developing potential, according to Jennifer, now that she'd been able to talk him into putting away his slide rule, at least on Friday nights.

But Jennifer, too, had blossomed, and now that Maxine had agreed she could stay with Del until she finished high school, there was talk about Jennifer being voted class president next year. She couldn't wait to be Kay's maid of honor at the wedding, and she was excited at being included in all the plans. The only thing she hadn't been able to talk her father or her future stepmother into was allowing Daisy to be flower dog and Duffy to carry the rings. But they were all going on vacation together— as soon as Kay and Del got back from the honeymoon, wherever that might be. Oh, and she had decided she didn't want to be called Pat after all. Perry thought Jennifer was a beautiful name, so delicate, so feminine; so from now on, Jennifer it was going to be.

"It's beautiful," Kay said, staring down at the locket and trying not to cry. Quickly, she handed it back to Del. "Here, help me put it on, for good luck."

Del was just clasping the locket around her neck when the big doors opened and Kay's name was called. At that, she turned to Del in panic again.

"You said you had a professional opinion," she said. "Tell me what it is, quick!"

But now that her moment had come, the man who before would have been armed with market surveys and theories and survey reports, who would have taped and rehearsed her and guided her through every syllable and gesture to prepare, just smiled and kissed her tenderly on the lips. He'd learned a few things, too.

"My professional opinion?" he said with a grin, giving her a little push in the right direction. "Go in there and knock 'em dead, kid."

HISTORICAL

CHRISTMAS

STORIES · 1991

Bring back heartwarming memories of Christmas past
with HISTORICAL CHRISTMAS STORIES 1991,
a collection of romantic stories
by three popular authors.
The perfect Christmas gift!

Don't miss these heartwarming stories,
available in November
wherever Harlequin books are sold:

CHRISTMAS YET TO COME
by Lynda Trent
A SEASON OF JOY
by Caryn Cameron
FORTUNE'S GIFT
by DeLoras Scott

**Best Wishes and Season's Greetings
from Harlequin!**

XM-91R

Reach for the stars with

Harlequin Superromance®

in a new trilogy by award-winning author Pamela Bauer

Family ties...

Seventh Heaven (title #481)
Kate Osborne feels she needs to watch out for her daughters. But it seems she isn't the only one watching! Police Commissioner Donovan Cade appears to have a telescope trained on her oldest daughter's bedroom window! Protest leads to passion as Kate discovers Donovan's true interests.
Coming in December

On Cloud Nine (title #484)
Kate's second daughter, Juliet, has old-fashioned values like her mother's. But those values are tested when she meets Ross Stafford, a jazz musician and teaching assistant... and the object of her younger sister's affections. Can Juliet only achieve her heart's desire at the cost of her integrity?
Coming in January

Swinging On a Star (title #487)
Meridee is Kate's oldest daughter, but very much her own person. Determined to climb the corporate ladder, she has never had time for love. But her life is turned upside down when Zeb Farrell storms into town, determined to eliminate jobs in her company—her sister's among them! Meridee is prepared to do battle, but for once, she's met her match.
Coming in February

SPB

Harlequin Superromance®

COMING NEXT MONTH

Take 4 bestselling love stories FREE

Plus get a FREE surprise gift!

Special Limited-time Offer

Mail to Harlequin Reader Service®

In the U.S.	In Canada
3010 Walden Avenue	P.O. Box 609
P.O. Box 1867	Fort Erie, Ontario
Buffalo, N.Y. 14269-1867	L2A 5X3

YES! Please send me 4 free Harlequin Superromance® novels and my free surprise gift. Then send me 4 brand-new novels every month, and bill me at the low price of $2.96* each—a savings of 33¢ apiece off cover prices. There are no shipping, handling or other hidden costs. I understand that accepting the books and gift places me under no obligation ever to buy any books. I can always return a shipment and cancel at any time. Even if I never buy another book from Harlequin, the 4 free books and the surprise gift are mine to keep forever.

*Offer slightly different in Canada—$2.96 per book plus 49¢ per shipment for delivery. Canadian residents add applicable federal and provincial sales tax. Sales tax applicable in N.Y.

134 BPA ADL3   334 BPA ADMH

_____

Name   (PLEASE PRINT)

_____

Address   Apt. No.

_____

City   State/Prov.   Zip/Postal Code

This offer is limited to one order per household and not valid to present Harlequin Superromance® subscribers. Terms and prices are subject to change.

SUPER-91   © 1990 Harlequin Enterprises Limited

HARLEQUIN®
OFFICIAL SWEEPSTAKES RULES

NO PURCHASE NECESSARY

1. To enter, complete an Official Entry Form or 3" × 5" index card by hand-printing, in plain block letters, your complete name, address, phone number and age, and mailing it to: Harlequin Fashion A Whole New You Sweepstakes, P.O. Box 9056, Buffalo, NY 14269-9056.

   No responsibility is assumed for lost, late or misdirected mail. Entries must be sent separately with first class postage affixed, and be received no later than December 31, 1991 for eligibility.

2. Winners will be selected by D.L. Blair, Inc., an independent judging organization whose decisions are final, in random drawings to be held on January 30, 1992 in Blair, NE at 10:00 a.m. from among all eligible entries received.

3. The prizes to be awarded and their approximate retail values are as follows: Grand Prize — A brand-new Mercury Sable LS plus a trip for two (2) to Paris, including round-trip air transportation, six (6) nights hotel accommodation, a $1,400 meal/spending money stipend and $2,000 cash toward a new fashion wardrobe (approximate value: $28,000) or $15,000 cash; two (2) Second Prizes — A trip to Paris, including round-trip air transportation, six (6) nights hotel accommodation, a $1,400 meal/spending money stipend and $2,000 cash toward a new fashion wardrobe (approximate value: $11,000) or $5,000 cash; three (3) Third Prizes — $2,000 cash toward a new fashion wardrobe. All prizes are valued in U.S. currency. Travel award air transportation is from the commercial airport nearest winner's home. Travel is subject to space and accommodation availability, and must be completed by June 30, 1993. Sweepstakes offer is open to residents of the U.S. and Canada who are 21 years of age or older as of December 31, 1991, except residents of Puerto Rico, employees and immediate family members of Torstar Corp., its affiliates, subsidiaries, and all agencies, entities and persons connected with the use, marketing, or conduct of this sweepstakes. All federal, state, provincial, municipal and local laws apply. Offer void wherever prohibited by law. Taxes and/or duties, applicable registration and licensing fees, are the sole responsibility of the winners. Any litigation within the province of Quebec respecting the conduct and awarding of a prize may be submitted to the Régie des loteries et courses du Québec. All prizes will be awarded; winners will be notified by mail. No substitution of prizes is permitted.

4. Potential winners must sign and return any required Affidavit of Eligibility/Release of Liability within 30 days of notification. In the event of noncompliance within this time period, the prize may be awarded to an alternate winner. Any prize or prize notification returned as undeliverable may result in the awarding of that prize to an alternate winner. By acceptance of their prize, winners consent to use of their names, photographs or their likenesses for purposes of advertising, trade and promotion on behalf of Torstar Corp. without further compensation. Canadian winners must correctly answer a time-limited arithmetical question in order to be awarded a prize.

5. For a list of winners (available after 3/31/92), send a separate stamped, self-addressed envelope to: Harlequin Fashion A Whole New You Sweepstakes, P.O. Box 4694, Blair, NE 68009.

PREMIUM OFFER TERMS

To receive your gift, complete the Offer Certificate according to directions. Be certain to enclose the required number of "Fashion A Whole New You" proofs of product purchase (which are found on the last page of every specially marked "Fashion A Whole New You" Harlequin or Silhouette romance novel). Requests must be received no later than December 31, 1991. Limit: four (4) gifts per name, family, group, organization or address. Items depicted are for illustrative purposes only and may not be exactly as shown. Please allow 6 to 8 weeks for receipt of order. Offer good while quantities of gifts last. In the event an ordered gift is no longer available, you will receive a free, previously unpublished Harlequin or Silhouette book for every proof of purchase you have submitted with your request, plus a refund of the postage and handling charge you have included. Offer good in the U.S. and Canada only.

HOFW · SWPR

HARLEQUIN® OFFICIAL SWEEPSTAKES ENTRY FORM

4-FWHSS-4

Complete and return this Entry Form immediately -- the more entries you submit, the better your chances of winning!

■ Entries must be received by **December 31, 1991.**
■ A Random draw will take place on **January 30, 1992.**
■ No purchase necessary.

Yes, I want to win a FASHION A WHOLE NEW YOU Classic and Romantic prize from Harlequin:

Name _____ Telephone _____ Age _____

Address _____

City _____ State _____ Zip _____

Return Entries to: **Harlequin FASHION A WHOLE NEW YOU,**
P.O. Box 9056, Buffalo, NY 14269-9056 © 1991 Harlequin Enterprises Limited

PREMIUM OFFER

To receive your free gift, send us the required number of proofs-of-purchase from any specially marked FASHION A WHOLE NEW YOU Harlequin or Silhouette Book with the Offer Certificate properly completed, plus a check or money order (do not send cash) to cover postage and handling payable to Harlequin FASHION A WHOLE NEW YOU Offer. We will send you the specified gift.

OFFER CERTIFICATE

Item	A. ROMANTIC COLLECTOR'S DOLL (Suggested Retail Price $60.00)	B. CLASSIC PICTURE FRAME (Suggested Retail Price $25.00)
# of proofs-of-purchase	18	12
Postage and Handling	$3.50	$2.95
Check one	☐	☐
Name		
Address		
City	State	Zip

Mail this certificate, designated number of proofs-of-purchase and check or money order for postage and handling to: **Harlequin FASHION A WHOLE NEW YOU Gift Offer,** P.O. Box 9057, Buffalo, NY 14269-9057. Requests must be received by December 31, 1991.

ONE PROOF-OF-PURCHASE

4-FWHSP-4

To collect your fabulous free gift you must include the necessary number of proofs-of-purchase with a properly completed Offer Certificate.

© 1991 Harlequin Enterprises Limited

See previous page for details.